Marco's *Next Move*

By: Janice Broyles

MARCO'S NEXT MOVE
By Janice Broyles

Published by Late November Literary
Winston Salem, NC 27107

ISBN (print): 978-1-7375561-2-1

Copyright 2022 by Janice Broyles
Cover design by Sweet N' Spicy designs
Interior design by Late November Literary & Sweet N' Spicy designs
Available in print or online. Visit latenovemberliterary.com

All rights reserved. No part of this publication may be reproduced in any form without written permission of the publisher, except as provided by the U.S. copyright law.

This is a work of fiction. Any brand names, places, or trademarks remain the property of their respective owners and are only used for fictional purposes.

Janice Broyles.
Marco's Next Move/Janice Broyles, 1st ed.

Printed in the United States of America

Dedicated to all social workers and the children they help.

CHAPTER ONE

I stared at the math test but couldn't focus. After math class was lunch, and it couldn't get here fast enough. My stomach growled loudly at the thought of instant mashed potatoes and Salisbury steak. When my stomach growled again, some kids around me stopped their work and glanced my way.

Stop it, I ordered my stomach silently. *You're embarrassing me.*

My stomach responded so loudly, several kids started laughing. The teacher shushed them, and then my stomach grumbled again as if in defiance.

I'll grumble when I want to, it said.

Stupid stomach. It always betrayed me and at the worst possible times.

Ms. Sanders opened up her top drawer, grabbed something, and came toward me. Since she placed me near the front, she didn't have far to walk. She slipped a packet of cheese crackers on my desk. "Did you miss breakfast?"

I didn't look up, and I didn't nod. She already knew the answer. She knew that my foster parents overslept nearly every morning. She knew I lived in their trailer with half their floor rotting out miles outside of town. I'd have to leave before six in the morning if I was going to walk to school. And she knew that I stayed up late babysitting their other three foster kids while they went out drinking. She knew all that. All the adults in the school knew that. So, I grabbed the crackers without saying a word, ripped the packet open, and began eating.

Thirty minutes later, my stomach had been temporarily silenced and my math test sat completed. Ms. Sanders saw my finished test, so she approached me again and picked up the paper with my scribbled answers. She set it back down and whispered, "Good job. Another perfect score."

When the bell finally released class to lunch, Ms. Sanders called me to her desk and asked if I completed any of my missing work. I didn't answer, and I certainly didn't stop. It was lunch time, and this was the only meal that I was guaranteed every Monday through Friday.

"Marco." Halfway down the hall, someone called my name. I kept moving, zeroing in on the cafeteria. "Marco. You're needed in the office."

Almost there.

"Marco." Ms. Sanders stepped in front of me.

Okay, she moved fast. "It's lunch," I complained, looking past her to the long line already forming.

"The office just called my room and said you need to get down there."

"But lunch…"

"I will go get you lunch and bring it to you."

I nodded, "Okay, but don't forget the chocolate milk."

"Got it." She motioned for me to turn around.

I practically stomped to the office. *Can't a guy get some peace?* As soon as I opened the office door, my grumpiness disappeared. "Dad?"

"Hey there, Marco." He extended his arms, and I ran into them, hugging him as tight as I could.

It'd been three months since I'd seen him. Three months since the jerk-face Mr. Harvey came and took me away.

"They said we can use the office meeting room," Dad said. "Come with me."

I followed him to a small room used for parent meetings. When I first moved in with the foster parents, I had to sit in here. Still, I took a seat across from Dad and smiled at him. "I didn't know if I was going to see you again."

"Of course, man. No one's going to keep me from you. I promise."

My smile grew. I could see the redness in Dad's eyes and how his hand twitched, but he looked showered and shaven.

Ms. Sanders came in and set a lunch tray down in front of me. "As promised." She gave me a wink and stepped out of the room.

"Go on and eat," Dad said. "You're skin and bones."

I didn't need any more of a push. I shoveled the mashed potatoes and gravy into my mouth in giant bites.

Dad ruffled my thick, curly hair. "You need a haircut."

I shrugged and moved on to the Salisbury steak. As I finished the meal and chugged on my milk, the door opened and Mr. Harvey stepped inside. I immediately frowned.

"A few more minutes, please?" Dad asked.

Mr. Harvey smiled and nodded. "Of course." He looked at me and said, "Hello, Marco. Good to see you."

"*Not* good to see you," I muttered after he left.

"Hey, be polite."

"I don't like him."

"Mr. Harvey's a good guy. He's looking out for you."

"Then why am I living in a trailer that smells of cat pee and with part of the floor rotted through?"

"It's hard for families to take teenagers."

"I'm only twelve, and none of this would have happened if he would have left me with you."

Dad studied his hands. They wouldn't stop shaking, so he sat on them. "Listen, Marco. I'm going to give it to you straight. I need to get clean. A couple of months ago, I got in trouble with the cops for trying to steal some medication from the pharmacy. They caught me with a wad of cash and some other stuff. That's where I've been."

"Locked up?"

"Yeah. I wanted to tell you, but I was embarrassed. I told Mr. Harvey not to say a word. It was only for twelve weeks, but I've got to do six months in a rehab facility, and then two years of probation."

"You said you weren't gonna steal anymore."

"I know, and I'm sorry." Dad finally looked at me. "I love you, kid. You're the best thing I've ever done. And I'm messing up. I got to get right. That means we've got to do this, okay?"

I thought of staying another six months in that stinky, rotten trailer and felt near tears. Dad and I always had to move from one squat to another, but we were at least together. "They don't feed me," I said quietly. "They lock their cupboards."

Dad's jaw set in an angry line. "They're not feeding my boy? I'll take care of it." Then he shook his head. "You know what? That doesn't matter anymore because you won't be staying there."

"I get to leave?"

"Yeah, you're going to be staying with my mom. Your grandmother."

"Who?"

"It's your grandmother, and I kept you from her for a lot of different reasons. But she's good, and she'll be good for you. I promise."

"I have a grandma?"

"You do."

Mr. Harvey stepped into the room again. "I'm sorry, Lance. We have to get you reported into the facility."

"I don't want to be with anyone but you," I complained. "I'll be good. I won't bother you."

"It's not that simple. I can't take you where I'm going."

"Why would they separate you and me? We're a team. We take care of each other."

"We'll always be a team, but we have to do it their way. I've got to get things together."

I shook my head, becoming angrier. I couldn't imagine living with some lady I'd never met.

"This is just temporary, Marco. We'll be together again. I promise."

I kept shaking my head. I couldn't say a word because I was too focused on not crying.

"I've got a duffel bag here with all your books and some more of your clothes. You forgot a bunch of stuff when you left last time."

"I didn't have time to pack anything."

"I know. Do me a favor, hold on to your books, okay? It's important to me that you have them." He gave me a long, hard look. "Do you understand what I'm saying?"

Not exactly sure why he'd be insistent on me keeping my books, I finally nodded because he seemed to be waiting for it.

"Good. Now give me another hug. It's gonna have to last until I can see you again."

I hugged Dad as tightly as I could. He'd been in jail this entire time, and I had no idea. I was upset he kept it from me, but not as upset at the thought of having a grandmother I knew nothing about. And now I would show up on her doorstep?

"Be good," he said in my ear. "And be respectful. Don't let that smart mouth get you in trouble."

"I'll try."

Dad gave me a quick squeeze, then released me. He stepped out of the room and quickly left the office. I ran after him, trying to catch up as he headed outside. I saw the two cop cars pulled up at the door. I watched as one of the officers cuffed Dad and directed him to the back of the car.

"Dad!" I yelled, running to him.

The police officer shut the door but kindly stepped out of my way.

A tear leaked out, but I blinked the rest back.

"Keep reading the books," he said through the window. "And don't forget I love you."

The car started, and before I could say anything else, the cop drove off, taking my father with him.

CHAPTER TWO

"Talk to me, kiddo," Mr. Harvey said. He's tried to talk to me since we left school, but if he thinks I've got anything to say to him, he's stupider than he looks.

We drove in silence for a while. The duffel bag sat in my lap for some time. Eventually, I unzipped it to see what Dad had packed. He packed the few t-shirts I owned, plus his own oversized Michigan sweatshirt. I loved that sweatshirt. Other than that, there were just a handful of my books. He didn't pack over half of them.

One of my favorite books, *The Starship Enterprise*, was in there. I pulled it out and looked through it. The pages were all mangled and a few were missing, but one of the motel managers from last spring was going to throw it out from their lobby table, so I took it. I'd read the book at least twenty times. I wanted to get the rest to the series but reading wasn't too high on Dad's priority list, so neither were books.

One time I found Dad leafing through it. It had been one of the days I had gone to school. "Did you see this?" he asked and opened the book to one of the back pages where a set of numbers had been scribbled.

"No," I said and went over to study it. "These numbers weren't in there before."

Now in Mr. Harvey's car, I flipped to the page and ran my finger over the numbers. Dad said it must be a code that unlocked a mysterious treasure. He made me vow not to touch it, but to leave it there, that way when we found the treasure, we'd be ready. Not that I believed him. I found the marker he used to write the numbers the next day.

No, the numbers didn't fool me. He probably needed to hide them.

In the last couple of months, Dad started to change. He acted nervously and kept talking to me about emergencies. "We need to be prepared," he explained. We talked about our emergency location in case something happened. "You remember where we meet if we get separated, right?"

I slammed the book shut.

"Whatcha reading back there?" Mr. Harvey tried again.

I wanted to point out that I couldn't possibly be reading since the book was closed. But I wasn't talking to him, so I set the book beside me to illustrate that no reading was happening here. Dad asked me to be respectful, but keeping my mouth shut was as close as I'd get to that.

"I'm a reader, too. Mostly John Grisham or Tom Clancy. Ever read any of their books?" He paused. "I'll have to pick you up a few. You'd like them." He paused again, only to keep talking, "Television gets kind of old after a while, don't you think? Nothing like a good book, that's what I always say."

I stayed silent.

"I overheard what you said about your foster parents. I will look into it, and make sure they do not take in any more children. Being with them at least put a roof over your head. I couldn't have you in the streets while your father sat in jail."

I glowered at him, and then stuck my chin out and turned to stare at the window. Dad gave me a roof over my head! I wanted to yell it, but I refused to say anything. What did Mr. Harvey know? It's always been Dad and me. Dad was far from perfect, but living with those nasty foster parents let me know it could be worse. If I was being honest with myself, living on the streets with Dad was pretty close to being as bad. It wasn't always like that though. Dad and I used to have a trailer of our own. Until the drugs. He became an addict. I was only a kid. The biggest difference between him and the foster parents was his love for me. Dad loved me, and I loved him.

"You hungry?" Mr. Harvey asked, pulling into a burger joint.

My stomach grumbled in response. Stupid stomach. I twisted in the seat and glared out the window, ordering my stomach to be quiet. I refused to give him the satisfaction of knowing my stomach was hungry again.

"Tell you what," he continued. "I'm going to go in and get me a double cheeseburger with some fries and a strawberry milkshake, and I'll get a second one just in case I'm hungry later. Okay?"

"Chocolate," I said. My grumbling stomach seemed to have a

mind of its own.

"What was that?" He leaned back into the car.

"I said chocolate. You know. Maybe a chocolate milkshake?"

He nodded his head, his thick eyebrows crinkling together as if contemplating the fate of the universe. "Good call," he said. "If you feel like coming in, go for it. There's air conditioning inside."

The heat clung to me, even with all the windows rolled down. September in Detroit is a beast with thick humidity thrown it to make it *really* miserable. But toughness demanded sacrifice, so I stayed in the car.

Mr. Harvey held two bags and two extra-large shakes as he came out of the fast-food restaurant. I nearly drooled. Then he just plopped the second bag right beside me along with a super huge milkshake. "Hey, Marco, you don't mind holding that for me, do you?"

That's when I saw my reflection in the car's mirror. I quickly looked away, embarrassed at my dirty appearance. But it was more than that. I looked half-starved and…unkept. Dad was right. My hair was matted and too long. Dad told me once that I looked a lot like my mother with big brown eyes and light brown skin, but in the one picture Dad had of her, she didn't look like this.

Mr. Harvey slid behind the driver's wheel. "You don't want any?" he asked, noticing the untouched bag. As he started the car and backed up, he added, "Help yourself."

That was all the encouragement I needed. I gulped down the food in large bites, not even registering what kind of sandwich he had bought me. I even licked the wrapping paper and shook the bottom of the bag to see if any fries had fallen. When I looked over, sucking on my milkshake, Mr. Harvey watched me out of the corners of his eyes. His eyes darted toward the road as soon as we made eye contact.

"What are you looking at?" My defiance was firmly in place again.

"Nothing," he said. "You feeling full now?"

"Yep." Since the food eased my hunger pangs, I felt more talkative. "So, where do you think you're taking me?"

"To a relative. We want to help your dad, Marco. As soon as he gets better, you two can be together. It's best for everyone if you allow that to happen." He gave me a pointed look.

"I do help him. We were doing fine too until you showed up and ruined everything."

At the next red light, he turned to face me. "You're only twelve, with an entire life ahead of you. You need to focus on yourself. He needs to clean up for himself." Changing the subject, he said, "You're in seventh grade, right?"

I shrugged and didn't answer.

"According to your school records you missed 50 days last year, and this year you've already missed nine."

I shrugged my shoulders again. It bothered me, but what could I do? I couldn't tell him that I didn't attend school because I stayed up half the night worried about if Dad would come back alive or not. Instead, I said, "School's boring."

"Your test scores were off the charts," Mr. Harvey continued.

"You scored well past the high school level in reading, writing, and math. Ms. Sanders told me in the office that when you'd show up, you would catch up all of your assignments at lunch, and your English teacher told me you're reading higher-level texts that most students shy away from."

"So, what's the problem?"

"Your father needs to get help. Then you can go home."

"What home?" I thought of the mean people who were my foster parents. Would they send me back there? Where would Dad and I live when he got out of rehab? But none of that mattered. Dad and I would figure it out because we were a team.

"But I do have good news. We already contacted the middle school in your grandmother's town. She's going to make sure you don't miss any school." He glanced at me with a wide grin.

I folded my arms and scowled. *That's what you think.* My Dad and I were good at running. We left places and situations at the drop of a hat. The only reason I hadn't left those foster parents was that I had no idea where Dad was. I stayed until I could learn what happened. But now that I knew where Dad was, sticking around with my dear old granny wasn't going to happen.

"I know what you're thinking, Marco. But you can't run away from this."

Wanna bet?

"It's a court order, which means that they can send you to juvie if you decide to be difficult."

"Let me get this straight," I said, with irritation and just a tad bit of desperation leaking out into my words. “You’re going to force me—against my will—to go live with some stranger who is probably more jacked up than my dad, and if I decide to hit the road, then I’m the bad guy? That is messed up on so many levels.”

“This relative is not jacked up. And if she is, you let me know. If your dad sobers quickly, it won’t even be for long.”

“How long we talking?”

“I’m not sure. That’s up to your father.”

My heart sank. Dad had tried to get clean so many times I’d lost count.

Mr. Harvey zoomed past trucks as he made his way up the highway. “Think of this as an opportunity. An opportunity for your father to focus on getting better, and an opportunity for you to focus on yourself. Things are about to change, Marco, but in a good way.”

I scoffed and looked back out the window. I stopped believing in empty promises a long time ago.

CHAPTER THREE

“Marco, we’re here.”

I sat up fast, rubbing the sleep out of my eyes.

“Did you have a good nap?” Mr. Harvey asked as he unbuckled his seatbelt.

Then I remembered.

I remembered Dad at the school, and then him being escorted in the cop car away from me, and suddenly I was very cranky. “I wasn’t sleeping,” I snapped. “I was only resting because I was bored out of my mind.”

“Really? Who knew boredom could make a person snore so loudly?”

I made a face at him. “Leave me alone,” I muttered and glanced out the window. “What kind of dump is this?” I asked testily. My day just kept getting better and better. “You know, if leaving my dad wasn’t traumatic enough, being sent to the boondocks will do the trick.”

“Hey now,” Mr. Harvey warned. “What are you talking about? This is beautiful Northern Michigan. You don’t see trees like this down in Detroit."

"You can say that again." It was like Mr. Harvey parked the car right smack dab in the middle of a spooky forest. Complete with creepy old cabin too. My heart took a nosedive.

"There's a lake just down the road," Mr. Harvey was saying, "and the fall colors are breathtaking."

I stared at him like he was speaking Chinese. "Say what?"

He opened his door and pointed toward a huge clump of trees. "There's a lake right over there. We passed it on the other side."

"So? I don't swim."

"It's easy to learn."

I opened my door and stepped outside, ignoring him.

"I see nothing but trees and an ugly cabin," I grumbled. And there *were* trees. Lots and lots of them. I glanced across the dirt road. I glanced down the dirt road. Yep. Lots and lots of trees.

And it gave me the heebie-jeebies.

"I know it's not much to look at," Mr. Harvey started. He must have read my face, "but she is your grandmother, and we're excited she agreed to take you in."

I stared at him in my *you've got to be kidding* expression, and then fixed my gaze on the heap of logs that took on an extremely misshapen outline of a house. It couldn't have been bigger than any of the trailers I'd lived in, the roof needed work with patches sticking up perpendicular to it, and one window frame had no pane whatsoever, just plastic taped over it. And then there were the trees!

I'd never seen so much green before in my life. I couldn't see another house down the entire stretch of dirt road.

"Please tell me this is a joke." I swallowed and tried not to panic. "We're in the middle of nowhere!"

"Not true. Right down the road, there are a couple of other houses, and the town is just a few miles away."

"Town?" I asked, a sinking feeling in my stomach. Tears suddenly threatened. I stopped crying years ago when I realized that it never made the problems disappear. But this…this was too much. First, seeing Dad taken away by the police, and now this.

I forced the tears back as I headed to the dirt road. I forced the tears back. I refused to look like a baby. I'd been in horrible predicaments before. That was the pathetic plot of my life. I would get myself out of this one too.

"Marco, it's not so bad," Mr. Harvey said. "Your father grew up here." I heard him open the car door. I stopped, took a few deep breaths, and turned around. He held the duffel bag. I couldn't leave without my books. I slowly walked back to him. Besides, where would I run away to? The forest? Not happening. The trees were seriously creeping me out.

"There is no way you, or whoever you work for, would have approved this house for me to live in," I argued. "Then again, after the last place you dumped me off in, this cabin fits the bill."

Mr. Harvey closed his eyes and exhaled. "I understand that this doesn't look the best, but this cabin is nicely maintained on the inside. The new window will be in this week, and the roof will be repaired too. She has a room just for you. Plus, she lives on the outskirts of Otsego County, which means that you will be attending one of Northern Michigan's top school districts."

The screen door to the cabin swung open and some white woman started waddling over in our direction. She looked like a butterball turkey with a mound of red hair bunched on a human head and an ugly skirt around a waist the size of a hula hoop.

"Please tell me that's not my grandmother."

Mr. Harvey shushed me and said, "No. That's Ms. Wright, your new social worker."

My quick comeback halted on my tongue. "What?"

"Look who's here," she yelled over, clapping her chubby hands. "We've been waiting for you, sweetie."

The emotion boiled in me like hot lava. "So, you're ditching me too?" I asked Mr. Harvey. "Just take me from my dad. And then leave me? With *her*?" I breathed ragged breaths to try to keep the tears from coming. I. WILL. NOT. CRY.

"I'm not ditching you, Marco." Mr. Harvey lightly touched my shoulder.

I pushed his hand away. "Save it. You and your excuses go shove it for all I care."

"Listen to me. I'm not ditching you."

"Yes, you are!" I argued. "What do you call this?" I waved my hands at the surroundings. "And what do you call her?" I pointed at the fat lady who finally made it over to us.

"Hello, hello, hello," she sang cheerfully. When she smiled her eyes squinted shut so I couldn't see them. And her earrings were too big.

"I'm Ms. Wright, but you can call me Eleanor." She extended her hand, but I could only stare at her fat fingers, which reminded me of sausages, which reminded me I was hungry again, which reminded me of all the other times I'd been hungry, which reminded me of my father.

I simply glared at her, fists clenched, teeth gritted, and chanted in my head, *nerves of steel…nerves of steel.*

"Give us a minute," Mr. Harvey said quietly to her. She nodded briefly, her smile still in place, forced and fake.

She murmured she'd meet us inside. She gave me one last glance before waddling across the small clearing to the cabin.

"Marco."

I didn't look over. Instead, I told myself over and over not to care.

"Marco." Mr. Harvey stood in front of me now, looking down at me with that horrid look of sympathy. "I'm not ditching you."

I didn't say anything.

"Do you believe me?"

"Whatever," I said and shrugged. I would show him how much I *didn't* care. "Say what you need to say to make yourself feel better."

"You're angry."

"No, I'm not."

"You have a right to be."

"I'm not angry, so drop it."

"You're very important to me."

"Whatever. I don't care. Leave me with turkey sausage lady."

Mr. Harvey's mouth twitched into a semi-grin, but he quickly recovered. "Ms. Wright will only be working *with me* because Detroit is four hours away."

"Four hours?" How long had I zonked out? "How am I going to see Dad?" my voice level raised with each word. "Who's going to take care of him? He needs me!" I shouted. My breaths became ragged again and those stupid tears would not go away. I put my fists to my eyes and pressed against them as if that motion would shove the tears back down into my tear ducts.

"As soon as your father gets better, you will see him again. I promise. Just stay here for a little bit. Get to know your grandmother. She's excited to meet you."

"Sure, she is," I said sarcastically. "That's why I've never met her. Because she's so excited I'm her grandson."

"Sometimes family situations are complicated, but she is excited."

"My family situation was just fine until you decided to barge in and ruin everything," I said.

Mr. Harvey started to say something but stopped himself. I watched him and waited, wanting him to tell me that we could go home. He finally said, "Come on, let's go meet your grandmother. I'll be right beside you."

My argument vaporized into the forest air, as my feet moved automatically behind him. I did look around to contemplate running off, but the forest intimidated me. Who knew what lurked behind the trees?

With my imagination in overdrive, I thought I saw something. Maybe some ghost or psycho killer. I picked up speed and stepped on Mr. Harvey's heels, falling into him. He turned quickly. "You okay?"

Terror clutched my insides. I looked back at the forest, then back at Mr. Harvey. "I'm cool," I whispered.

"You do realize Otsego County is probably the safest place to live in all of Michigan, don't you?"

"What? I'm not scared?"

Once on the small porch, I pulled down on my shirt, but I couldn't make it any longer. I might have been short for my size, but the t-shirt was a size or two too small. Mr. Harvey knocked on the screen door, and I wondered if I should have changed shirts. I only had a few to choose from, but I'd been wearing this one for the last several days. Then again, who cares? Maybe this lady will hate me enough to send me back. Even the rotted-out trailer seemed better than this.

Another white lady came to the door, much thinner than the other one, a pair of reading glasses perched on top of her head. I inhaled sharply in surprise. Her dark blonde hair had a lot of white mixed with it, but it reminded me of Dad's. And her face. It was like looking at a female version of Dad. The lady looked at me, her eyes widening in surprise, her mouth hanging open.

But it didn't seem to be an excited surprise. More like you're-not-what-I-was-expecting kind of surprise.

"Yes, I know. I'm black," I said sarcastically.

"Ms. Fuller?" Mr. Harvey gave me a warning glance. "It's nice to put a face to the voice on the other end of the phone." He chuckled, but it died off pretty fast.

She never took her eyes off me but squeaked and clutched her chest.

At that point, I was tired, annoyed, and scared, and I had had enough. "Didn't anyone teach you that it's rude to stare?"

"This is Marco." Mr. Harvey interrupted anything further I was about to say and rested a hand on my shoulder. "He's excited to meet you."

I looked at him in surprise. "I never said that. You told me she was excited to meet me."

"Marco," Mr. Harvey said between clenched teeth. "Please use manners."

"It's fine."

We both turned to face the woman who had just spoken.

"He's right. It's rude to stare. I just wasn't expecting..." She trailed off not finishing her thought and continued to watch me. She opened the screen door and motioned for us to come in. "It's nice to finally meet my grandson."

I walked inside completely speechless. She agreed with me?

"I've been hoping to meet you for quite some time," she continued.

Once again, I didn't know how to answer that. I had a grandmother who *wanted* to meet me?

"This is the living room." She kept going, as if she was afraid of any awkward pause. "It's pretty open and nice. It leads right into the kitchen, as you can see. Right down this hall, there are two bedrooms and a bathroom. It's not the biggest place, but it fits my needs. And sorry about the roof. And the window. It should all be replaced soon."

My grandmother expected me to say something, but all I could do was nod. The living room seemed roomy enough and opened into a small kitchen area. The first thing I noticed was how clean it was. I'm talking c-l-e-a-n. The only parts that looked remotely cluttered were her small kitchen table with a laundry basket on top and the piles of books that surrounded a big recliner that sat near the plastic-covered window.

"You like books?" I asked. I wanted to examine each one of them but stayed in my spot near the door. "I could never get enough books. The ones I got I had to steal…you know what, never mind."

The adults nervously chuckled at that. Mr. Harvey had a smile plastered on his face, but his eyes warned me to behave. I shrugged at him as if to say, *What are you going to do about it?* It was his fault I was here in the first place.

“I have to admit I’m quite the voracious reader,” she said. “What’s the one you’re holding?”

I showed her *The Starship Enterprise*. “There are more books to the series, but I only have this one.”

“I bet the library would have some of the others. We’ll have to get you a library card. That way you can read books without stealing.” Her voice trailed off, and she coughed into her hand.

Library card? Rows of books waiting for me to read? Then I reminded myself I wasn’t staying. *Don’t get attached.*

“Ms. Fuller,” Mr. Harvey interrupted. “Marco probably wants to clean up from the long trip. Why don’t we show him his room?”

And there it was. The awkward pause. My grandmother nodded and added, “That sounds nice, and then maybe a shower?”

I would have smart-mouthed her again, but I wanted some time to myself to think. And take a shower.

My clothes in the duffel bag were all filthy. Dad and I weren’t too big on using the laundry mat because it cost too much money. We would wash our underwear in the sink of wherever we were staying and call it good. Luckily, Mr. Harvey handed me some clean clothes from a bag he had brought. I followed my grandmother down the narrow hallway while Mr. Harvey stayed in the living room with Ms. Wright. She dropped my duffel bag in a darkened room, opened a small hallway closet, and handed me a towel.

“That’s your bedroom where I set the bag, but let’s clean up first. Bathroom's right there."

I went inside the bathroom, which just happened to be about the size of a closet.

My grandmother looked me over before closing the door. "And just throw the clothes you have on in the garbage."

I wanted to say something sarcastic to rebuff the blunt comment, but I couldn't. Instead, I asked, "You're my dad's mom?"

She smiled sadly and nodded. Reaching her hand out to me, she nearly touched my cheek before dropping her hand quickly. "Make sure you scrub really hard."

Sighing, I rolled my eyes and shut the door in her face. My clothes peeled off me. Oh, yeah. I knew I smelled funky. The water poured down hot before I jumped in. It soaked through me, rinsing off layers of grime. Unsure of when I last took a bath, I scrubbed as hard as I could.

As the scum washed off my body, I sort of felt like it was a rebirth. Like a preacher, I heard once talking about being "born again." Maybe this was what it felt like.

Not that I wanted to be here. Or that I liked anyone in the other room. And I knew I wasn't going to stick around for long. As soon as the opportunity presented itself, I would high-tail it out and head back to Detroit. But if that was my grandma, maybe I should try to make a good impression. Then I could go get Dad, and we could come back to visit. If nothing else, I needed to find out why Dad never talked about that woman in the other room.

When I finished and put on the clean clothes (which was very hard to do, I might add. I kept bumping into the wall), I opened the bathroom door to sneak to my room.

I turned the light on and noticed a nice bed on the left side of the room with a nightstand beside it. There was also one dresser and a nice-sized window that looked out at the trees. That's when I heard their whispered voices.

They probably didn't want me to hear. I tip-toed down to the end of the hall and listened anyway. Maybe I'd find out how Mr. Harvey found me in the first place.

"I can't believe him. That is not the same Lance that I raised." The older woman whispered fiercely at Mr. Harvey like it was his fault.

"I don't know what to tell you."

"Tell me he's getting help."

"Lance has to go through a minimum of six months rehabilitation. This is a good thing. But he is a grown man, Ms. Fuller. I have Marco to look after. Right now, his care and upbringing are what matter to me."

"He was only seventeen for God's sake. He kept everything a secret. Then was just gone. Like that. No warning, no nothing. And now it's like I'm losing him all over again!" My grandmother seemed to be crying.

"That's not Marco's fault. Look at it from his point of view. Every few months, he ups and moves. Last year he didn't even complete a full year of school. He was too busy making sure his father hadn't died from the drugs he had taken the night before." Mr. Harvey's hardened voice relaxed, "He needs a new start. Both of them do."

"This is the first time I've laid eyes on him! And look at him." I heard her voice catch again. "Why wouldn't Lance take care of him? Feed him? Clean him?"

My gut twisted as I listened. I didn't want to hear anymore, but my feet couldn't move. Did I look that bad? I glanced down at the clean outfit I had on. The pants were a bit short, but at least the shirt was long enough. But my arms were thin, really thin. I guess I never noticed that before. Still, I didn't like they were talking about my dad like he wasn't a good parent. He might have issues, but I had never slept outside. Never.

Still, there was nothing I could do but stand and hear the rest. The tears that had threatened before were long gone. Only a dull ache in the deepest part of me remained.

"Now you have a chance to know him," Mr. Harvey said, quieter now. I had to strain to hear him. "He's a great kid. A little rough around the edges, but he's smart. A little mouthy, but brilliant…and funny."

"That's exciting," Ms. Wright jumped into the conversation without whispering.

"Lance's smart too. Well, he used to be," my grandmother said. "How did you figure out where they were?"

I held my breath.

"Lance called us about Marco. He got arrested for stealing pharmaceuticals and called me as his one phone call. I took care of things for him and found a place for Marco to stay temporarily. It's Lance's intention for this separation to be temporary. He told me that he refuses to give up parental rights. But there's a ton of hoops he has to jump through first. That day, if it happens, is a long way off."

My mouth dropped open, and my heart seized, as the betrayal hit me like a hammer right in the chest. Dad? He called Mr. Harvey? No. He wouldn't have done that. We were a team.

I stepped out from the hall and glared at them. My grandmother had tears in her eyes. I pretended that didn't bother me. At that point, I hated all of them. Maybe even my father, too. "This is just perfect," I said to Mr. Harvey. "You lied to me. I don't want to be here. I want my dad."

My grandmother's pained expression zeroed right into my heart.

"I haven't lied to you Marco," Mr. Harvey said.

"Yes, you did! You said I could go back to my dad. You said that he'll get help."

"What I said," Mr. Harvey interrupted. "Is that your dad has the choice to get help. He wants you back, Marco. We have to believe he's going to get the help he needs."

"He probably made the hard decision of calling Mr. Harvey because he wants to give you a chance to meet your grandmother,"

Ms. Wright said. "Now he can focus on getting help. This can be a good thing if you remember to keep a stiff upper lip."

"So, let's leave the kid with someone who has never met him. And where've you been for the last twelve years?" I stormed into my bedroom, slamming the door for emphasis.

I didn't want to stay with my grandmother. I needed to get back to Dad. Plain and simple. He had some explaining to do. I paced back and forth, wanting to punch something.

Maybe I could call someone and ask them to take me. Unfortunately, I didn't think there was anyone I could call who would want to take me four hours south. For that matter, who did I know that even had a car?

The despair felt just as powerful as the betrayal. I fell on my bed and stared at the ceiling, willing myself to be tough.

"It's a shame. A shame, shame, shame," I heard my grandmother say. What does that mean? Should I be ashamed to be me? Or, is it a shame what happened to me?

"Hey, kiddo," Mr. Harvey said as he leaned against the now open door.

"Doors are closed for a reason," I said still staring at the ceiling.

"Your room is nice," he responded. I wasn't going to admit to Mr. Harvey that this was the best bed with the best window I'd ever had. He had ruined my life. If the earth opened up and swallowed him whole, I wouldn't even feel bad. I'd probably smile down at him and wave.

“Are you going to be okay?” He walked over to the bed.

“I’ll be fine. I’ve been in worse situations before.” I turned over to face the wall.

“I’ve got to get back, but please give her a chance,” he said, heading out of the bedroom. Stopping, he added, “And I mean both of them. Ms. Wright is a nice person too. And your grandmother is concerned about her son just as much as she’s concerned about you. That’s the conversation you were eavesdropping on. It doesn’t mean she doesn’t want you. It should probably be her who tells you this, but she has tried to reach out to your father several times. Even hired a private investigator to try to find him when you both went on the run. So, give her a chance.”

I’m not sure how long I stared at the wall, but I waited until Mr. Harvey had left, and then some. Boredom hit, and I sat up and grabbed the bag with what little clothes and books I had.

All of it needed to be burned. Even the books Dad gave me were ripped and falling apart. I picked up a thick Stephen King book we bought for a quarter at a church rummage sale and flipped through it. I would read the horror story to Dad on the nights he stayed in. I started reading halfway through and paused to examine the page. The letter “L” had been written on the bottom corner of the page. That was new. I’d read the book enough to know that letter had never been there. I turned the page and spotted the letter “P” in the same spot as the other letter. I turned another page. “H.” The next page had “E.”

Dad had written those letters on every page.

H.E.L.P. H.E.L.P. H.E.L.P. H.E.L.P. H.E.L.P. H.E.L.P. H.E.L.P.

I dropped the book.

Dad was asking for my help. He made sure to give me these books. Why? What was I supposed to do? His words in the police car replayed in my mind. *Keep reading the books, and don't forget I love you.*

The sun had yet to go down, so I knew if I was going to move, it'd have to be now. When I thought the coast would be clear, I went to the window and opened it. The forest still freaked me out, but Dad needed me. He wrote that because he knew I'd find it. I still needed to figure out how I was going to help him, but I wouldn't find the answers hours away from him. I popped the window's screen, grabbed the duffel bag, lugged it over and out the window, and jumped outside.

I escaped situations before. And I was about to do it again.

CHAPTER FOUR

A couple of things I didn't foresee in my first runaway attempt up north. Like the fact that a duffel bag filled with books would weigh about a thousand pounds. Or that it would be a good idea if before jumping out a window I remembered to put on my shoes *first*.

I dragged the bag around a large garden and stopped at the edge of the forest. I toughed it out and walked past some trees. Until a branch snapped. My shout reverberated against the trees and seemed to come back to me. I ran back to the clearing.

If I could deal with Detroit, I should be able to deal with the woods!

"If you're going to run away, you might want to try the road instead of the woods. You only have a few hours of light left. It's pretty dark here at night."

I slowly turned to see my grandmother on the other side of the garden. She knelt by some plants, pulling up weeds. A big hat covered her face, so she had to look up to see me.

I turned back to face the forest. This was the first time I'd been caught so quickly trying to escape. I hoped I wasn't losing my edge.

"Your father ran away when he was seven. We weren't living here at the time. This was our summer cottage. We raised him about two hours south of here. Anyway, he decided to move into the treehouse in our backyard." My grandmother laughed slightly at the memory. "He sneaked inside all day long to make a sandwich or pour a glass of juice. When the sun set, I went to check on him, and I couldn't find him in the treehouse. I was a little worried. I checked the neighbors' house and walked the length of the street. And the whole time do you know where he was?" She didn't wait for me to answer. "Lance was right in his bed snoring away."

I stood somewhat embarrassed at being caught and yet fascinated that she knew my father. Most people who knew my father didn't exactly have warm, fuzzy stories to tell about him.

"As I was saying, if you're going to run away, the road's the best way to take. Especially since I don't have a treehouse."

"I don't want Ms. Wright to find me walking on the road." Why was I telling this woman my strategy?

"She's already gone." My grandmother stood and swiped the dirt from the knees of her overalls. "She left with Mr. Harvey. Said she'd stop by tomorrow when you were more settled."

I stayed quiet and listened. Bizarrely, I liked the sound of my grandmother's voice. I'd read about voices as smooth and sweet as honey, and I used to think that was a bunch of rubbish. But that's how her voice made me feel. Like warm honey streaming down to my toes. But I might be losing my marbles too. This place was doing weird things to me.

"If you take the road now, there's a good chance you'll escape. You might want to put on shoes though. Dirt roads are a killer on bare feet."

She picked up her tools and walked away from me to the edge of her cabin. Over her shoulder, she added, "Or if you're hungry, you can always stick around. Get a warm meal and a good night's sleep. Then escape in the morning when you're feeling more refreshed."

And with that, she rounded the cabin and was out of sight.

My mind knew that her strategy was nothing more than reverse psychology. And it would not work. I even scoffed at the idea. A warm meal? A good night's sleep? Whatever. Dad was asking for my help. That mattered more than a warm meal.

But my stomach grumbled at the very thought. "Traitor," I whispered to it.

The bed *had* been comfortable.

I shook my head back and forth to clear it. "Stay strong," I ordered. "Go find Dad."

If I could find a bus station, steal someone's wallet, I could purchase a one-way ticket to Detroit. Then I'd find out what rehab place he was at and stage a break-out.

Yes, that's what I would do. But I needed my shoes. I left them in the bathroom.

I lifted my duffel bag to the opened bedroom window. Then I reconsidered. It was heavy. I decided to leave it on the ground, I climbed up and into my room. The aroma of whatever she cooked smelled overwhelmingly good.

I stopped and inhaled. I couldn't remember the last time I had a home-cooked meal.

Standing there I also observed how quiet it was in comparison to the noise of the inner-city. No cars sped by, no semis blared their horns, no neighbors in the next room shouted at each other. I didn't even hear a television. I heard an occasional bug rapping against my window, birds chirping, a chainsaw somewhere in the distance whirring, and a stranger in the kitchen clanging pots. That was more distressing than the lack of noise.

I snuck to the bathroom to retrieve my shoes. The bathroom had already been cleaned; my old clothes were gone. Wow. She was fast.

I put on my shoes nearly shaking with the temptation of food. But no matter how tempting the smell or the hunger I felt, that lady—my grandmother—made me nervous.

"You coming?"

I looked up and over my shoulder. My grandmother stood at the end of the hallway near the kitchen holding a steaming bowl of something. "Yeah," my mouth said before my brain could alter the response. I quickly recovered. "But I'll have to go soon."

She nodded seriously. "I understand."

"No offense or anything."

"None taken."

"It's just my dad needs me. I have to make sure he's all right."

The pained look on the lady's face stopped me. Still, she held up the bowl. "Homemade chicken noodle soup. It was Lance's favorite." She turned and went back into the kitchen.

I swallowed my nerves and ventured to the kitchen. She stood at the stove hovering over a pot. I took a big gulp.

As if sensing my presence, she walked to the round kitchen table, removed some clutter, and set down some soup and grilled cheese. "Come take a seat," she said, her back still facing me. "You've got to get some meat on those bones."

Doing as she said, I sat in the only vacant chair and began shoveling the sandwich down my throat.

"Wait a second," she said. "Remember to say grace."

"Say what?" I asked with a mouthful already in my mouth.

She grinned at me as she leaned against the counter. "That's right, mister. Take a second or two and thank the good Lord for your meal."

I blinked in surprise and wondered if I should swallow the mouthful I had already put in my mouth. "Thank you, God, for my meal," I said, then looked at her to make sure that met her approval.

She gave a slight nod. "Now you can dig in."

I remembered to chew with my mouth closed, but I'm sure I looked like a chipmunk with my cheeks puffed out from big wads of sandwich. I pretended not to notice her staring at me. Instead, I focused on the food.

After I started slurping down the chicken noodle soup, my grandmother snapped out of her silent gaze. "When's the last time you ate?"

"This afternoon, thank you very much," I said, a little too snotty.

"Didn't he feed you?" she asked, shame coming out with each word. "Well, just looking at you answers that question." She turned back to the stove, so her face could no longer be seen by me.

I looked down at my soup. I didn't want to talk bad about my dad, but I had to admit, he often forgot I was there, let alone give me food. But I wasn't going to tell my grandmother that. "I didn't ask to be fed," I said. "And if I was hungry, I found food all by myself."

Looking over her shoulder, she asked, "Would you like some more?"

"Yeah," I said, grateful she didn't press the issue.

"Yes, please," she corrected me, but she didn't make me repeat it. She slapped several pieces of cheese onto thick bread, threw the bread together, and slathered it with butter.

"So how come I've never met you?" I asked while waiting for my sandwich. She had already refilled my soup bowl. She stopped and looked at me with her lips pursed together. It made me uncomfortable. "I didn't mean anything by it, I was just wondering, that's all."

She finished flipping the grilled cheese sandwich and placing it on my plate, sliced it in half. The cheese oozed out. I devoured it.

She removed a laundry basket full of towels from the other chair and sat next to me, her lips still tight and pursed. “I don’t know why,” she finally said. “Once Lance left home, he never looked back. He hasn’t been in contact with me these twelve years. I never even received a baby picture of you. I found him when he was living on Seventh Street. I drove down and had some gifts for both of you. You would have maybe been one. He stood on the porch and wouldn’t let me in. Said a few ugly words to me, then slammed the door in my face. I just stood there, holding the gifts. I left them on the porch and drove back. I even sent out Christmas cards and presents until about six or seven years later, they started getting returned. I tried to keep tabs on him, but he didn’t want to be found. I kept believing that one day he’d want to see me.”

I had a grandmother who had tried to send me presents? Why would Dad completely cut her off? “Did you know my mom?”

“She was standing at the front window, holding you, when I came with the presents. She looked very sweet and beautiful, but she never came outside.”

“Maybe you should have kept trying,” I said, thinking about the years of hunger and emotional upheaval I endured when it would have been nice to have a little bit of normal to lean on. Maybe Dad could have received help early on. Maybe my life wouldn’t have been so awful. Upset at her lack of effort, I said, “Maybe things could have turned out differently if you found us and brought us back home.”

“I did the best I could. I was going through my own ordeal,

and it was too much trying to handle a rebellious son." She lifted her head and looked straight at me. "There. That's my answer. It may not be a good one, but it's the only one I got."

We sat in silence.

I wanted to talk back to her. To tell her to shut up and yell at her a little, but I couldn't. It might have been because I felt drained of any emotion after dumping it all on Mr. Harvey. But it was something about her. I didn't want her to have a bad opinion of me especially when I would be leaving soon.

"For the record, I tried several times to meet my grandson," she said quietly. "And I'm so sorry about your mom. I didn't know she had passed away until Mr. Harvey told me."

I glanced up at her, a knot in my throat.

She pushed herself away from the table and walked to the sink. After filling it with suds and water, she furiously scrubbed the dishes. Like cleaning those dishes would clean off the guilt on her conscience.

I couldn't figure out anything else to say, so I changed the subject. "What happened to the window?"

Her gaze turned and fell on the front room window with plastic in its place. "Oh that," she waved her hand like she was swatting a fly. "I'm so embarrassed. Sears was supposed to deliver another one this week, but they haven't yet. Anyway, some nutso kids came onto my property and threw rocks at my window. Most of the rocks just chipped it, but a big, nasty one broke right through it."

"Why would kids throw rocks at your window?"

For a second, her face appeared grim, but then she shook herself and smiled. “Who knows? There have always been kids coming down this road to do crazy stuff. Next time, I’ll catch them. Then they’ll be sorry.”

She left the kitchen not long after that. I could tell already she enjoyed sitting in her brown, overstuffed recliner and reading. She had these romance novels stacked around her, dozens of them, her own fortress of fantasy. “I know you’re thinking of taking off, but I’m serious about waiting until the morning. We’re supposed to get a doozy of a storm tonight. I’d get a good night’s sleep.” She positioned herself there in her chair and opened a book.

A storm? I peeked out the screen door. The sky had grown overcast and the wind had picked up since before the meal. If the trees weren’t creepy enough before, they now swayed as the wind blew through them. They rustled back and forth angrily. Something banged past the cabin and I jumped inside my skin. I turned to see if she noticed. She was already laid back in the chair, feet up, mouth open, and snoring like there’s no tomorrow.

Feeling a bit panicked, I walked back to my room and shut the door. The window still sat propped open with no screen. The wind shoved through the window knocking over the lamp.

I gathered my courage and leaned out the window to drag up my duffel bag. It was too heavy. I debated leaving it there, but rain might leak through it. My books were my only valuable possessions, so I hopped out of the window. The trees with their branches and leaves seemed to inch closer whispering to each other to come eat me.

The stupid bag was too heavy! I kept turning around to watch the trees all the while lifting the bag over my head to get it inside.

That's when I heard the moaning. Low and deep.

With every last bit of strength, I shoved the bag through the window and lifted myself to get inside. Something hit my leg. I yelped in surprise and fear, falling headfirst into the bedroom.

"What's going on?" My grandmother stood at my opened door holding her romance novel like a weapon. Yeah, right, lady. Like that would ward off the forest of ghosts and killers.

My heart beat wildly. "Outside," I said not even trying to hide the panic. "There's something outside."

"Are you sure?"

"Something hit my leg."

She looked down at my leg. "Well, the wind's blowing, Marco. Sometimes debris flies up with a storm like this." Still, she went to the window and looked outside. Then she picked up the screen and snapped it in place. "Stay put tonight, sweetie." She pulled down my window and latched it into place.

"Is the forest haunted?" I asked, wanting to change the subject. Few people called me a term of endearment. None of them meant it. But her words seemed sincere, and that made me uncomfortable.

"Nope. Don't think so. And I own about twenty acres of land, and I've walked every inch of it."

"By yourself?" I asked in amazement.

She looked at me and smiled in amusement. "Yes, by myself. You're just not used to it, is all. So, stay put, and get a good night's sleep."

I didn't need to be told again. Escape would be my objective in the morning.

When she left the room, I picked up the Stephen King book, only to set it back down. I wouldn't be reading that tonight, thank you very much.

Instead, I grabbed the only book Dad had ever given me as a Christmas present. After I opened it (wrapped in the Walmart bag), he said it was the hardest book he ever read in high school. He said it would challenge me, but he knew I could do it. That was last Christmas. I'd read the book—*The Adventures of Huckleberry Finn*—too many times to count. And not just because Dad gave it to me, but because Huck always got himself out of every situation. Mostly by lying and running away, but still.

That's the book I wanted to read tonight.

But as I situated my pillows on the bed and leaned against them, the day's events took their toll. I continued thinking about Dad and where he was and what he was doing. I missed him terribly, so I unzipped the duffel bag, pulled out his Michigan sweatshirt, and pulled it over my head. It needed to be washed, but I didn't care. It smelled like tobacco from his brand of cigarettes. Even with the angry forest and blowing wind and Huck Finn waiting with his adventures, I was comforted by the sweatshirt and dozed into a dreamless sleep.

CHAPTER FIVE

I woke up to the aroma of pancakes and bacon. Then I pinched myself.

It had happened before. Waking up thinking I smelled pancakes, bacon, maybe even some scrambled eggs, only to have reality slap me in the face with nothing. What started as a sweet dream quickly became a nightmare.

Hunger could play some mighty awful tricks on a kid. It was the worse trick of them all. I would wake up seriously drooling over the phantom smells, my stomach gnawing my insides.

But when I woke up this morning, the amazing smell didn't disappear once reality set in. It didn't hit me that I woke up in an old cabin with a grandmother who made me nervous, or that we were surrounded by possessed trees. Nope. The only thing I thought about was following my nose to the food.

"Good morning, sleepyhead," my grandmother said as I walked into the kitchen. She flipped pancakes on a large griddle. "Take a seat, sweetie. Hope you're in the mood for a big breakfast."

I sat in the chair and eyed the food closely. She piled pancakes onto a plate with some bacon and set it before me. "Syrup and butter are on the table."

After I loaded the pancakes with butter and half the syrup in the bottle, I opened my mouth to shovel in the first bite.

"Don't forget to say grace," she said from the stove.

"Thank you, God, for this food," I said quickly. On a whim, I added, "and thank you, Grandma," before devouring my first bite.

She brought me another stack of pancakes and bacon and sat down with her plate. "You're welcome." She paused and raised an eyebrow at the sweatshirt I still wore. "Where'd you get that?"

"This?" I glanced down at the sweatshirt. "It belonged to Dad. I was kind of missing him last night."

"That sweatshirt actually belonged to your grandfather. I always wondered what happened to it." Grandma took a sip of her coffee and changed the subject. "Did you sleep well?"

I had so much food in my mouth I could only nod.

"I purchased the mattress and comforter set as soon as I found out you were coming."

"Where do you sleep?"

She pointed toward the recliner. "Right there. My bedroom is the one across from you, but I use that more for my sewing machine and projects. I've been in a recliner for so long, I don't even have a bed!" She laughed at that.

I felt a little bad that she bought that nice bed for me and now I'd be leaving. "Well, you can always use my bed if you need one."

My grandmother watched me carefully. "You're right," she

said, nodding. "Good thinking. And if you ever want to visit it'll be right here for you."

I stopped eating and sat back. Something in the sound of her voice hit my heart. I felt terrible. "You want me to visit?"

"I would love for you to…*stay*."

I looked down at the floor.

"You could always give it a week," she kept talking. "Think of it as a vacation. A chance to get to know your old Grandma."

I thought about Dad. He needed my help. He wrote the message in one of my favorite books.

Even though I realized my grandmother might be someone I wanted to get to know, I couldn't leave Dad hanging. "I can't," I said. "I don't want Dad to die. He needs me."

My grandmother smiled sadly again. "I'm sorry, Marco. A twelve-year-old boy shouldn't have to take care of his parent. And maybe if I had been a better parent to him, he would have been a better one to you."

She sure knew how to ruin a good breakfast. But I couldn't blame her; well, maybe I did a little. I wanted to change the subject. "Tell my body I'm twelve. It'd be nice to grow."

"A couple of weeks of good nutrition, and you may start growing some inches."

The phone rang. She went into the front bedroom to answer the phone. "Marco, it's for you."

Me?

I walked into the front bedroom and traveled through the maze of her projects.

"Sorry about all the clutter," she whispered. "I like to call it organized chaos."

Taking the phone, I mumbled, "Hello?"

"Hello, Marco. How'd you hold up through the night?" Mr. Harvey asked.

"Fine, I guess." I couldn't tell him about leaving. He wouldn't be too thrilled with that idea. "Have you heard from my dad?"

"He's in rehabilitation, but I can't disclose the location."

"Why not? I'm his son. Don't I deserve to know?"

"He asked me not to tell you. He's worried you might run away."

"But he asked for my help." I felt confused. "Why did he write the word help in my book? Maybe he's lying to you, and he needs me to save him."

"Marco, this is what I know. And I'm going to trust you with the whole truth."

The pancakes threatened to come back up as I squeezed the phone and gritted my teeth.

"Marco? You still there?"

I didn't say anything. But I didn't hang up either.

"Your father called us. Asked us to come and take you away from him. Said that his mother would be an excellent candidate for you to stay with for a while. When he talked to me, it was really hard for me to understand him because he was sobbing so hard. That tells me it wasn't an easy decision for him. It also tells me that you are exactly where your father wants you."

My shoulders had tightened and my jaw clenched as I fought back the hurt. Dad didn't need my help? Then why did he write that? But how could I help if I stayed with my grandma? "What do I do now? This place is freaking me out." I felt bad saying that in front of this nice woman, but I wasn't thinking too rationally.

"Stay put," Mr. Harvey warned. "I'm serious, Marco. Don't try any of your shenanigans. It becomes a police issue if you try to run away."

"Oooh, I'm so scared," I said with attitude.

"I'm serious," he said again in a stern tone. "There are a lot worse places to stay. Trust me. Your grandmother has a clean home and a room just for you. You haven't had it this good, so relax and enjoy it. I'm going to contact the rehabilitation center and see if they will allow you and your father to exchange letters."

I didn't say anything. I didn't like being bossed around, but I liked the idea of writing him letters.

"Now Ms. Wright is going to stop by today to check in on things. Please try to be nice."

"Why? Will she sit on me?"

"Marco," he warned.

"What? It's a legit question. Her fake smile has to wear off sooner or later."

"Just be nice. Got it?"

I ignored him and handed the phone back to my grandmother. I left the room, walked out the front door, and sat on the porch step.

There was no wind, which helped make the woods not as creepy. The air smelled really good. At least it didn't stink like Detroit.

"Want to go for a walk with me?" Grandma stepped past me off the porch. "It's Saturday, so there's no school. Thought I'd show you around a bit."

I eyed the woods warily.

"You won't be alone, I promise. Plus, I always carry my Swiss army knife," she took one out of her pocket.

"I guess," I said, unconvinced it was a good idea.

She led me directly across the front of the clearing to a narrow path that led right into the woods. "This takes us to the lake," she said and started walking down the trail.

I tried not to follow too closely, but I couldn't help looking over my shoulder every few seconds. A bird flapped his wings right over us, and I ducked for cover. "How do you know someone's not camped out back here, ready to jump out and stab you."

"Why would someone do that?"

"Because there are psycho murderers out there, and this is the kind of place they like to hang out."

"Better not be. It's my property, and I will guard it."

I snorted a laugh. "With what? Your Swiss army knife? No

offense, but you're like sixty? They'd probably take you down."

"Hey! I'm only fifty-five, thank you very much. And you've never seen me with a gun. Trust me, I can outshoot anyone in this county and probably in the state."

Once again, I wasn't convinced, but I didn't say anything. If she wanted to live in la-la land, that was her business.

We didn't walk too long before the path opened up into another clearing where I saw a beautiful lake with a small beach.

"This is one of the reasons why we bought this property. Stan, that would be your grandfather, he loved to come out here and fish every day. He did it too up until his death."

"My grandfather died?" I asked quietly. "Does Dad know?"

"Yeah, sweetie, he knows. That's the main reason he left. He didn't know how to handle his grief. We all deal with it in different ways I guess."

"He probably loved him a lot," I said to myself.

"He did," my grandmother agreed. "They were very close. I bet that's why he's kept that sweatshirt all these years."

"I wish I could have met him. I wish I could remember more about my mom too."

Grandma turned and smiled brightly at me. "Stan would have loved having a grandson."

I nodded, wanting to believe her. It would have been cool to have a grandpa. Mr. Harvey was the only guy, other than Dad, who had ever been somewhat nice to me.

"Boy, our family is a mess," I said out loud.

Grandma started laughing. The sight of her made me start to laugh.

"What a nice smile my grandson has. And you know what? No family is perfect. We just got to do the best we can."

I sat on the sand and stared at the water.

"Do you swim?"

I shook my head. "I've never tried. This is the first time I've ever been to a lake."

"You'll have to learn. Swimming's fun. So's fishing." She sat next to me.

"Maybe," I said and shrugged my shoulders. I could only imagine giant fish chomping on my feet while in the water. "Mr. Harvey's sort of right. It's pretty to just sit and watch the water. But don't tell him I said that all right? Wouldn't want him to get too cocky."

Grandma shook her head. "I won't say a word. So, tell me about yourself. We have twelve years of catch-up to do."

"There's not much to tell," I said, suddenly feeling shy. My life consisted of taking care of Dad and finding food. Sometimes school was thrown in the mix. That was about it. Pretty pathetic.

"You like books," she prompted. "What's your favorite kind? Science fiction?"

"I like reading all kinds of books. I'm not too picky. It's kind of hard to get books around where I'm from. When I find one, I read it."

"What's your favorite food?"

"Anything. When you're hungry, you don't care."

Grandma studied me for a few minutes, making me uncomfortable. "I…" she began. "I'm not sure how to fix…this…but I promise you, Marco, I'll never not be a part of your life again." She grabbed my hand and squeezed.

My mouth became dry, and I could barely swallow. I stared at Grandma's hand, wanting desperately to believe her. "Could you take me back to him?" I asked. "Maybe we could sit down and talk to Dad together."

"As soon as the authorities tell us he can have visitors, that's exactly what we can do. But I need you to try to be patient. We'll figure this out, but we need to do it together."

I didn't know what to think or say, so I continued watching the lake. My brain couldn't figure out what to do next. Should I run? Should I stay?

"If I said I'd pay you five dollars, would you jump in?" Grandma pointed at the dock.

"I'd do pretty much anything for money." But my stomach did a nervous flip at the thought.

"Come on," she said, standing up. "Let's put our feet in."

The water was cool against my feet and the sand squished under my toes. I ventured out a bit further, working my way up to my knees.

"Your father and his friends would come down here almost every day in the summers and jump off the dock." Grandma stared off, smiling at the memory.

I tried to imagine Dad with friends. "I wish I could've seen it."

Grandma took me another way back to the house. She identified birds for me, pointed out different types of trees, even showed me a few survival skills like tying a piece of clothing around a branch to show I'm close by. By the time we walked back into the clearing, Ms. Wright stood outside her SUV talking on her cell phone.

"Is it already three o'clock?" Grandma asked.

"What's she doing here?"

"Probably wanted to make sure you're okay. That's what social workers do."

"Yeah, well, I don't like her."

That stopped my grandmother in her tracks. She looked at me curiously, "Why?"

"I don't know. She tries too hard. And she's always fake smiling at me. And, I don't trust her, I guess."

"I understand your reasoning, but at least be respectful. She's worked hard with me so that I would be ready for you. She's a smart cookie."

"She needs to lay off the cookies if you know what I'm saying."

She shook her head. "That was not appropriate. Or nice."

Well, I thought it was at least a *little* funny. But I could tell that me grinning or laughing at my joke wasn't what Grandma wanted.

Ms. Wright met us at the porch and tentatively smiled at me. "How are you doing, Marco?"

I bit my tongue and told myself to be polite. "I'm fine. Why's everybody asking me that all the time?"

Well, I *tried* to be polite.

"A lot of people care about you," she said.

As my grandmother let her into the cabin, I thought about her last statement. You'd think I would be encouraged by it, especially after the nice walk I had with my grandmother. But it only made me feel sad. And the more I thought about it, the more alone I felt.

CHAPTER SIX

After I made small talk with Ms. Wright—who still tried my patience with her over-the-top niceness—I excused myself from the kitchen table.

"Can I watch some T.V.?" I asked my grandmother.

"I don't have one," she said as she handed Ms. Wright a glass of iced tea.

"Say what?"

"I haven't had one in years."

"How do you not have a television? There are more T.V.s in American homes than working toilets."

"Then aren't you glad we at least have a working toilet."

Ms. Wright and Grandma laughed at that one. I scoffed. My joke about the cookies was funnier. "What am I supposed to do?"

"You could walk down the trail to the lake again. It's an easy path. Or you could read. That's always entertaining."

I didn't feel like reading. "I'll go for a walk, I guess. But we've got to talk about this not having a T.V. business."

Outside wasn't near as creepy as it was before my

grandmother took me for a walk. But just the same, I didn't want to walk the trails just yet. Goosebumps sprouted just thinking about walking back into the woods. Instead, I walked to the dirt road and decided to go in the direction Mr. Harvey said were houses.

"I can't believe there's no T.V.," I muttered. "Just dump me in the middle of nowhere with nothing to do and nowhere to go." I slowed as I heard the sounds of the forest. The dirt road was wide enough for maybe a car and a half, but the trees hung over it like a massive green canopy.

The goosebumps came back with a vengeance. I turned to walk back but stopped myself. "You've gone into crack shacks. Stop being afraid!" Mentally pushing myself forward, I kept walking toward the direction of other houses. I reached down and picked up a large stick that had fallen from a tree. It wasn't much, but it would offer some protection.

A noise filled my ears and grew louder, and I looked all around to try to make it out. "It's bugs," I told myself. But if it was, then it was some huge bugs. The buzzing intensified until it rumbled so loud in my ears, I covered my head and prayed for deliverance.

Just then a dirt bike jumped out of the trees and nearly collided with me. The driver quickly turned the wheel, spitting gravel and dirt. Soon another two dirt bikes jumped out of the woods, spitting dirt and gravel in my direction. They revved the engines and sped past me down the road.

And I let out the breath I'd been holding. "Cool," I finally whispered to myself. I wanted one of those dirt bikes.

After following the direction of the dirt bikes, I noticed the trees weren't so thick and a stop sign stood several yards in front of me.

And there next to it holding a yard sale sign stood a girl watching me.

I stopped for a second wondering what to do. Finally, I decided to approach her. She had a tan complexion and dark braided hair with bangs, and she stood an inch or two taller than me. Then again, everyone was taller than me.

"Hey," I said. "What's up?"

I noted her smile and green eyes. "I've never seen anyone come from down that road before. At least not on foot."

"Yeah, well, my Mercedes is still at the dealership."

Her smile widened.

"What about you? Why are you holding a yard sale sign?"

"Because we're having a yard sale." She stuck the sign into the ground to prove her point.

Feeling embarrassed, I tried again. "Which one's your house?" Now that I was at the stop sign, I saw Mr. Harvey had been right. There were several houses on roads leading in at least three directions. I wondered if my grandmother owned her whole road past the stop sign because that was the only spot where there weren't other houses.

The girl pointed directly across from us. "There. With all the junk in the yard."

She pointed at a long trailer with a built-on room in the front. And yes, the entire yard housed a scattering of lawn ornaments, overgrown weeds, and two disassembled cars. A large, multi-colored totem pole stood beside the front door. “That’s cool,” I said pointing to it.

“Thanks. My Dad carved and painted it. We’re Chippewa. Well, he is. My mom’s family is from Ireland or something.”

“Cool,” I said again.

The garage door had been swung open and tables and boxes of junk lined the driveway.

“Can I take a look at what you’re selling?” I might not have any money, but I wanted to hang out with this fascinating girl for a few minutes more.

“Don’t be too excited,” she said with evident boredom. “It’s just a bunch of junk.”

I headed toward her house. When I got there, a disheveled-looking woman, with a cigarette dangling from her mouth, cussed into her cell phone. She waved at me then screeched, “Gertrude!”

“I’m right here,” the girl said in a huff from behind me.

“Go get the rest of the stuff from the backroom, and knock off that attitude before I knock it for you.”

The girl—Gertrude?—looked over at me and rolled her eyes. “I’ll be right back,” she said and went into the garage.

My investigation began. I sorted through boxes of records and CDs and just discovered a box of books when the girl came back outside. She dropped two garbage bags full of clothes at the woman's feet. "Don't expect me to go through all that," Gertrude told her. "And I can't carry the T.V. It's too heavy. Have Ricky do it."

The girl sat on the ground next to me. I'd piled some Louis Lamoure Western novels on my lap. It wasn't my favorite genre, but it would do. "Gertrude?" I asked. "That's the weirdest girl's name I've ever heard. And trust me, I've heard some pretty weird names."

"I know. My dad's brilliant idea. Gertrude is after my grandma." She played with her shoe strings while I kept rifling through some old books. "What's your name?"

"Marco."

"That's kind of weird."

"Yeah, my mom picked it out because it sounded international. That's what my dad told me at any rate. But kids always ask if my last name is Polo."

Gertie started laughing. "I play that game in the water sometimes. Marco! Polo!"

"I've never played that game, but I've never really gone swimming before. It's a water game?"

"You've never gone swimming?"

I didn't answer because I didn't want to talk anymore about my life.

"It's a game where one person is it, and they have to close their eyes in the water and yell out, 'Marco!' The other players run around, splashing the person who's it, and they yell out, 'Polo!' It sounds silly, but it's fun. We'll have to play it sometime."

A loud buzzing sound—much like before—began to pierce the air. The three dirt bikes ripped across their front yard, coming to a halt right near the front door.

I stood and set the books back in the box. "Who are they?" I asked as they jumped off the bikes and took off their helmets.

"My brother, Ricky, and his two idiot friends."

They were older guys, maybe sixteen-ish, and they had already spotted us.

"Ricky, go and get the television for the yard sale," his mother commanded. She puffed on another cigarette.

"Who's Gertie's boyfriend?" he asked his mother while sneering over at me.

Guy looked like a ferret. Beady eyes, pointy nose, weak chin, dark stubble that could pass for whiskers.

"He's none of your business," Gertie responded. "So shut up and go get the television."

Ricky's eyes narrowed. His two cronies warned Gertie to step back. Impressively, she folded her arms across her chest and stood her ground. "Watch your mouth, little sis, or you'll be sorry."

"You can't do anything. Mom's here."

"She ain't always going to be here, so watch your back."

Their mother yelled at them to shut up and ordered Ricky downstairs for the television, to which he muttered, "Yeah, yeah, yeah."

"I hate my brother," she whispered to me. "He acts like he's all that, when he's nothing but a loser."

The other two guys came over to us. They both had oily hair to their shoulders, stubble on their faces, and B.O. stains on their t-shirts. Oh yeah, classy.

Two choices presented themselves to me. I could be a complete smart aleck, or I could leave well enough alone. I decided it would depend on how they handled me. Maybe they came in peace.

"Hey, Gertie, what's a black kid doing on your property."

So, they didn't come in peace.

I went to say something, but the girl grabbed my arm.

"This isn't 1950, Lars, so get a clue."

She pulled me back to the road.

"Where are we going?" I asked confused.

"You're going to wherever you came from," she answered. "Those guys are trouble. And once they mark you, you're doomed. So, get out of here."

"I'm not scared of a bunch of—"

Gertie shushed me. "Seriously. Go away. Now."

"Can I come back later?" I wanted to get to know her. And I still had to check out the rest of the stuff. When I glanced back at the two guys, their attention had already turned to Gertie's mother, who giggled from their attention.

"If you want to risk it, but I wouldn't." With that, she turned and walked back to the yard sale.

Not knowing what else to do, I started back on the dirt road that led to my grandmother's house. I told myself I would see if she could loan me a few dollars, then I would return to the yard sale. It wasn't about the girl. The first girl to be nice to me in the history of *ever*.

About halfway back into the forest of ghosts and killers, I heard the buzzing. My instinct knew the danger. And it knew it was coming in my direction. I picked up speed and ran, but I couldn't outrun the dirt bikes.

They circled me, spitting dirt in my direction. All three of them stopped in front of my path.

Ricky took off his helmet. "You leave my sister alone. Got it?"

I clenched my fists but knew better than to say anything. In my experience, white guys were the biggest bigots of all. Ricky might have been some type of Native American like Gertie, but the other two were as pasty as they come. So, I nodded. He must have been satisfied because he gunned the engine and blasted through the trees, the other two following him.

Ms. Wright's big SUV came down the narrow road. I moved to the side as she slowed down. "Your grandmother's waiting for you," she said with a smile after rolling down the window. I could feel the blast of air conditioning from inside. "I'll check up on you soon. Oh, I almost forgot. Here. Is this the series you were talking about?" She held up two *Starship Enterprise* books from the series.

"Where'd you get them?" I took them from her and ran my

hand over the covers.

"I stopped by the library today. I knew your grandmother didn't have a T.V., and I remembered the book you had in your hand yesterday."

It was the second and third book in the series. I had wanted to read them for a long time. I finally glanced up at her. "Thanks. Does the library have the rest of the series? I think there are a total of twelve books."

"They had a few others. I thought these two books would be enough to get you started until you got your library card." She paused. "If you need anything else, don't hesitate to ask. I'm here for you, Marco."

Her words seemed sincere, so I kept my mouth shut and only nodded.

"Oh, one more thing," she said and turned to rummage through her bag. She pulled out a giant chocolate bar and handed it to me. "When I get stressed out and discouraged, I like a little chocolate."

A quick comeback played on my tongue, but I was touched by the gift. I couldn't remember the last time I had a chocolate candy bar. I opened it up quickly and broke off a piece, shoving it in my mouth. "Thank you," I said, remembering to be polite. "Do you want a piece?"

Her smile grew. "Aren't you sweet? No, hon. I'm on a new diet, but thank you." She waved me goodbye and slowly drove away.

I continued walking back to my grandmother's house with the

two books in one hand, the chocolate in the other, and thinking about dirt bikes and a pretty girl named Gertrude.

CHAPTER SEVEN

Grandma's snores hit my ears as I walked up to her front steps, so I quietly shut the screen door. After I threw out the crumpled wrapper, I stood and looked around, wondering what to do. I headed to my bedroom, fell onto my bed, and opened up the second book to the *Starship Enterprise* series.

Soon the heat got to me. At least in the motels we stayed at, an air conditioner sort of worked. Grandma opened the windows this morning, and fans blasted throughout the cabin, but they blew nothing but hot air.

No television.

No air conditioner.

No Dad.

No friends.

I thought about Gertrude and smiled at her name. If only her stupid brother hadn't got up in my business. I envisioned karate chopping him into little pieces.

As my boredom only increased, I remembered Gertrude—Gertie—said something about selling a television. I jumped up.

"Yes!" My grandmother had to have money somewhere.

My investigation began. I searched in all the usual places for a purse or wallet. After the front room and kitchen came up purseless, I set my sights on the other bedroom. The telephone was in there, maybe she kept her loot in there too.

I tip-toed inside the bedroom across from mine. Old newspapers and magazines had been stacked in piles along the walls. Flipping through some, I noticed dates going back into the 1960s. But why so many? An older-than-the-hills sewing machine sat ready for use with five wicker baskets full of different types of material. A single wooden chair that looked more dilapidated than usable leaned against the sewing machine with some sort of costume sprawled across it.

I studied the costume. Soft orange material rounded itself on wire with two holes at the bottom and one at the top. A black hood attached itself to the top hole with green scraps sewed to an orange oval. I knew it was a pumpkin, but what I didn't know was who it was for. It couldn't have fit me, and I'm short for my age. Plus, faded spots in the costume showed me that it wasn't made yesterday. This costume was old.

"Dad," I whispered aloud, touching the costume material. It had to be my father's costume. I swallowed the lump in my throat and tried to envision him as a young innocent child in a Halloween costume. Halloween. A holiday I hated because I never had a costume. I did enjoy the classroom parties and stealing kids' candy bags the night of trick-or-treating, but Dad never walked me door to door. Feeling myself get upset, I set the costume down.

I reached a long, narrow closet and slid the door open. A large trunk had been shoved in the back corner. I dug into it and found photo albums and a big, lumpy package wrapped in white sheets. The sheets easily unraveled, revealing a wedding dress.

"Marco?"

I froze. Then I heard the footsteps. I wrapped the sheets around the wedding dress and shoved it into the chest as fast as I could.

"Marco?" my grandmother called, walking closer to the bedrooms. I heard my bedroom door open and close. "Are you back yet?"

Having no other choice, I stepped into the closet and slid its door closed. This couldn't be good.

The second bedroom door opened.

"Marco?"

I didn't move, didn't breathe.

The long pause unnerved me. I could feel her eyes penetrating the room and hoped that she didn't have radar vision. Soon she shut the door.

I wasn't caught, but I knew I had to wait to leave the room or my grandma would know something was up. So, I slid open the closet door as quietly as I could and turned the pages of two photo albums I had discovered.

I lost track of time as I became entranced at this other life my father had led before having me. Pictures of Christmases with tons of presents. One showed him grinning with an action figure in his hand. There were pictures of Dad with his friends. Dad at birthday parties. Dad's arms around a cute Labrador puppy. Dad with Grandma eating ice cream cones. Dad with what must have been my grandpa racing go-carts. One picture showed the three of them standing in front of this cabin, only the cabin was new and beautiful.

I closed the second photo album and thought for a long time. What made Dad move to Detroit? What happened that he walked away from this life? This seemingly perfect life? A part of me was angry that he threw it away. A part of me was jealous because I had never experienced most of what was in those pictures. But the biggest part of me wondered if I was the reason. Placing the photo albums back where I found them, I took the few pictures had confiscated and slid them in my back pocket.

I couldn't hear Grandma anywhere in the cabin, so she must have stepped out. If I was going back for the T.V., I'd have to move fast. Not knowing how long I had, I continued searching for hidden places where money could be found. I tip-toed over to the phone, which sat on a desk, and as silently as possible, slid open the desk drawers.

"Jackpot," I whispered, knowing a wicked grin was on my face. Grabbing a thick wallet, I opened it up and counted seventeen dollars. That would have to be enough. Still not hearing anything, I took it as my cue that the coast was clear. I shoved the money in my other pocket, set the wallet back in the drawer, and silently closed the drawer.

Inching the bedroom door open, I looked both ways before leaving the room and shutting the door behind me.

I walked out into the living room, but Grandma's recliner was empty. Then, the front screen door slammed shut.

"Where were you?" she demanded.

"Um," I started. Think, think. "I must have just missed you."

"You were outside?"

"Yes. Yes, I was. I heard you calling me, so I walked in, but you weren't here," I lied.

My grandmother studied me closely. I just stood my ground and tried giving my most innocent smile.

"How about a late lunch?"

Lunch?

The money was burning a hole in my pocket, but I wasn't about to say no to food.

The television could wait until after lunch.

"Sure, let's eat."

CHAPTER EIGHT

Grandma could cook. It might have been fried bologna sandwiches and reheated soup, but still. I almost felt guilty about stealing her money.

"Did you check out the area?" She poured me a second glass of the most perfectly sweetened lemonade in the world.

"Sort of," I said between gulps. "I'm going to go explore for a little while longer." I didn't say anything about the yard sale. More knowledge meant more questions.

She smiled in surprise. "Of course. I'm glad you're feeling more comfortable."

Comfortable enough to steal seventeen dollars.

I mentally shook off the guilt. She wouldn't mind. Especially when she saw the new T.V. I brought back. Maybe I'd even buy her a romance novel as a gift. I saw a few of those in the book boxes.

"Do you want company? I could always go with you."

I set my bowl and plate in the sink. "Nah," I said as nonchalantly as I could. "I've got to toughen up."

"Right," she nodded. "I see you're not taking your duffel bag, so that's a good sign."

She winked at me, but I didn't see the joke. I was staying for the time being because Mr. Harvey didn't leave me a choice. I shrugged, "I guess I'm staying for a little while."

"Sounds like a plan."

I took off before she could ask any more questions. As I jogged back down the dirt road, I hoped the three guys weren't around. I didn't want any hassle. And I could only shut my mouth for so long. Eventually, I would speak up.

On the way back to Gertie's house, I kept checking over my shoulder for the dirt bikes, but I made it there unharmed. They weren't at the house either, so I took that as a good sign.

I didn't see Gertie or her mother, so I searched for the T.V. One day I hoped to have one of those flat-screen televisions. The kind that mounted on the wall. Those were sweet.

"You're back."

I looked up as the screen door slammed shut. My stomach acted all fluttery and nervous. "I wasn't finished shopping."

Gertie glanced around. "All right, but you better make it quick."

I grabbed a romance novel. "For my grandma."

"That crazy lady from down the road?" Her eyes widened. "I heard she's got chopped up body parts buried all over her yard."

"Grandma?" I snorted. "That's funny." Still, I swallowed and paused. I had just met her. Maybe she was a secret ax murderer.

"She lives all alone in that creepy cabin. I don't know," Gertie shrugged, but I had a feeling she did know. She knew a lot more than she was telling. "So, is that all you're going to buy?"

I would have to ask her questions later. "I was just looking for the television that I thought you had for sale."

"It's over there under the tarp." She pointed in the direction of junk I had just snooped through.

Under the tarp sat my television. It wasn't a flat screen, but it seemed sturdy. "Does it work?"

She came over to me and bent down. She strained to pick up the television set, so I grabbed the other side of it and helped place it on a card table. "Thanks." She plugged it into an electrical outlet against the side of the garage.

I turned the dial and static quickly filled the screen. I flipped through channel after channel, but static was my only program selection.

"See?"

"See what?" I was disappointed in finding a television with no working channels.

"It works," she said.

"What do you mean 'it works'? It's all static!"

She grabbed the antenna from the ground, set it on top of the T.V. and fiddled with it, then tried the channels again.

"Ha! See?" I exclaimed like I had just proven a point. "It's still all static."

She raised her nose in indignation. “Fine. Don’t buy it then.”

“Maybe I won’t,” I said, sticking my nose up too.

The dirt bikes sped down the road toward the house. Gertie and I looked at each other in panic. She shoved me down. “Get under the tarp.”

“What? I’m not scared of no white--”

“Just stay in there!”

The bikes stopped. I heard the gravel crunch as they headed over to Gertie.

“Where is he?” Ricky asked.

“I don’t know who you’re talking about.”

“Come on, Gertie,” One of the other guys said. “Where’s the little black kid?”

“You guys are delusional, now leave me alone.”

Then it was quiet. I strained to listen, but there wasn’t anything to listen to. I couldn’t sneak out from under the tarp because any movement would make the old material rustle.

I heard someone shoving someone else.

“Stop it, Ricky!”

“Make me.”

“Knock it off!”

I couldn’t have that. There was a damsel in distress. I threw the tarp off me. “Leave her alone!” I bellowed.

Everyone turned to me simultaneously. I took off toward the road, running as fast as my short legs could carry me. Why couldn’t I be any taller? Or stronger? Or faster?

A hand grabbed my shirt and pulled me down.

“Well, well, well, looks like someone needs to get his hearing checked.” Ricky picked me up off the ground but didn’t set me down. “Check his pockets.”

Now I really kicked. Two of them had to hold me down while one found the seventeen dollars in my pocket. “Give that back!”

Ricky whistled. “We’ll take that. Next time, you’ll think twice before stepping on my lawn.”

“Maybe he’s one of those special kids who can’t comprehend,” Ricky’s friend said with a laugh.

“Wow, that’s hilarious. Where’d you dig that one up?” Suddenly I knew I had to fight. For vindication. For my pride. For Gertie. I threw myself at Ricky, tackling him to the ground. I got a few punches in before his friends grabbed me again.

“Mom!” Gertie yelled. “Ricky’s beating up a customer!”

A screen door opened, and I was dumped onto the ground.

“What’s going on?” Gertie’s mother asked.

“This kid was starting trouble,” Ricky said.

“Whatever, Ricky. He’s just a kid who wants to buy the T.V.”

“What’s wrong with you?” The mother glared at Ricky. “Don’t you have the police on our backs enough?”

Ricky muttered some choice curses before shoving past the junk and into the trailer.

“I told you to stay under the tarp,” Gertie said.

I couldn't believe my ears. "I was defending you!"

Her hands rested on her hips again. "I can take care of myself."

"Fine, whatever," I said as I stomped off. "You and your broken T.V. can go shove it."

I stormed down the driveway vowing never to rescue a girl again and furious for leaving without the T.V. All I got out of that whole situation was some dirt up my nose, empty pockets, and a bruised ego.

"Hey, wait a second!" I heard the girl yelling at me, but I kept marching. "Wait!" she shouted. "You forgot the romance novel."

I sighed and turned around. I couldn't leave empty-handed. Still, I didn't walk toward her. I let her come to me.

"Here," she said, shoving it at me.

Placing it under my arm, I turned and kept walking. "That's the most expensive book I have ever bought."

"You're welcome, you little ingrate!" she said.

That made me stop again. "Tell me about it," I said, facing her. "It stinks when someone doesn't say thank you."

"Okay, okay," she sighed. "Thank you for trying to stick up for me. Even if it was stupid."

"It wasn't stupid," I said. "I knew exactly what I was doing."

"Mmm-hmmm. And what exactly was that?"

Why do girls ask so many questions? Especially when I wasn't prepared with a clever answer? "It took their attention off of you."

We stood watching each other. I didn't leave because I didn't want to be the first one to turn my back. She'd have to turn first.

"By the way," she started. "The T.V. does work, it just doesn't get any channels."

I shook my head. "A working television with no working channels."

Then she smiled. Her teeth were perfectly straight and white, and when she smiled, she had this one dimple. "We hooked up a DVD to it, and the movies worked fine. Plus, we hooked up an Xbox and that worked too."

"So, if I don't have a DVD or an Xbox, then it's pointless to get the T.V.," I argued.

The girl bit her lip and stared at me. "Probably."

"I'll take it, but you got to get the money from your brother."

"No problem, I'll just tell Mom he stole it from the till. Why do you want it anyway if you can't use it?"

Because I'm on a mission, I wanted to tell her. *That having a T.V. was a start.* All I said was, "Let's get the T.V."

I learned fast that televisions, especially the older, boxier kind, weighed a ton. She wheeled out an old toy wagon. I maneuvered the heavy television onto the wagon and pulled the handle. It was still heavy.

"I'll walk with you," she offered. "Then we can take turns pulling it."

Secretly, I was thrilled, but I had to act cool. "Aren't you afraid my grandma might cut you up?"

"I'm a fast runner. She'd never catch me."

I wanted to refuse. I wanted to say I could do it by myself. But those words never came. Instead, I thought of walking down the road with her and said, "Sure."

I lugged it down the driveway and onto the road, sweat trickling all over my body. Gertie tried to make conversation, but I was focused on getting to my grandma's cabin without dying.

"Let's try this," she said, coming over to my other side and grabbing the handle. "We'll both pull together. That ought to lighten it up."

We pulled it down the road at a decent speed and ended up at my grandmother's quicker than I expected.

Finally stopping, I fell to the ground. "That was a chore."

She fell next to me. "I know. How would you have done it, if I hadn't helped?"

"I could've done it," I started.

"Ingrate," she muttered.

That made me laugh.

Gertie smiled.

"You have nice teeth." My stomach dropped to my feet. Did I just say that?? I couldn't think of a way to recover.

"Thanks," she said, giving me a weird look. "I got my braces off right before summer. My mom says my smile cost her a fortune, so I'll tell her the investment paid off. Not that she paid for it. The tribe did." She paused, "What about you? You've got nice straight teeth, too."

"No braces for me," I said. I left out how I couldn't remember if I'd ever even been to a dentist. "But I brush them all the time."

She laughed. "Brushing your teeth doesn't make your teeth straight." Gertie did a quick survey of the place. "Rumor has it the place is haunted with all the murdered souls." She pointed at the broken window.

"The window's supposed to be here any day this week," I said, defending the same place I begged Mr. Harvey not to leave me in. "Besides it's not my grandma's fault that some kids threw rocks at her window."

Gertie became very quiet. Abruptly, she stood up. "I've got to get back before my mother goes nuts." She reached out her hand and helped me up.

"It was nice meeting you," I said.

"Yeah, I'll see you in a couple of days. I'm assuming you'll be on the same bus."

"Are you at the middle school?" I asked. I hoped that she went to the middle school so that I had at least one familiar face.

"I'm in seventh grade," she said.

"Me too! I'll save you a seat on the bus," I offered. I hoped she wouldn't say she didn't want to sit with me.

Instead, she said, "Sure. Until then."

After she left, I dragged the T.V. into the house.

"What the Sam-hill is that?" my grandmother asked, standing

at the door with her book still in her hand.

"It's a television," I said, grinning from ear to ear. "Oh, here. I bought you a novel."

Grandma's mouth dropped open for a second before she stammered, "Th-thank you, I guess. Where did you get all this? You didn't go through someone's garbage, did you?"

"No, I went to a yard sale, and I met a girl. Her name is Gertrude."

Grandma's mouth set in a firm line. "I know who the Blackstone's are. They're not good stock. That boy of hers causes trouble."

I thought of Ricky. "Yeah, but Gertie's nice. She's different from the rest of them."

Grandma helped me carry it to my room. After we got the antenna situated, we turned the knob on the television.

"It's static," she said.

"I know, but if I get a DVD player or a game system, it works fine. Well, that's what Gertie said."

Grandma shook her head and clicked her tongue. "Well, maybe if you get good grades in school, we'll see about getting you one of those things you just said." She went to leave, then turned and asked, "How'd you pay for it?"

The question caught me off guard. "Uh…" I didn't work well under pressure.

"Marco? How'd you pay for it?"

I licked my lips, and my eyes darted around. Why couldn't I think of anything?

She went into the second bedroom, straight to the desk. I closed my eyes and waited for her to realize who her grandson really was. A thief.

CHAPTER NINE

When she came back to my room, she was holding her wallet. “How much was in there?”

“Seventeen dollars.”

“Do you have any left?”

I couldn’t tell her Ricky stole the money because she might not let me see Gertie. I shook my head.

“Seventeen dollars for a broken television?”

“And a romance novel.”

Grandma looked down at her wallet and started chuckling. But when she looked up at me, any smile was gone. “Do not ever, and I mean *ever*, steal from me again. Do you understand?”

I nodded.

“All you have to do is ask. If I have it, I don’t mind helping you out. But we’re not going to start this relationship with you being a thief. Am I clear?”

Her face was stone.

I bit my lip to keep it from trembling. Dad never got mad at me. He’d go into raging drug fits occasionally, but he never got angry when I stole stuff. But Grandma made me feel guilty, and I didn't like it.

"Well, I can just leave," I said, trying to keep my voice from not shaking.

"You would rather leave than just try and be honest?"

"If you're going to yell at me, then I'll just go." I was a man. I could do this. But why did she have to look at me like *that*? "All I did was buy a television!" I cried out. "And I bought you a book. I was trying to be *nice*!"

My breaths came in huffs, and I turned away. I was getting too emotional.

"All I'm asking you to do is be honest. Can you do that, Marco? I'm not angry. I'm not yelling. It's important though that you understand you don't have to steal from me. You're not going to starve here. And if you want something within reason, I will work hard to get it for you. Okay?"

I still faced the wall, but I nodded. I felt bad about taking her money, but I didn't know what to do with the feelings I had.

"All right, well, we best get to work."

I turned around now that I was composed. "Work? On what?"

"You owe me seventeen dollars. Let's go." She left the room. I heard the front door open and close. "I'm *waiting*!" she yelled from outside.

I wondered if she would just come and drag me, so I headed out.

"Over here," she called from the side of the house.

Once there, she walked me to the backyard. Three large gardens took up the majority of space.

"These are all my vegetables," she said, pointing out the rows. "Over there, I've planted strawberries. And see there, the blackberries are ripe and ready to be picked."

Grandma turned, walked to an outdoor shelf, and came back with gloves and a large basket. "You're to pick the blackberries and fill up this basket and there's another one like it on the shelf. Wear gloves or your hands will get scratched. When you're done with that, I'll need your help weeding over there by the cucumbers."

I stood shocked. "Say what?"

"You heard me. Go, earn back my money."

For the next two hours, I picked blackberries—I ate about half of them—then helped Grandma weed and hoe the garden. The blackberry part I didn't mind so much. The weeding part was horrible. Sweat trickled down into my eyes. I even swore under my breath a few times, but Grandma at least pretended not to hear.

I did wonder a time or two if I was going to accidentally dig up a body part. I really hoped not.

Finally, and I mean *f-i-n-a-l-l-y*, she checked her watch and said, "Whew! I'm pooped. Since you've worked off your debt, how about some dinner?"

I dropped the hoe and started walking away.

"Put it back where it belongs."

Sighing, I went back over, picked it up, and took it to one of the shelves. She took off her large hat and swung her arm around my shoulders. “You did good, kid. I’m proud of you. How about I make some blackberry pie for dessert. I even have some whipped cream we can put on top.”

So, I might have been a little mad at her, but I nodded vigorously at the idea of pie.

“Let’s go wash up, then I’ll get started.”

As I dried off from my shower, I could smell something delicious. I opened the door and inhaled deeply. The cabin might have been stuffy, but the pie was making me drool. That wasn’t the only smell. I walked to the front door where Grandma stood grilling chicken drumsticks. Barbeque!

“I’ve never had a barbeque in my life,” I said out loud.

Grandma’s smile turned into a frown, but only for a second. Turning back to the grill, she said, “Go, check on the pie, but don’t leave the oven door open for too long.”

I didn’t really know what to look for, but the pie seemed fine, so I went outside. Now that it was evening, it was cooler outside than in the house. “It seemed okay to me,” I told her. There were aluminum foil bags scattered on the grill. “What’s that for?”

“Those are grilled potatoes with butter soaked in them.”

Heart attack. Might. Just. Have. Heart. Attack.

Grandma grinned. “Well, I’ve figured out the way to get you to do whatever I want. Just cook you some good food.”

"Yep. Eating from dumpsters isn't what it's cracked up to be," I joked.

Grandma paused from flipping the chicken. She didn't look at me, but she started, "You…" then she shook her head. "I can't believe my grandson had to find food in dumpsters."

"Not all the time," I defended. Once again, I made Dad look bad.

"This is ready. Want to eat out here?"

We sat at an old, weathered picnic table whose wood had turned gray and splintered, but I didn't care. The chicken melted in my mouth, the potatoes were laden with melted butter, the corn on the cob couldn't have been sweeter. I didn't say a word the entire meal. Grandma could have told me to slow down, but she let me be.

I knew that most people ate better than me, but I never really imagined this. It made me sad to think Dad couldn't even try to cook for me, or even buy me groceries regularly. It wasn't like Grandma was rich, yet she had food.

"What are you thinking about?" Grandma asked.

I shook my head. I might have been hurt, but I didn't want to get Dad in any more trouble. "Stuff," I muttered.

"Once the pie has cooled, we'll have a nice dessert."

"Can I call Mr. Harvey?" I wiped my hands and mouth on a napkin.

"Of course, you can. Do you know the number?"

"Yeah, he gave it to me."

"You know where the phone is. Go make the call, and I'll take this in the house."

I rose from the picnic table, but stopped and said, "Thanks for dinner, Grandma. That was the best food I've ever had. After I get off the phone, I can help with the dishes."

Her eyes watered and she smiled tightly, nodding at me. "You're most welcome. And don't worry about the dishes."

I went into the second bedroom and dialed Mr. Harvey's phone number.

"Hello?"

"Hey," I said quietly.

"Marco! How's my man doing?"

I couldn't say anything at first. I thought of Grandma's watery eyes and me stealing her money and Dad not feeding me, and I got this big lump in my throat.

"Want to talk about it?" he asked. "Why don't you start with what you did today?"

I coughed then mumbled, "I went to the lake."

"Well, that's cool."

"Yeah, and I went to a yard sale."

"Anything good?"

"I met a girl and bought a T.V."

"Both necessities in life, I dare say."

"I worked in Grandma's garden."

"No way! Did you die?"

He pulled a laugh out of me. "It was torture."

"I bet."

There was a pause before I asked, "How's Dad?"

"He's still in rehab, and from what I hear, he's detoxing."

"How bad is it?"

"They didn't give me too many particulars, but from my knowledge, detoxing takes several days and is not always pleasant. The body is wanting the drug." He paused, then added, "The rehab place he's at is very good. They are taking care of him. I promise."

I should be there with him, but I didn't say those words out loud.

"Marco? It's going to be all right."

I hung up without another word. I stared at the phone, then went into my room. Grandma had opened my window and put a fan in it, making it a lot cooler. I fell onto the bed, grabbed the second book in *The Starship Enterprise,* and picked up where I left off. I needed to get lost in another world so I could stop thinking about my own.

"Will the fan keep you awake?" she asked from the door.

"No, I like it." I didn't look up from the book. I didn't want her to see me upset. Since I was on my belly, she'd have a hard time seeing my emotions.

"How's Mr. Harvey doing?"

"Fine."

"Any news?" she asked with some hesitation.

Now I glanced up. It dawned on me that she might be worried about her son. “Mr. Harvey said Dad’s detoxing. I saw it in a movie once. There’s a lot of sweating, shaking, and screaming.”

Grandma looked thoughtful. “Sometimes Hollywood doesn’t get it right. Detoxing can be tough, but Lance is tougher. He’ll be fine. I know it.” When I didn’t say anything, she said, “Well, I’ll let you know when the pie is ready.”

I set the book aside and took out the pictures from my back pocket that I had confiscated earlier that day. I stared at the picture of my father for a long time. At first, I hadn’t recognized him, he looked so young and vibrant and alive. His blondish brown hair curled around his ears and flopped into his eyes, and his smile filled his whole face. His eyes weren’t dimmed and glassed over from drugs but seemed to be full of mischief like he knew a funny secret and wasn’t telling. The other pictures were of Dad, Grandma, and a kindly-looking man. They were standing next to Mickey Mouse. Dad looked a little younger than me, but in the snapshot, they all seemed so happy.

I placed the pictures inside a book and set it on the bedside table. But now and then, I’d stop reading, and I’d take them out to look at them. Later that evening, after two slices of pie, the pictures ended up on my pillow as I dozed into sleep.

CHAPTER TEN

I woke up Sunday morning with Grandma standing over me. "Let's go fishing."

"Now?" I rubbed my eyes.

"No, tomorrow," Grandma said with a chuckle. "Yes, now. Come on, get up. The fish are biting. It'll be great."

It didn't feel super great, but I stumbled out of bed anyway. After I dressed and splashed some water on my face, I went into the kitchen. "I'm ready, I guess."

Grandma handed me a small glass of orange juice. I downed it and handed it back. She handed me a brown paper bag and a hot cinnamon roll on a napkin. "There are more cinnamon rolls in the bag. I've got a thermos of water. Fishing poles are outside. Follow me."

I took a bit of the cinnamon roll and ended up eating half of it by the time I made it outside to Grandma. "These are good."

"Let's go." She handed me a fishing pole.

The two of us walked the trail to the lake. "Why are we fishing so early?"

"Fish bite best at different times of the day. This is a good time to catch some."

I ate another cinnamon bun before we made it to the lake. I followed Grandma onto the dock, and we walked to its edge.

For the next two hours, Grandma taught me how to fish. It was a little boring while we waited for fish to bite, but eventually, we caught a couple.

"Reel it in!" Grandma said excitedly. "This will make our fourth fish!"

"It feels big," I said, keeping the line as taut as I could while reeling it in.

"Oh, look at that!" Grandma grabbed the line as a big fish dangled from it. "It's a walleye."

"You were right. The fish are biting!"

Grandma helped me unhook it and drop it in the cooler. "We'll have fried fish for lunch. How's that sound?"

As we walked back to the house, Grandma said, "After we fry these up for lunch, what do you think about getting a library card? That way, you can check out the books you want to read."

A library card felt kind of permanent, but it also sounded nice. I liked to check out books from the school library.

Grandma seemed to sense my hesitation. She added, "If you have to leave, I'll return the books for you."

"Promise?"

"Absolutely. I would hate for you to owe thousands of dollars in library fees." She looked back at me and smiled.

"Ha, ha, you're so funny."

"Aren't I though?"

Two hours later, the fish was filleted and fried. "These are delicious," I said, dipping a piece in tartar sauce.

"I try to fish at least once a week. I like living off the land. It makes me feel connected to it."

"I do feel bad for the poor fish." I examined a piece before popping it into my mouth.

"Whatever I catch and keep, I eat. Never kill for the sport of it." She placed her plate in the sink.

I did the same and picked up my book to continue reading. I settled in on the couch.

Grandma leaned against the counter and watched me. "You'll be going to school tomorrow."

"Thanks for the reminder," I muttered. "That's not exactly a mood booster."

Not missing a beat, she said, "Your clothes are ridiculous."

I dropped the book and stared at her in surprise. She grinned and looked a little mischievous. "And you're one to talk. Your t-shirt doesn't even match your shorts." I made sure to put in an emphatic "hmmph!" to prove my point.

"Pink and green match!" Still, she examined her outfit closely. Then, she restated it, "It matches!"

She acted so indignant that I started to laugh. Grandma tried to keep up her sour puss expression, but even she started to chuckle.

"The only reason I said your clothes are ridiculous is because I want to take you to Walmart to get some new duds. I realize it's not a fancy place to shop, but they've got some decent things there. Maybe after the library, we'll see what they have."

That stopped me in my tracks. "Really? You want to take me shopping?"

"I remember what it was like in school," she said. "And I don't want my grandson looking like he doesn't have any taste."

"I have taste," I defended myself. "I just don't have any money."

"All I am saying is since I get money from the state to buy you clothes and stuff, I thought we'd do that this evening."

"You get money for me? I didn't know that." I wondered if Dad ever received money for me. If he did, I never saw a penny of it.

"Would you like some new outfits, maybe new shoes?"

"Would I? Can I get some jeans? Ones that are long enough?" My excitement bubbled over. "Oh! What about Air Jordans? Can I get a pair?" I didn't give Grandma a chance to answer. I jumped up from the couch, placed the book in my room, and put on my shoes.

When I came out, she had changed into a white short-sleeved shirt. I stifled a smile.

"What?" she asked. "I just decided that I wanted to wear a white one."

"At least it matches."

We took her beat-up Chevy hatchback that had more rust than

paint, which proved challenging with its sputtering engine. I could have spent hours in the library, but my excitement at the prospect of new shoes trumped the excitement of books. After checking out a stack of five books, we eventually ended up at Walmart.

Entering the store, I didn't even try to mask my excitement. Grandma had me run to the dressing room with arms full of clothes, then run back to get more. I'd put a t-shirt in the cart, she'd take it back out. She'd put in a sweater, and I would sneak it back out, hiding it underneath stacks of khakis.

We did agree on several items. All in all, I ended up with some jeans (two blue and one black), a pair of khakis, a Detroit Pistons jersey (way cool), another Michigan sweatshirt (Dad's was cool, but the new one was way cooler), one dressy sweater (You never know when you'll need one), and several t-shirts that actually fit me. One said *It's only funny until someone gets hurt, then it's hilarious*, and another one said in big letters, *Genius at Work*. The others were graphic tees, but still pretty sweet. The coolest part of the day happened to be trying on shoes. They weren't Air Jordans, but still! I didn't know shoes could fit this well.

Grandma also bought me a backpack with some pencils, notebooks, and folders.

"Are you ready for school now?" she asked, as we carried the bags to the hatchback.

"Yeah, and I didn't have to steal any of it!"

Grandma's eyes widened. "And that's good."

Waiting for her to unlock the car doors I added, “Thanks, Grandma. I’ve never had a pair of new shoes before.”

She stopped what she was doing and watched me for a minute. “No problem. At least now my grandson won’t look so ridiculous,” she said with a smile and a wink.

“Yeah, too bad we couldn’t pick up some stylin’ clothes for you,” I replied.

“I don’t care what you say,” she said, opening the door. “I am the queen of fashion.”

I placed the bags in the back seat and rolled down my window. The heat poured out, and neither one of us wanted to sit in a sauna. Even in Northern Michigan, September was a miserable, sweat-drenched haze, and Grandma did not have air conditioning in her car.

“Do you have something against air conditioning?”

“Yes, it’s against my religion.”

“Say what?”

“Just kidding.”

“I was going to say that’s some messed up religion.”

“There’s one more place I want to go,” she said, braving the heat and getting in the car.

We drove through town, which took all of about two minutes, and then parked in front of a little barbershop.

“Well, well, well,” I said under my breath, but just loud enough for her to hear.

“What?” Her face was the mask of innocence. “I know these

guys, and I just want to say hello. And, if by some chance, a razor falls on your head, then—" She left it unfinished.

I didn't live in an alternate universe; I needed a haircut in a big way. My hair grows in this huge dome around my head with massive curls. I washed it out yesterday, but there were huge tangles in it.

"It won't be too bad. I'll even buy you dinner when it's all finished."

The bell jingled on the door as we entered. Three older men buzzed away at some hapless souls, while one barber sat in his own barber's chair flipping through a newspaper and waiting for the next customer. He peered at me from over the paper, and as he did a full scan of my hair, his eyes widened in surprise. The older man looked at me for a minute, but mostly he stared at my hair.

Unluckily for him, I was the next customer.

He pulled himself out of the chair and gave a nervous smile. It was more like a grimace.

"What would you like me to do with it?" he asked slowly, touching the top of my hair in bewilderment.

My grandmother piped in, "I want it off, all off."

My gulp did not go unnoticed. "Can I change my mind?"

"It'll be over before you know it," Grandma retorted and pushed me toward the chair.

Piles of my hair began to fall to the floor in huge black clumps. Even my grandmother watched in fascination. Catching her gaze, I told her, "I want a nice dinner for this."

She stayed true to her word. I walked into Big Boy restaurant feeling like a bald shrimp, but I was eating in a sit-down restaurant.

"Don't you feel free?" she asked me. We slid into a booth and flipped open the menus.

"I feel scrawny."

"Well, you look very handsome. It's a big improvement."

"Well, I'm not so hot anymore." I rubbed my hand over my head for the hundredth time. "Did he leave any hair at all?"

"Yes. It's just really short. Trust me, it looks nice. Now I can focus on those gorgeous brown eyes of yours."

I smiled to myself, thinking about Gertie. I wondered if she would think my haircut looked nice.

"What's with the smile?"

I shrugged.

"Come on, tell me. What's got you smiling like that?"

I glanced around and saw people looking over at us. "You promise not to say anything?"

Grandma crossed her heart with her finger.

"It's Gertie."

Now Grandma raised her eyebrows.

"She's really pretty, that's all. That's what I was thinking about."

"I don't know her very well," Grandma said. "But I do think she's cute. She's probably smitten with you."

"Why would say that?"

“Because you’re a good-looking young man, that’s why!”

I rolled my eyes. “You have to say that. You’re my grandmother.”

“I don’t have to say anything.”

The waitress set our food in front of us.

Grandma said grace for both of us. I kept looking around at all the people still watching us.

“Why do I feel everyone’s looking at me?”

“They’re not looking at you. They’re looking at me.”

I wanted to ask why, but something made me stop. It had been too good of a day, and I didn’t want to pry into her past and ruin all of her efforts.

From fishing to going to the library, to buying new clothes and shoes, and then getting my hair cut, it had been a busy day. Even with the traumatic hair chopping episode, no other person had ever spent so much time on me. I dug into my burger feeling pretty close to happy.

CHAPTER ELEVEN

Later that evening, Grandma and I sat in the living room, trying to read. We had a fan blowing right on us, plus the ceiling fan spun on its fastest cycle. All both of them were doing was stirring up a lot of hot air.

"You need an air conditioner," I said, giving up and setting down the third book in *The Starship Enterprise* series.

"Why? There are only about two weeks that I need it. If that. You'll see. This heatwave will be over soon." She stopped reading and used her book as a fan. "You could always go swimming."

"There's a pool?"

"Yeah, nature's pool, otherwise known as a lake."

I made a face. "I can't swim. You know that."

"It's shallow for quite a distance. Your Dad used to run the length of the dock and jump in and the water still wasn't over his head."

"I don't have swim trunks."

"So? Bring me out one of those old pair of pants, and I'll make them work."

I wasn't entirely sold, but she shooed me into my room. I grabbed the ugliest pair with faded knees and worn back pockets and brought it out. I handed them to her.

She already had a pair of scissors in her hand.

Someone knocked at the door, and I ducked. Grandma raised her eyebrows.

"Sorry," I muttered. "A knock at the door was never a good thing."

Her face turned to an unreadable expression.

The knock came again.

The door was already open to let in any outside breeze. That's when I saw Gertie, peering inside.

"Gertrude?"

"Just call me Gertie," she reminded me.

"Want to come in?" I walked over and opened the screen door.

"Your hair."

I rubbed my bald head. "It's gone."

"Yeah, I can see that."

"Glad to see you still got yours."

She laughed.

"So, you want to come in?"

She seemed unsure. "That's all right. I was just coming over to see if you wanted to ride bikes."

I noticed her bike on the ground. My face fell. "I don't have a bike."

"We're getting ready to go swimming," Grandma said, coming up from behind me. "Would you like to come?" Grandma handed me cut-offs.

Gertie acted shy around Grandma. She wrung her hands and kept looking from me to her. "I guess I could go get my bathing suit. You don't mind?" she asked me.

"Why would I mind? I'm about to die from this heat."

"Your head's probably cooler," she teased.

"My head is, but my body's not."

"I have this big inner tube we can jump off," Gertie said, then jumped off the steps to her bike. "I'll be right back. Don't come to get me," she said quickly. "I'll come to you. I don't want my stupid brother doing anything to you like last time."

"I can handle myself," I said, but she had already begun pedaling off.

"What happened before?" Grandma asked.

"Nothing important. Her brother doesn't want me talking to Gertie."

"That whole family is messed up," she said under her breath. "And they call me crazy…"

"Gertie's not messed up." I took the shorts and went into my room to change.

"You're probably right. But I don't want you around those boys. They are pranksters. They're the ones who broke the window."

I stepped out of the room in the cut-offs. "Why does that not surprise me?"

"I think we have an inner tube in the shed from years ago. Let's see if it's any good."

Grandma headed outside, and I followed. She had a large, oversized shed that housed a ton of gardening tools and supplies. She pulled a chest out from under one of the tables and opened it up. But my attention was diverted to the looming rifle that hung on hooks on the farthest wall. I didn't like guns. Hearing gunshots in Detroit was a daily sound. Almost like background noise. Until it came too close. One time in the fourth grade, a bullet shot through the glass of our classroom, shattering the window and scaring all of us. "Drop down!" the teacher had screamed. Luckily, there were no more shots, and the bullet flew past our heads.

"Look at this!" Grandma said with a whistle. "We've hit the jackpot! Marco?" She must have followed my gaze. "Oh, don't worry. It's not loaded."

"Do you use it?"

"I can. Normally, I'll do a little deer hunting in November, or I'll have to take care of a pest that gets onto the property. You'll have to go hunting with me."

"Deer hunting? Why would you do that? And what kind of pests?"

"Because venison is good. And because it helps control the deer population. And lots of pests. Skunks, squirrels, field mice, possums, raccoons, deer, bear…"

"All those animals are around here?" Maybe there was a good reason to be afraid of the forest.

"Where do you think those animals live?" She stood, holding two deflated pieces of plastic.

"Not in Detroit."

"I found a raft *and* an inner tube. Come on, let's go inflate them." She handed me the two deflated items, then reached down, grabbed some kind of device, and left the shed.

Once outside I noticed she locked the shed with a key that hung around her neck. That's when Gertie came pedaling up to us with an inner tube hanging diagonally around her. "If I wasn't hot before, I am now," she said and set her bike down.

I was wary about going to the lake now that it had officially been revealed to me that creatures lurked behind the trees. Sure, I knew animals had to live somewhere, but the idea of a bear watching me from the other side of a bush was not reassuring. But neither Grandma nor Gertie acted worried or bothered, and I wasn't about to act unmanly. If they could handle it, so could I!

Grandma handed me the inflated inner tube. "Check that out," she said, smiling widely. "Good as new." She wiped the sweat from her brow.

"Thank you," I told her. "Are you coming with us?"

"I wasn't going to, but a dip in the lake does sound nice. Why don't you two go on ahead, and I'll catch up in a little bit."

Gertie still had her tube around her, so I placed Grandma's

inner tube around me and headed in the direction of the trail. I hoped I remembered how to get there. I wanted to impress Gertie. But I had to run to keep up with her, so chances are, she already knew where it was.

We entered the trail area, and I swallowed back my fear. "You ready for school tomorrow?"

"It's school. I deal with it. What about you?"

I didn't answer. Just thinking about school had me breaking out in goosebumps.

"I wouldn't be nervous," she said, rightly understanding my silence. "The kids can be idiots, but they're not vicious."

"Yeah, but you're probably the same skin color as they are. If they treat me the way your brother treats me, then it's going to suck. Big time."

"First of all, I'm not the same color. Not exactly. Not only that, but my brother hates me, and he takes it out on anyone who tries to get close to me. I never bring friends over. And it's not just because I'm embarrassed by all the junk we have everywhere."

"Why does he hate you?"

"Because I'm the reason his dad's in jail."

We reached the clearing that opened up to the beach. I glanced behind me, surprised we walked the trail so quickly. Gertie had helped me keep my mind off scary things. "His dad's in jail?" I asked. "What'd you do to put him there?"

Gertie brought up her arm and let her hand cover her eyes like a visor. She didn't look at me, only stared at the water. "Let's go swimming," she finally said.

I didn't push. I knew what it was like to keep secrets. "You first."

Now she turned to me. "You're not afraid of the water, are you?"

"No, but I can't swim. It's not like I ever had the opportunity to swim before."

"This lake is super shallow. Only the middle is deep. You'll be fine." She dropped her inner tube and ran into the water before diving in. When she popped up, the water was only at her waist. "See? It's shallow!"

I dropped the inner tube walked into the water and headed toward her. The water was cool around my legs.

Gertie ran at me and splashed me.

"Ha, ha, ha," I said and kicked up a spray of water at her.

We ran after each other, trying to douse the other in a fountain of water. Pretty soon, I was out far enough, that the water hit past my waist.

"Watch this," Gertie said. She plugged her nose and fell back into the water. She didn't come up at first. I put my nose as close to the surface of the water as I could. She waved at me from below.

When she came up, I was impressed. "You were down there a long time."

"I counted a minute. Can you beat that?"

"You want me to put my head underwater?" I looked at her like she was some kind of crazy.

"You won't drown. It's too shallow. Besides, I'd pull you back up. A tough guy like you can easily handle this."

And there were the words. I wanted to tell her it was an act. I didn't think I was so tough. But another part of me wanted to prove to her that she was right. That I could be tough. I followed her lead and plugged my nose. Then, taking a deep breath, I closed my eyes and fell back into the water.

I didn't last long. I kept wondering if I opened my eyes if a big fish would be staring back at me. But when I pushed myself back up, breaking the surface of the water, I couldn't stop grinning. "Yeah, baby!"

"That was fifteen seconds."

"You counted slow."

Gertie and I stayed in the water the entire evening. Grandma had already come, swam, and left, and we still stuck around, unwilling to leave.

"I never imagined that I would leave Detroit and end up living in the woods," I mused out loud.

The two of us were chilling on top of the inner tubes, floating near the dock.

"You've never been up here?"

I stared up at the sky, already dimming from the soon-to-be setting sun. I could see the faint outline of the moon. What would I have been doing right now if I was still in Detroit? I'd probably be in that nasty trailer, trying to break into one of their cabinets for some food. I never would have imagined myself floating on top of a lake with a bunch of crickets making noise around me, a new friend floating beside me, and feeling so relaxed I could have fallen asleep. "I've never left Detroit until two days ago."

"Will you tell me about where you came from?" she asked. "You just kind of showed up."

"I'm visiting my grandma. Dad wanted me to come up north because…" I didn't want to say the truth. It made my stomach twist in knots. Instead, I said, "Because we're so busy all the time with Dad working and stuff."

"Yeah? What's he do?"

"He's…a pilot. Travels all over the world. He decided it would be easier to live with Grandma for a while until they can give him a better flight schedule."

"Wow," Gertie said. She had turned her head to look at me, her eyes big. "That would be so cool."

"Yeah, he buys me souvenirs and stuff."

"What's the coolest souvenir he's ever bought you?"

"I don't know. There's been a lot."

"Do you have a mom?"

"She died. I think. I don't know much about her." There. At least *THAT* was the truth.

"I'm sorry. That sucks you don't have a mom."

"It's been me and Dad."

"Now that I've met your grandma, she doesn't seem that crazy. And if your dad is letting you stay, you must be safe enough."

Now I looked over at Gertie. "My Grandma's not crazy. Stop saying that."

"I'm not saying that. I'm saying that she doesn't act the way everyone says she acts."

"Who's everyone?"

"Everyone." Gertie motioned with her hand. "I guess a long time ago she was running from house to house, no shoes on, her hair a mess, wanting to know who took her baby. They had to call the cops on her. That's what my mom says, at any rate. But she's known to exaggerate."

I didn't say anything because I was thinking about Grandma running from house to house, wondering where Dad was. I felt bad for Grandma. Why couldn't Dad have tried to talk to her? Why'd he just up and leave?

Suddenly, I was done swimming. I flipped over onto my belly and used my arms to paddle to the shore.

"Hey," Gertie said, catching up. "Are you okay? I didn't mean to make you upset."

"I'm fine, just tired. You ready to head back?"

"Yeah, I guess," she said with a shrug, trudging out of the water. "I wish I could float on the inner tube all night. That way I wouldn't have to go home."

I pulled the tube out of the water and grabbed the towel Grandma left for me. "You can talk to me about your family if you want."

"No," she said, wrapping her towel around herself and slipping into her flip-flops. "I can't. Come on. It'll be dark soon." She took her inner tube and started toward the trees.

Later that night, after I showered and got ready for bed, I realized I hadn't had that much fun for as long as I could remember. The whole day seemed to be taken from a fairy tale.

And I felt guilty. Was I already forgetting about Dad?

I walked to the living room where Grandma sat, reading a novel. She glanced up and raised her eyebrows. "Everything all right?"

I didn't say anything. All I could do was press my lips together to keep the guilt from bubbling out of my body.

She pushed herself into an upright position. "Marco? What's wrong?"

Finally, I blurted, "Can I call Mr. Harvey again? I know I talked to him the other day, but maybe he heard something, and he got busy and forgot to call." That would help. I could check on Dad.

"Of course." She glanced at her watch. "It's nearly ten, but he said we could call anytime."

I itched with impatience as Grandma pushed through the clutter of the front bedroom to the phone. "I've been thinking about getting one of those cellular phones," she muttered to herself.

Grandma handed me the phone that was already ringing through. I bit the inside of my cheek, hoping he'd pick up the phone.

"Hello?"

"Mr. Harvey? It's Marco."

"Hi, Marco. What's up?"

"How's my dad? Have you heard from him?"

"Not yet, but I found out that you can write letters back and forth. I think it'd be a good idea for you to write him."

"Yes, I can do that." I looked at Grandma and smiled. I told her, "I can write letters to Dad."

She gave me two thumbs up.

"Hey," Mr. Harvey said brightly. "How's it been up north? Your Grandmother told me that you all went shopping today. Did you get some new duds?"

"Duds? Who calls them duds?"

"Clothes. Shoes, pants, shirts."

"Yeah, it was kind of cool. She made me get my hair cut."

"Are you ready for school tomorrow?" Mr. Harvey asked.

"No, not really."

"You'll be fine. Show them how brilliant you are."

"Will you call me the minute you hear anything about Dad?" I asked, changing the subject back to him. "I don't care if it's at three in the morning."

"Yes, Marco, of course."

I hung up and went to my room, shutting the door. I took the pictures I had found of my dad and sat on the bed, staring at them for a long time. My imagination worked overtime. I envisioned him shaking horribly from the drug detox. It didn't seem right that I was having such a good time. How could I be laughing and shopping and making friends when Dad could be in agony?

I didn't want to think about how far apart we were. I didn't want to think about how I got here in the first place. I didn't want to think about him needing help and having no one there.

I didn't want to think about that. But I did anyway. I thought about it all well into the night.

CHAPTER TWELVE

"Rise and shine, sleepyhead," Grandma sang.

I rubbed my eyes, checked my alarm clock, and rested my head back on the pillow. "Five more minutes."

"Get up before your eggs and bacon turn cold." She yanked the covers.

"Hey! That's not very nice," I grumbled and curled myself into a ball. The last time I looked at the clock had been 2 a.m. and then I had nightmares about Dad that kept waking me up. And now I paid for it.

"Don't make me pour water on you," she said.

Admitting defeat, I stretched and trudged out of the bedroom. The smell of Grandma's cooking drew me to the kitchen.

I guzzled the orange juice and dug into my toast. "Mmmm. Do I get this every morning?"

"Don't count on it," she said. "Today is a big day. Tomorrow, you'll get cereal."

Even with my grandmother's prodding, I had to hurry the rest of the morning to catch the bus. I threw on a new t-shirt, a pair of new jeans, and then laced up my new shoes. Grandma stood waiting with a lunch bag in hand. “Here,” she said, passing it to me. I grabbed it and ran out the door.

I climbed onto the bus and breathed a sigh of relief. No one else had been picked up. The driver, a heavyset lady with ten earrings and a nose stud, gave me a peculiar stare. “Good morning to you too,” I said as I made my way to the back.

I took a seat in the back and glanced at my lunch bag. “Wow, there’s a first time for everything,” I thought out loud. Peeking inside, I saw a thermos, sandwich, chips, some cookies, and an apple. The school lunch had always been my one constant meal of the day. Sometimes I would look around and watch kids eat lunch from their lunchboxes and wish that Dad would do the same for me.

That made me think about last night, and the nightmares, so I closed the lunch bag and looked out the window. Normally, there was a way to check up on Dad. I knew where he would go when we had to hide. That didn’t do me any good with Dad stuck in rehab.

The bus stopped, and I looked up to see Gertie climb aboard. We both smiled. I shimmied over as she sat beside me. Thoughts of yesterday at the lake came flooding back.

Gertie picked up where we left off. In a few minutes, we were joking and arguing over who paddled the fastest while on the inner tubes. Then she drew a map of the school and showed me where everything would be. She also did a running tally on all of the teachers. She listed teachers to avoid, cranky teachers, teachers who let kids do whatever they wanted, and those teachers who assigned too much homework.

I didn't see the point in instructing me on teachers when I didn't get to pick which ones to have. I said this to Gertie, but she just shrugged and said that ignorance isn't always bliss.

As the bus filled up, Gertie would stop and greet a couple of girls, but then she'd turn to me and we'd start talking again. A couple of kids glanced over my way, but more out of curiosity than anything else. When the bus pulled in front of the school, I was surprised at how packed the bus had become.

"Well, here goes," I whispered, as everyone piled off.

"Relax," Gertie whispered back. "It'll be a piece of cake."

She walked with me to the office, which just happened to be on the other side of the building. The crowd of kids pushed and pulled their way through the doors and halls, and I had to push and pull with them. I couldn't help noticing the sea of white faces. Back in Detroit, it was the complete opposite, and I was one of the majority. Not here. Not in this town.

Once we reached the office, Gertie said she had to leave. "Maybe I'll see you in class. If not, then we can sit together at lunch."

I wanted to hug her. Somehow the day seemed more bearable just knowing I had at least one friend.

As the crowd separated us, a student shoved me out of the way. "Move it," he said. His hair covered his eyes and fell to his shoulders. The other boys he walked with snickered and moved on.

"Sorry," I muttered, but he didn't hear. Feeling jostled, I opened the office door and pushed myself into the crowded room. The small quarters were crammed full of students, parents, teachers, and secretaries all running around with last-minute things to finish.

When I approached the counter, I asked the frazzled secretary for my schedule. Her face sagged with wrinkles, and sunspots speckled her diminishing hairline, making her appear meaner than Shakeed's rottweiler at the last motel I stayed at.

Without saying a word, she pointed toward an office door that held a sign, George Harrington, School Counselor. Then, she screeched, "Next!" in a high-pitched, squeaky voice that sent shivers down my spine. Yikes. What planet did that one come from?

Mr. Harrington was no better. When I walked inside his office, he acted surprised to see me there. "Can I pick up my schedule?"

His brows creased together in apparent irritation. "Shut the door," he commanded. His long arms folded across his broad chest resting comfortably on his paunch of a belly. His bald scalp shone from the ceiling's bright light, and his outdated suit pulled against his heavy body.

After a couple of minutes of studying me, he asked, "Where are you from?"

"Detroit."

He nodded his head like he knew the answer. If he knew the answer, then why'd he ask the question?

"I've met with your grandmother and your social worker, so

I'm aware of the situation." He looked at me and raised his eyebrows. "We don't want trouble, understand? Keep your nose clean."

What was the deal with school counselors? Did they take a class on how to be jerks? I hoped they wouldn't make me see him regularly. I'd much rather chew on broken glass.

"We don't deal with shenanigans, so think twice before stirring up trouble." He raised his eyebrows and stared at me with what I assumed was an intimidation tactic.

I resisted the urge to roll my eyes. I wanted to say something like, "Is this the welcome wagon? Because if it is, you suck at it," but I knew better than that. Instead, I said, "I won't be any trouble."

He seemed content enough with my answer, so he pulled my schedule from his computer. "You have Mr. Oliver for the first hour. The gym's just down the hall and to the right. Room numbers are outside the doors."

Not knowing what else to say, I grabbed my schedule and nodded at him. Once outside the office I examined it and groaned. Gym, Language Arts, Math, Spanish, Science, and Geography. It didn't matter how many schools I'd been in, somehow they all managed to be the same. And somehow, I always got stuck with gym first. At least they didn't stick me in choir. Every school I attended so far had stuck me in that awful class. What made them think I'd want to be with a bunch of girls who wanted to be singers but sang so flat even the tires lost air?

I endured first and second hours at snail speed. Mr. Oliver, who's also the basketball coach, stood tall with large arm muscles. The girls giggled among themselves and batted their lashes at him. He reminded me of one of the smarmy men that always showed up to give Dad drugs (You'd be surprised how normal those people look), so I didn't like him right from the get-go. Thankfully, he only had me watch badminton today.

Second hour I met Mrs. Watson who had a nice smile but liked to clap her hands a lot. I think she did it to get our attention, but it was only more distracting.

My third-hour teacher looked young enough to be one of these kids' older sisters. She told me how glad she was that I was in her class, then handed me a glitter pencil and a calculator as a welcome present.

I described my teachers to Gertie at lunch.

"What's the math teacher's name?" she asked.

"Miss Dantsy."

"The other two I've had before, but not her. She must be a new teacher," Gertie commented. We carried our lunches to a vacant corner table and sat down.

"She looks like she just graduated high school," I said between bites of my sandwich.

"Yeah, well my math teacher smells like dirty laundry and has nose hairs that stick out."

"Mr. Oliver, the gym teacher, seems like an idiot."

"No, he's cute!"

I stared at her in mock horror. "Please stop. You're killing me." I began again, "I also have Martinez for Spanish, and I've got Mrs. McKenzie for science and Mr. Fitzgerald for Geography. I haven't had the last two classes yet."

Just then, the same kid who had shoved me outside the office walked over to our table. Neither one of us wanted to look up. Deciding to appear tough, I stared him square in the eyes. He flipped his long hair, but he was only looking at Gertie.

"Hey, Gertie," he said. I glanced over at Gertie, but she still had her head down.

When she looked up at him, her sharp gaze could have cut ice. "What do you want?"

"I was only coming over here to tell you that Ray still has the hots for you." He pointed in the direction of Ray. I immediately spotted him because he was making kissing motions at Gertie.

"Leave me alone," she muttered.

"Well, if you change your mind, just let Ray know. He's always had a thing for trailer trash." He walked back to his table.

Gertie's face hardened. "He hasn't liked me since last year when Ray was my science partner. Ray asked me to be his girl, but Tim wasn't having any of that."

"No way," I said, with a mouthful of chips.

"Yep, Ray turned into a big jerk and started being rude. So, I told him to hit the road. Ever since then, they've tried to start trouble."

The laughter from the other side of the cafeteria seemed to

echo in my ears. Before better judgment had the chance to make an argument, I was up and out of my seat.

"Marco, what are you doing?" Gertie called after me, but I was already on my way.

I set my face and marched to them. I pretended to be Arnold Schwarzenegger ready for combat. I'd watched the late-night movie of Terminator. I practiced his stone-cold face many times.

"You're in the wrong part of the cafeteria," Ray said. "Losers sit over there."

All the guys laughed and so did I. Then I stopped, and put my hardened face in place again. "Not funny."

The four guys at the table stood up. I noticed a teacher on his way over, so I talked fast. "You can all get up if you want to, but I'll be quick. The next time you choose me or my friend to pick on will be the time my fist lands in your face."

"How old are you?" Tim asked. "Like ten? I could squash you like a mosquito."

The guys jeered, then went to sit down. Wanting them to take me seriously, I grabbed the chair of one of them, and before he could sit down, pulled it out from under him. He landed flat on his butt.

The whole cafeteria silenced. Then the giggling started. Soon, everyone was laughing. I turned around shocked to see the scene had held everyone's attention. Including the teacher.

"Do you think you're a wise guy?" the teacher asked, looking right at me.

"No, sir," I said straight-faced. "It was…an accident. I didn't know he was going to sit down."

The teacher, who had a thick mustache and thinning hair, turned his attention to the boys. "Tim, you going to cause trouble with the new student?"

Tim feigned complete innocence. "This kid just comes over and starts something, and you're gonna blame me? Whatever." He flipped his hair for emphasis.

Right then I would have loved a pair of scissors to cut his obnoxious long hair right off his forehead. But I had to focus on the teacher.

"Another incident and you're going to Mrs. Snider's office. Got that?" He looked at me and the table of bullies. We all murmured in agreement. He acted satisfied and walked away.

Tim whispered, "You just waged war against the wrong guy."

"Bring it on," I whispered back, even though I had to stand straight and on my toes to almost, sort of, reach his eye-level. I strolled over to my seat with my head high. Arnold Marco Schwarzenegger cowers to no one. I thought Gertie would be smiling, but nope. Her hands covered her face.

"You shouldn't have done that." We left the cafeteria and headed down the hall.

"You know, you really should start thanking me when I come to your rescue," I said.

"Not when you just made the worst enemy you could make,"

she hissed. "You may have a big mouth and a whole lot of attitude, but you have puny muscles and Tim will annihilate you!"

"Hey!" I said insulted. "I do not have puny muscles! And for what I lack in height, I gain in skill."

The bell rang, and we had to part ways. Some kids would glance at me in the halls, or steal a look in my direction during my science and geography classes, but no one else tried to start anything.

During the bus ride home, Gertie shared with the other kids what happened at lunch. They were all riveted and eyed me with curiosity. When it stopped at Gertie's house, she threw her backpack around her shoulder and said to me, "Well, I'll say one thing."

"What's that?"

"You're definitely going to make this year interesting."

I kept up the Arnold act until I stepped into Grandma's cabin. Once there, and my guard down, I took off my shoes and curled up on the couch. Grandma set her book down and gazed in my direction.

"One of those kinds of days, huh?"

I nodded. "Do you have any workout equipment?"

"Does this body look like it works out?" Grandma asked another question. "Why do you want workout equipment?"

I wasn't about to tell her what Gertie said about me and my puny muscles.

"You could always do push-ups and sit-ups. That's a good place to start, and they require no equipment." She stood and went into the kitchen. "I'm going to get started on dinner. Why don't you relax and start your workout regimen in the morning?"

But I didn't answer. I was already dozing off.

CHAPTER THIRTEEN

The end of the second school week finally came, but I was in a nasty mood. Acting like Schwarzenegger every day took a lot of work, not to mention I had started my push-up and sit-up regimen. I could only do nine push-ups and seventeen sit-ups, and my puny muscles had been complaining about how sore they were.

"Earth to Marco."

I heard Gertie and peeked open one eye. "Hmm?"

"We're almost home. Time to wake up."

"Thanks. It's been a killer week."

"Yeah, I get it. It's tiring being so tough." She elbowed me and grinned.

"Exactly." I was too tired to come up with a witty comeback. "At least I got those punks off our back." I would catch Tim glancing back at me in math class, or he and his buddies would look at me and whisper at lunch, but no one had started anything. But that didn't make me feel good. It felt like I had lit the fuse to the stick of dynamite and was waiting for it to explode. Something was going on with them, and whether I admitted it or not, it made me nervous.

“I know. That’s been nice. Maybe you don’t have puny muscles after all.”

“Ha, ha.”

“It’s weird. Tim and I were friends back in elementary school. He used to be nice. Then a couple of years ago, I don’t know, he got this attitude. I think maybe his parents divorced. Anyway, all the girls have crushes on him. They love his long hair.” She flipped hers, mimicking Tim.

“Oh yeah? *All* the girls?”

“Well, not all. Not me. Especially not me.”

“And you said Ray was your boyfriend last year?”

“For a little while. Until Tim sabotaged us. The jerk.”

“Maybe he likes you.”

“Shut up.” She rolled her eyes.

“No, I’m serious. Maybe he was jealous of you and Ray.”

“Or maybe he’s a jerk and likes to do jerky things.”

“Well, maybe that too.”

The bus pulled up to Gertie’s. “Want to hang out this weekend? I can ride my bike over.”

I perked up. “Yeah, or I can come over to your place. I want to watch T.V. somewhere.”

Gertie crinkled her nose. “I don’t want you at my house. It’s embarrassing…”

The bus driver shouted, “Gertrude! Move it!”

“We’ll talk later,” she said and got off the bus.

I watched Gertie maneuver through the mounds of junk in her yard to the trailer's door. She reminded me of one of those flowers growing in the middle of a junkyard. She didn't fit the picture of the rest of her family. For one thing, she was always super clean. Her clothes smelled like laundry detergent, and her hair always smelled like really pretty girly shampoo. She had told me at one point that she refused to have a dirty house and cleaned and vacuumed the whole thing herself. Besides the bedrooms. She said she wouldn't touch anyone else's bedroom.

If there'd been anything good about this week, it had been her. It wouldn't surprise me at all if Tim crushed on her.

As soon as I stepped off the bus and onto our yard, I noticed three things: the brand-new window that had been installed, Ms. Wright's big SUV, and Mr. Harvey's Taurus pulled off to the side. I wondered if Dad had come with him, and the thought had me sprinting to the door.

Maybe he missed me so badly, he dumped the drugs in record time. I threw open the screen door and scanned the room. But only Mr. Harvey and Ms. Wright sat on Grandma's lumpy couch. I let the screen door slam shut.

"It's just you," I said, not hiding my disappointment.

"Hey, Marco. Nice to see you too" Mr. Harvey gave a wry smile. "You are Marco, right? The kid I'm looking for had long, curly hair." He used his hands to make a dome around his head.

"Very funny. By the way, nice tie. Was the clown store

offering discounts?"

Grandma gasped. "Marco! Use your manners!"

But Mr. Harvey laughed. "My aunt and uncle work for the circus, and they sent it to me as a gift. I left the red nose at home."

I tried not to smile, but it was hard. Mr. Harvey had pretty decent comebacks. "So, what brings you up to Hicksville? Checking up on me?"

Mr. Harvey walked over to me and patted me on the back. "I've heard good reports about you, that's all. And I missed you. Thought I'd come to say hello. Ms. Wright wanted to say hi, too."

"So, you're coming to check up on me."

"How's school going?" Ms. Wright asked with her smile up to her ears.

"It's school. Nothing special."

"He made a friend." Grandma handed me a lemonade.

"Nice," Ms. Wright said.

Why was she acting all surprised? I had already talked about Gertie to her just two nights ago.

Mr. Harvey sat back down, so I followed him and sat on the arm of the couch.

I kept staring at his crazy tie. "Seriously, Mr. Harvey, you have got to get yourself some better ties. Why is it super wide on the bottom?"

"That's the style."

"No. No, it's not."

“Marco thinks he knows fashion,” Grandma said. “But I’ve had to teach him a thing or two.”

The adults laughed.

“Grandma, you’re wearing overalls.”

Now they really laughed.

They stayed while Grandma made dinner. Ms. Wright grilled me with at least another hundred questions, and I tried to be polite. Finally, I had enough. “No more questions, Ms. Wright, okay? I’m tired.”

“Look at you.” Mr. Harvey interrupted me from saying anything more. “It’s been about two weeks, and your face is fuller. Don’t you think?” He turned to Ms. Wright.

“I’m going to buff up.” I showcased what little muscles I had.

Mr. Harvey acted impressed.

“I can already do nine push-ups.” I felt the need to show him, so I dropped down and pushed out ten push-ups before falling on the floor.

Once Ms. Wright had left, Mr. Harvey asked Grandma if I could take him for a walk.

Grandma looked at him knowingly. “Of course. Dinner will be ready in about ten minutes.”

As soon as we were outside, he said, “Why don’t you show me the lake?”

I stopped at the edge of the trail. I remembered how to get there, but the trees and I were not quite best friends yet. “How about walking on the road?"

"That sounds good, too."

We walked a little while before Mr. Harvey said, "I have to tell you something."

"Okay. Spit it out."

"It's about your father."

I stopped. "You've been here all this time, and now you finally say something?"

"We felt I should talk to you alone."

"Why'd I have to make nice conversation? Why couldn't you have been like, 'Hi Marco. Good to see you. Let's talk.'"

"Because Ms. Wright needed to finish up her questions, and I didn't want anything getting in the way of that. I told her I'd wait until after she left."

"What is it you want to talk about?"

"Your father has gone missing."

I stopped walking.

"They already have a couple of leads, so please don't panic. I thought you should know in case he comes for you."

This shouldn't surprise me. Dad was slippery when it came to getting out of tough situations. "Did they let him walk out? Was he kidnapped?"

"He can't walk out, not on his own. The leads point us to two men pretending to work there. Surveillance shows them in your father's room several times. Then somehow, they cut the surveillance and disappeared. With him."

"He's not getting clean?" My heart dropped. I should have known Dad would have a hard time without drugs. He had enough contacts on the street, but none of them were smart enough to pretend to work for the rehab place. They were too strung out to put together more than a handle of coherent sentences.

"They found two orderlies, bound and gagged in the employee changing room. Their clothes had been taken."

"That wasn't Dad. He doesn't like to hurt people." My voice shook. "I don't want to talk about this anymore."

Mr. Harvey placed his hand on my shoulder. "I'm sorry, Marco. I promised I would be honest with you."

"I know."

"The police don't think your father hurt the men. They are investigated this as him being taken against his will."

If my heart hadn't been pounding fast enough before, it was now. "He's kidnapped?"

"Do you know who would want him out of rehab?"

"No. Most everyone likes Dad. He's a nice guy."

I thought of the book with H.E.L.P. on the corner of each page. "Dad's in trouble."

"Marco, I have a feeling you have a pretty good idea where your father might be."

"No, I don't."

"Don't the two of you have a secret location? A place to go

and wait for each other?"

How'd he know about that? Dad had a friend that worked at The Bridge motel, a little dive that we stayed in from time to time. We decided that if we ever got separated, we would hide by the motel's dumpster.

"How am I supposed to know where he is? It's not like I've got a running blog on his whereabouts." The new information unraveled me. Dad never did crime. Sure, he was a drug addict, and we would occasionally steal, but only when we needed to. I had never seen Dad with a weapon. Ever. Suddenly, I itched to find him, to make sure he was all right.

"I only wanted you to think about it and see if anything popped up. Any information could be useful."

"I don't know," I lied. My brain churned out ideas as to how to get downstate.

"How's life here with your grandmother?"

"It's fine, but if you think I'm staying long term, I'm not. I'm going back to Dad, and that's that." I paused, then added, "But I like Grandma. She's really nice. I want to bring Dad up here so that we can all be a family together."

"Oh, one more thing." He reached into his pocket and pulled out a card. He handed it to me. "I know your birthday's Monday, so I wanted to get you a little something."

I glanced down at the gift card and tried not to smile. With everything going on, I wondered if anyone would remember. "What's

Saturn?"

"It's another planet, you know that." I could hear Mr. Harvey's tease.

"Ha, ha, is this a one-way ticket?"

"It's the bookseller here in town. It's for twenty dollars. Not much, but you could maybe pick up two paperbacks. Anyway, I won't see you Monday, and I didn't want you to think I'd forget. Happy early birthday."

"Thanks," I said, still staring at the gift card. "Does Grandma know? About my birthday?"

"She received a list of your information, and I'm sure that was on it. Do you want me to tell her?"

"No." I looked up at him. "She's got a lot going on. It's no big deal."

"Turning thirteen is a big deal."

"No, not really. It's just another day." I asked, "Can I drive a dirt bike at thirteen?"

"I'd have to check."

Grandma called us to dinner. She had cooked a pot roast with mashed potatoes. I shoveled the food in my mouth, all the while thinking of ways to buy a bus ticket back to Detroit.

"It's a miracle I get him to say grace," Grandma joked to Mr. Harvey.

"He does look like he's put on a few pounds already."

"I'm right here," I said with my mouth full. "It's rude to talk about someone in the third person when that person is right there."

"If you're finished, go put your plate in the sink and get your homework done. Mr. Harvey will say goodbye when he's ready to leave."

I nodded, set the plate in the sink, and sulked to my room. Then it hit me. *Mr. Harvey!* I knew how to make it work. I sat on the bed and turned on the T.V. Static filled the screen, but I wasn't watching it anyway. I just needed something to fill the air. I couldn't take a duffel bag. It would be obvious. Instead, I dumped out the contents of my backpack, filled it with a couple of changes of underwear and another pair of pants and shirt, along with two pairs of clean socks. I had just enough room for a few books. I stuffed the two books inside with Dad's numbers and H.E.L.P.

Guilt hit me like a freight train. Grandma would be sad. But I was planning on bringing Dad back. I would somehow get her to listen to me. Still, I took a notebook, wrote Grandma a nice thank you note and a promise to come back, and set it on the table by my bed.

I walked out to the living room where they were talking. "I'm really tired. I think I'm going to crash."

"I'll call you in a couple of days," Mr. Harvey said. "And you call me if you remember anything that can help the police."

Mmm-hmm, yeah, don't think so, but I kept that thought to myself.

I leaned down and hugged Grandma.

She acted surprised. "Why thank you," she said and hugged

me in return.

Once in my bedroom, I shut the door and worked in overdrive. I stuffed the pillow under the blanket to look like a body, then turned off the lights. As quietly as I could I opened the window and pushed out the screen.

For a second, I hesitated. I thought of Grandma, of Gertie, of my new, more comfortable life. Something told me to stay. I found myself torn. A part of me wanted to stay. I had it good here.

But my Dad...

Did he run from the rehab center with help, or was he forced to leave?

If someone forced him to leave, who took him?

Where'd he go? Was he safe?

If I left now with Mr. Harvey, I could head to the motel. Maybe he was there, waiting for me. Then, I could convince him to come back up here. Maybe we could make a life up here. He could take me fishing, and I could introduce him to Gertie.

I jumped out the window with my backpack slung over my shoulder. I shut the window this time. I didn't want Grandma to figure anything out until I was already in Detroit.

It was already dark. I felt along the back of the cabin to the side of it until I could make out Mr. Harvey's car from the front porch light. He already stood on the steps, talking to Grandma!

Once again, my heart tugged with guilt, and I questioned my decision.

I didn't relish the thought of going back to a motel. Dad might not even be there, especially since he told me to come up to Grandma's house. And now, I had a nice, comfy bed right here. I had made a friend. I had all the food I wanted.

"Make a decision, Marco," I whispered to myself.

Ultimately, it came down to one point: Dad might need my help. Decision made.

I walked closer to the trees because the porch light didn't reach that far. I kept my eye on them while opening the back door of Mr. Harvey's car. Of course, he didn't have it locked. Then again, who would lock a ten-year-old, ugly, gray Taurus?

After crawling into the back of the car and quietly shutting the door, I huddled behind the driver's seat, telling myself this needed to be done.

I had told Grandma I couldn't stay for long. She already knew, so this wasn't like I was running away. And I would come back. First, I needed to make sure Dad was okay. But the longer I sat huddled in the back, the more I doubted going.

I should just tell them about our hiding spot. Then they could go and see if he's there.

Torn with what to do, I visualized two columns in my head. One was for the *Pros*, and the other was for the *Cons*.

What would be the pros of telling them?

My Grandma would want to know.

She's the only one who's ever bought me new shoes and stuff.

Mr. Harvey would be happy, but I don't care about him too much.

Maybe if they caught my dad, he'd go back to rehab where he could get clean.

If they caught him, at least I'd know he was alive.

What are the cons of telling them?

They would find him.

Put him in jail, instead of rehab.

I'd have to wait even longer to be with him again.

His messages were in my books. They're meant for me.

The time for indecisiveness was over. Mr. Harvey slid into his seat and started the car. But as the car reversed and pulled out onto the dirt road, I was already questioning it.

CHAPTER FOURTEEN

I heard Mr. Harvey fiddling with the radio. Suddenly, music blared from the speakers, and Michael Jackson's voice came through, belting out, "Beat It."

It surprised me that Mr. Harvey would 1.) listen to music this loudly 2.) listen to Michael Jackson (he seemed more like an easy-listening kind of guy) and 3.) would start belting out the lyrics with amazing accuracy.

Mr. Harvey slowed the car as the song ended. Was he at the stop sign?

"What is this?" he murmured.

I heard the passenger window go down.

"Can I help you?" he asked. "Is everything all right?"

Before any words were spoken, my gut twisted at who he was talking to. I sat upright as Gertie said, "Yes, I'm fine. Thank you."

Her face, even in the dark, looked puffy and red, like she'd been crying a long time.

"Do you live close by?" Mr. Harvey asked. "I know you shouldn't get into a car with a stranger, but I can call someone for you and wait until they get here."

"I live right there," she said. It looked like she was trying to keep her tears at bay, but she wasn't being very successful.

Even though I wasn't on the seat, I could make out Mr. Harvey's facial expression. He didn't know if he should leave or stay.

"I'm just getting fresh air," she said, wiping at her eyes. "Were you coming from Marco's house?"

"Yes," he said, a little too excitedly, as if they now have this connection. "How'd you know?"

"Ms. Fuller is the only house down there."

"Right, right. So, how do you know Marco?"

"From school. I was thinking of walking over there and seeing if he wanted to play video games, but it's too late now."

"He did go to bed already."

"Really?"

I would have slapped my palm to my face if I could have stayed undetected.

"So how do you know him?" she asked.

Oh no! He wouldn't tell her…

"I'm a social worker that checks up on him. We're pals."

Pals? I almost snorted.

Should I give away my position for him to keep his mouth shut? Sure, it might not matter with me leaving and all, but it did matter! I didn't want Gertie knowing I lied. I especially didn't want her to know the truth.

"With his father gone so much? He told me how he's always traveling from one country to another. That would be so cool. Maybe I'll be a stewardess one day."

"A stewardess?" Mr. Harvey asked while I died in the back seat. "Wow. That would be a cool job."

"Yeah, well, I guess I'll go back in now. If you talk to Marco before I do, tell him I might stop over tomorrow to hang out."

I heard her walk away as Mr. Harvey rolled up the window. He didn't move the car, probably making sure she got in her house all right.

It hit me that Mr. Harvey wasn't like most men I'd ever met. Most guys I'd ever been around were the ones who would hang around Dad. And they were not so nice. Dad would never talk about it, but I knew. Addiction made him endure horrible things. It killed me inside, but he was so far gone, lost in the jungle of drugs.

But not Mr. Harvey. He was super nerdy and had a weird taste in clothes, but he genuinely seemed to care. That was who he was. He didn't take advantage of people. He looked out for kids. At that moment, I was glad I knew him. He would have taken care of Gertie if she had asked. Even if it meant him getting home even later in the night. Not that I would ever tell him any of that. It would be too weird.

"So, your father travels to different countries, huh?" he asked without moving.

And my cover was blown. I sighed. "How'd you know I was back here?"

"I saw you through my rearview mirror when you sat up real fast."

I pushed myself up and on the seat.

"You can't go back with me, Marco."

"I was only going to talk to Dad and tell him to come up here so we can stay with Grandma."

"How would you find him? I thought you said you didn't know where he could be?"

Busted. I had to get better at this lying business.

I sighed again and leaned my head back against the seat. "You don't understand, Mr. Harvey. No offense. You're a nice guy and all, but you don't get it."

"Yes, I do. I get it, Marco. You love your father. You're scared for him. You want to help him. There's a part of you that's hurt that he ever called your grandmother."

Wow, he's good.

"But the truth is that you are not quite thirteen. Detroit is a dangerous city, especially for a young guy with little to no parental protection. You need to go to school. You need to hope for a future. You need to be a kid, Marco."

My throat seemed to swell up, making it hard to swallow. "I stopped being a kid a long time ago. Most guys my age have already been jumped into their gangs. It's the way it is."

"It might be the way it is, but it's not the way it's supposed to be. Be a kid. A teenager. Have fun. Do crazy, but legal, things. You might find you like it."

I shook my head back and forth. He wasn't going to talk me out of it. "You don't know what it's like to worry about your parent. You probably had some mother who made cookies and a father who tucked you in and read from the Bible or something."

"My parents died in a car crash when I was eight," he said simply. "They were older parents, so I didn't have any grandparents to go to. The only one I had was in assisted living. I had no one, so they bounced me around from one foster home to another. Seven foster homes total. They weren't bad places. Most were good people trying to help out dysfunctional kids. But I never found a home. A place that was mine."

"So, what'd you do?" I whispered, shocked that Mr. Harvey was sharing such a personal story with me.

"Well, after messing up my teen years, drinking and smoking and being stupid, I decided that I was going to listen to the advice of someone who told me that I had the power to make a difference in someone else's life. So, I went to a community college at first, then worked my way into Oakland University, and I earned a degree in Social Work. I knew I needed to help kids like me. Help them find a home I never found." Mr. Harvey put the car into gear and turned it around.

"I'm sorry you lost your parents," I said quietly. "I don't want to lose the only one I got."

"I know you don't. If we knew where he was, we could help."

I stared at the darkness outside my window and felt so tormented inside I thought I might burst from the battle. "Will he go back to jail?"

"Possibly, but we don't know the whole story yet. He may not be the mastermind behind his leaving the rehab place. Maybe they'll allow him to go back and simply complete the six months."

Mr. Harvey pulled up at Grandma's.

"Don't tell Grandma," I said. "I don't want to hurt her."

"She probably sees my car lights, and if you didn't want to hurt her, then why did you sneak out?"

"You know why."

"What I know is that I wish I had a grandmother like yours who would have taken me in and fed me and loved me."

"Okay, okay, stop trying to make me feel guilty." I stepped out of the car.

Mr. Harvey rolled down his window as the porch light came on.

Great.

Grandma opened the front door and peered out. "Marco? What are you doing outside?"

"Just talking to Mr. Harvey," I said.

"Tell her the truth."

"I will…just not right now."

"Lying gets you in trouble with grandmothers and when trying to make new friends."

"Will you lay off with the guilt trip? You're laying it on pretty thick."

"So, why did you say he traveled out of the country?" he asked as he put the car in reverse.

"I don't know." I shrugged. "It's the first thing I thought of. I didn't want to tell her how messed up my life was."

"It looks like her life is a little messed up. I've got to get back. We'll talk later."

He started to reverse.

The truth. It bubbled up inside of me. I couldn't right all of my wrongs tonight, but there was one thing I could do.

I ran toward the car. "The Bridge motel!"

Mr. Harvey slowed and poked his head out the window.

I walked to his window and talked fast before I lost my nerve. "Whenever we got separated, we'd meet by the dumpster behind The Bridge. Dad's friends with Bobby, the night manager. He even throws Dad some maintenance work when he's sober enough to show up."

Mr. Harvey's face looked sad. "I'll contact the authorities and let them know, If we can find him, I'll try to talk to him for you."

"Tell him to stop being stupid!" I yelled. "Tell him to stop taking drugs! Tell him I know about Grandma and that I'm mad he wouldn't let me meet her!" I turned to storm back into the house, but it dawned on me I forgot my backpack in the car. I went back, opened the back door, grabbed my backpack, and slammed the door shut. "And tell him I love him," I said, before heading toward the porch light and to the grandmother who was waiting for me.

CHAPTER FIFTEEN

Grandma stood at the window, looking out. I stood there with my backpack, feeling like garbage.

"Did you see this?" She indicated the window. "It's nice."

"It makes the cabin look prettier." It was one of those bay windows that stuck out of the house. Grandma had put some pillows on the bottom of it, and it looked like a cozy place to relax.

"I've always wanted a window where I could curl inside of it and read." She turned to me. "We can share it."

I was feeling worse by the second. "I only wanted to make sure he was alive!" I blurted. "I was going to come back."

Grandma gave a small smile. "If I thought it would do any good, I'd drive you down to Detroit myself. Sometimes the hardest thing to do is to wait."

How long had Grandma waited to see her son? Almost thirteen years. I couldn't imagine going that long without seeing him. "Can I get myself a root beer?"

"It's in the fridge."

"What made you decide to come back?" She followed me to

the kitchen.

I poured a small glass of soda and took a drink. "Mr. Harvey found me."

"Ah, I see. Well, I'm glad you came back. I would have missed you, and I would have been worried."

I didn't know what to say, so I kept drinking from the glass.

The phone rang from inside the front bedroom. Grandma went to answer it. When she came back, she said, "That was Mr. Harvey. He contacted the authorities. Told them what you said. They're on their way now."

I set the empty glass in the sink and went to my bedroom and sat on my bed, hoping Dad would be there.

I didn't sleep well that night. I kept waking up to the phantom sound of the police breaking down the door.

Gertie's voice woke me up the next morning.

My bedroom door was shut, but Grandma's house wasn't big. I heard Gertie say, "Hey, Ms. Fuller. Nice window."

I groggily sat up and rubbed my face.

"Come on in, Gertie," Grandma called from the recliner. "Let me see if Marco's awake yet."

"He can't still be sleeping. It's almost noon! That guy last night said that Marco had gone to bed early."

I poked my head out of the bedroom. "I'm awake, but give me a sec. I need to brush my teeth."

When I stepped out of the bathroom and went back to my

room, Gertie was there with her head behind my T.V.

"What are you doing?"

"Setting up the Xbox."

"Xbox? Gertie, you rock!"

She pulled the game station from her backpack. "I think I remembered everything." She dragged out cords, controllers, and several games. "I brought a racing game, a football game, and some oldies but goodies. Take your pick." She handed me the games and continued attaching the necessary components of the game system to the T.V.

It didn't take long for us to be playing some Xbox football.

"I'll be out back for a little bit." Grandma peeked her head in.

Once she left, Gertie asked, "What's out back?"

"She has a vegetable garden," I said. "She grows tomatoes, cucumbers, peppers, and even a row of corn. She told me it keeps her busy. I said that if she had a T.V. she would have something to do. She just shook her head and said that mindless television watching wasn't her idea of keeping herself busy."

Gertie turned to me her eyes wide with disbelief. "Are you serious?"

"Why are you looking at me like that? Yeah, I'm serious."

"So, it's true?"

"What's true? And stop looking at me like I sprouted two heads."

"I heard that's where she buried her husband and that's why

her plants are so ripe every year."

Suddenly, Gertie had my undivided attention. "What?"

Gertie nodded her head. Her face looked grim like she was about to tell me bad news. "Rumor has it that she killed her husband and buried him in her vegetable garden. I didn't believe it was true, especially when I met you and saw that you lived here. Now I find out she has a vegetable garden. It makes a person wonder."

"That is the stupidest thing I've ever heard," I said with attitude. "My Grandma? Have you taken a look at her? Does that look like a murderer to you?"

"Looks can be deceiving, besides it might not be true. But why would the whole town think that?"

"Why would she kill her husband?" I questioned. "She told me he got sick and died."

"I don't know. All I know is that she went crazy. One day everyone saw her husband, and the next day he mysteriously disappeared. And then she was pounding on everyone's door asking for her son. She fell off the radar. Only coming to town for groceries. I mean, shoot, I've seen her more since I've been friends with you than I have my entire life."

"If she's so crazy, why do you come around?" I was mortified that the town thought Grandma was a psycho-murderer.

"Because you're my friend, and I don't know, being here is better than being at home." Gertie shrugged her shoulders.

I stewed over the news, mulling it around in my head, and in the meantime, not being too successful with the game at hand. When Grandma came back in, she said she had to do some grocery shopping and asked if we wanted to come. Neither one of us wanted to stop the game, so she left us, saying she'd be back in an hour.

Her car had no sooner pulled away when Gertie turned to me. "Show me her garden."

I acted like it was no big deal, but it was. I didn't like the thought of people not liking Grandma or thinking that she was a crazy murderer. But I'd also be lying if I said I wasn't curious. Gertie and I made ourselves sandwiches, then headed outside. There were three large gardens behind the house and to the left side closest to the forest. Grandma had tall wire fences to keep out the deer and critters around two of the gardens but the other one sat near the house, so it had a smaller fence around it with a funny-looking scarecrow. "I told Grandma that thing wasn't scary," I said.

Gertie laughed. "Maybe to deer and bear, it is."

I swallowed and glanced around at the trees. "Have you ever seen one?"

"Bear or deer? I see deer all the time. They're annoying, but when they see you, they run. I saw a bear once, but they like to stay in the woods. Just don't leave food outside. Sometimes if they're foraging or hungry, they'll venture out to garbage cans."

Gertie had started to walk around the gardens when I faintly heard the phone ring. It might be Mr. Harvey calling about Dad. "I'll be right back!" I headed around the front of the house.

I ran inside and stumbled over Grandma's stuff to the phone. "Hello?" I asked, out-of-breath.

"Hey, Jay, what's up?" Tim's voice came through the other end.

It surprised me. "Who is this?"

I knew who it was. Tim had an annoying, surfer-boy voice like he thought it would make him sound cool. But it didn't.

"It's Tim. From school. I got your number from my mom."

"How does she have my number?"

"She works at the central office."

"Why are you calling me?"

"I thought you might want to hang out."

I didn't say anything. My mouth had no words.

"You don't sound super thrilled, dude." He chuckled. "A bunch of us are going up to the skate park. Want to come?"

Skate park? I didn't know what skates it referred to, but I had no expertise with any kind. "Is this a trick?"

"No. Why would it be a trick?"

"I'm confused."

"Listen, we're going up to the skate park. We'll be there in a few. If you want to come, then come. If not, whatever. Oh, and don't forget your board."

When I hung up the phone and looked up, Gertie stood at the door. "I think Tim just invited me skateboarding."

"Why?"

"I don't know. He hasn't said one word to me at school."

"He's trying to annoy me. I know it." She crossed her arms and scowled. "He sees that you and I are friends, and so he's going to try to take you away from me just like he tried to do with Ray. He's a scumbag."

"Well, don't worry. He won't take away our friendship. Besides, I'm not going. Skateboarding wasn't super popular in Detroit. I don't even have a board."

"Ricky does. If you want to go, we can go get it." She paused. "Do you want me to come with you?"

"You want to go?"

"Only if you do. And if you want me to go. I want them to see that I'm not afraid to show up."

"Of course, I want to go. I mean, if I was going. Which I'm not."

Gertie smiled. Man, she had a really pretty smile.

"I don't get why he's calling me in the first place."

"You kind of have a tough guy reputation since lunch on the first day. If he's not trying to get to me, maybe he decided to be friends instead of enemies. Or, he wants something from you, or is playing a trick to get you back for what you did."

"It's probably the latter."

"Yeah, probably." Gertie leaned against the door jam, then stood straight. "Oh, I almost forgot! Come with me for a sec."

We walked back outside to the middle garden where Grandma

grew a lot of her vegetables. "Look," Gertie said. She pointed to the far corner of the garden. "See how the dirt's been newly turned? Like someone's been digging and then refilling?"

"Um, it's a garden," I said with sarcasm. "Digging is essential for planting."

"At the edge? Nowhere near the plants?" She grabbed my hand and pulled me over to the spot. Just on the other side of the fence, a new mound of dirt had been patted down somewhat, but it was still obvious that for some reason, Grandma had dug here.

"So?"

"It doesn't strike you as odd that she dug right here?"

"No, Gertie, and I don't like it that you keep accusing my grandma of bad stuff. I don't think you believe it, either. If you did, you wouldn't be over here. So, what gives?"

She didn't say anything at first. Then she shook her head. "If I told you, you'd be mad and might not be my friend anymore."

"It'd have to be pretty bad."

"It is," she sighed. "You know that broken window your grandma had?"

"Yeah."

"My brother and his friends did that."

"I kind of assumed they did. Why would I be mad at that?"

She took a deep breath. "I was…with them."

"So, you're trying to make yourself feel better," I said, becoming upset, which was exactly what she'd been afraid of. "If you find something back here then good for you, you broke an old lady's window for a good reason."

"I don't know what I'm doing," she said. "I think I'm trying to show myself that what I did was wrong."

"It was wrong. You broke an old lady's front window! Her recliner is right there."

"I didn't do it. I was just with them."

A part of me wanted to show her that Grandma was innocent. I opened the small gate and went inside the garden. I fell on my knees and started digging. Gertie was right behind me. She started digging, too.

I wasn't expecting to find anything, but I did. My fingers hit something flat and hard. I sat back quickly. *Please, don't let it be bones…*

Gertie and I looked at each other. She wiped at the dirt. "It's a lid."

I let out an audible sigh of relief. A lid meant it wasn't bones. I kept digging around the lid. Eventually we pried loose a large coffee can. "Ha!" I said, more relieved than anything. It's not like body parts could fit into a coffee can.

"What happens if it's his brain?" she whispered, staring at the can.

"Will you stop?" Before I could talk myself out of it, I pulled open the lid.

It wasn't body parts or a brain. It was a coffee can stuffed full of cash.

CHAPTER SIXTEEN

We never made it to the skate park. Grandma pulled up while we were still dumping the dirt back over the coffee can. Gertie insisted I move the can somewhere else. "I shouldn't know where this is," she said. "It feels like an invasion of privacy."

"It *is* an invasion of privacy," I said. "And if I move it, then I would have to tell my grandma that I found it."

I heard Grandma's door shut. "Marco?" she called from the front of the house. "Help me bring in the groceries."

"Our hands," Gertie said. They were covered past our wrists in the dirt.

I wiped them off as best as I could and ran around to the front.

"Hey there," Grandma said with a smile. "Glad to see you two outside on a nice day like today. We've got to enjoy it. When October hits, the weather becomes rather unpredictable. We sometimes even get snow."

"Like last Halloween," Gertie said, acting like we didn't just find a can of cash in the backyard. She took a bag of groceries from my hand. "It was a mix of snow and freezing rain. It was so cold."

After we dropped off the groceries in the kitchen and helped Grandma put them away, she said, "Well, how about some ice cream? I've got a coupon for Moo's Parlor on Fourth Street."

"Dessert before dinner? I say, yes!" Gertie grinned over at me.

Grandma waited for an answer too. All I could do was think about the cash I had found. That amount of money would have helped me live for months, maybe even a year if I spread it out good. And it was buried in a garden at my grandma's house.

"Marco?" Grandma asked. "You all right?"

"Yeah," I said quickly. "Ice cream's good."

"Well, go wash your hands. They're filthy."

Grandma didn't ask any questions, but I was still on edge nearly the entire trip up to the ice cream parlor. Why didn't Dad ever call Grandma? Grandma could have sent money to help. What bothered me more than that was my sudden anger at Dad. How many nights did I go hungry? How many nights did he leave me alone with only the motel room's faucet for a drink?

"Marco?" Gertie had turned around in the passenger seat and looked back at me. "Your Grandma's talking to you."

I saw we had already arrived at the busy ice cream parlor. "Looks like everyone had the same idea we did," I said, trying to recover. "Sorry, Grandma, what'd you say?"

She observed me from the rearview mirror. She knew something was up. I knew she knew. I could see it in her eyes. "I was saying that we can come back when it's not so busy."

"It's warm. It's going to be busy. Come on," I said, indicating for Gertie to open up the door and let me climb out.

It would have excited me. The ice cream parlor smelled amazing with homemade waffle cones and fudge being made in different parts of the building. But as soon as I stepped foot inside, I was even more on edge. Gertie's brother and a bunch of his buddies were there.

Ricky wasted no time. He came right up to Gertie and asked what she was doing hanging around a bunch of freaks.

"Marco is my friend. Now leave us alone."

"Just go sit down," Grandma said calmly to Ricky. "We're only getting ice cream."

Ricky glared at Grandma, then grabbed Gertie's arm. "Come on. I'll take you home."

Gertie jerked her arm back. "No. I'm fine."

They were making a scene.

He smirked at his sister. "So, you'll rat out some people, huh, but hang out with a psycho and her spawn?"

"That's enough," Grandma said, her voice low and hard.

"What are you going to do?" he taunted. "Cut me into little pieces? Bury me in the back?"

An older man came up to us. "Shirley? Everything all right? Is this young man bothering you?"

Ricky scoffed and muttered, "Whatever," before walking away. He and his group left soon after. I heard the threats, and it made me feel sick. Would they hurt Grandma?

"We're fine, Pastor Bob. Thank you." Grandma smiled at the man. "That's Gertie's brother, and he's a bit of a bully."

"It's a shame they didn't catch him when he broke your window."

"It's just a hunch I had," Grandma said. "But next time, I'll be ready. You can be sure of that."

"Well, we'd love to see you at Sunday service." He smiled at me.

"Where are my manners?" Grandma asked herself. "This is Marco, the young grandson I was telling you about at our last session."

"Nice to meet you, Marco." He extended his hand.

I shook his hand but was too distracted to be polite.

Grandma talked with him until it was our turn to order. I didn't feel like ice cream, and I could tell Gertie didn't either, but Grandma was trying so hard to keep the mood light, I forced myself to order. "Chocolate chip ice cream on a waffle cone, please." I stepped to the side.

Gertie passed on getting anything.

"Don't let your brother win," I told her.

"I'll take a scoop of strawberry ice cream on a sugar cone," she finally told the lady behind the counter.

"Marco?"

I turned to see Tim walk in with the other guys and nearly

groaned out loud. What was this? Hicksville Central? Did everyone get ice cream on a Saturday?

"Hey," I said, not sure what else to say.

Tim had his skateboard under his arm. "What happened, man? I thought we were gonna pound the pavement."

"We got busy."

The lady handed me my ice cream cone.

"Oh, you're with Gertie." Tim eyed her before looking back at me. "We'll talk at school." He turned and got in line without saying a word to her.

"I hate that guy," she said under her breath. "Actually, I hate almost every guy that's been in here tonight. Other than that pastor. And you."

Gertie held her ice cream but wasn't even trying to eat it. It had begun to drip onto her hand.

Once Grandma got hers, we went back outside to stand in the sun. As we passed, Ray made kissing noises at Gertie. She practically snarled at them.

"I can tell there's a full moon tonight," Grandma said, taking a big bite of a small banana split. "Gertie, you're not eating your ice cream."

That snapped her out of her gloom, and she started licking to keep up with the melting pink ice cream. "Sorry."

"Don't you worry about your brother or those boys," Grandma told her. "You keep being you. I'm glad Marco and you became friends."

Gertie smiled sadly.

I popped the last of the waffle cone in my mouth. I hadn't realized I had eaten it all.

Grandma dropped off Gertie even though Gertie acted unenthused. I felt bad for her, but I had my own issues going on in my head. We said we'd meet up tomorrow to play some more games on the Xbox, and then she left to run up to her house. Her mother stood at the door, a cigarette dangling out of her mouth, looking irritated. She started yelling as soon as Gertie got up her steps.

"Not a good family," Grandma said. "Poor girl."

"I'm figuring out that most families have issues."

"True."

We drove down the road in silence. The question that had burned a hole in me through most of the afternoon needed to escape. But then Grandma would know about me and Gertie digging through her garden.

"What's bothering you?" she asked, as we pulled onto the property.

"Just worried about Dad. And Gertie. Last night when I was in Mr. Harvey's car, Gertie was out on the road, crying. Her face was all puffy and swollen. I don't think she's happy there."

"That young lady has had it rough. She's more like you than you realize."

That piqued my attention. "How?"

Grandma seemed to weigh her words. “There was a while there when Peg, that’s her mother’s name, was back with Ricky’s dad. She goes from one man to another quite a bit. Anyway, Gertie was rushed to the hospital for some incident. The man was arrested, and Gertie was out of the home and in foster care for about a year. Peg got some help and got her daughter back. Now she’s with Gertie’s father. But it doesn’t look like it’s going well. And then there’s Ricky. He’s a bad seed.”

It felt like someone had squeezed my heart with a tight fist and was refusing to release it. “Gertie,” I whispered. What had happened that she had to go to the hospital? Something bad enough to put Ricky’s dad behind bars for a long time.

“Be careful,” Grandma said. “Gertie is a good girl, I believe it, but everyone has their limits.”

I turned and studied Grandma’s face. We still sat in the car with the windows down. “Where did you bury Grandpa?”

She smirked. “I wondered how long it would take for you to ask that question. Where’d you hear the rumor first? School?”

“Gertie said something…but she doesn’t believe it!”

“Hmm, is that why both your hands and arms were covered in dirt?” Grandma studied me with a look that said she was one smart cookie.

I gave a half-smile and tried to laugh. But it couldn’t get past my lips. “On a good note, we didn’t discover any…bones or…brains…” I pressed my lips shut.

Grandma watched me for another minute more, then she surprised me. She covered her face and her shoulders started shaking. I thought she had started to cry, which made me feel even more horrible. Then muffled laughter escaped from her covered mouth. She laughed…and laughed…and laughed… She had tears streaming down her face from laughing so hard. Then she'd look over at me and start laughing again. "Oh Marco," she finally said, wiping her eyes. "Thanks for the laugh." She patted my cheek before stepping out of the car. "Come on, we still have to make some dinner."

She walked to the cabin, as I pushed myself out of the car. "You never answered my question!"

"I'll answer you tonight," she said without looking back.

Why did that not make me feel super secure?

CHAPTER SEVENTEEN

"Here," she said, opening her arms to the large expanse of meadow.

At least I think it was a meadow. It was dark, and I was freaked out. So, other than for Grandma saying it was a meadow, I had no idea.

"I can't believe you didn't even bring a flashlight," I said for the third time.

"As I've already told you, I know this land like the back of my hand. Besides, it's a full moon."

"Well, I don't know the land. What happens if we get separated?"

"If you ever get lost in the woods, tie a piece of string or material around a tree trunk. If you're on the move, keep tying something around tree trunks or somewhere it can be seen. That way we can find our way to you. And, always, if you can, stay in one spot. That way, you're easier to find."

"That is not helping."

"I thought you wanted to know what happened to your grandfather?"

“Yes, but you could have told me from the safety and security of the *house*.”

“You lived in Detroit for your whole life, which is one of the worst, most dangerous cities ever, and you’re afraid of some trees?”

“No. I’m not too excited about what could be lurking *behind* the trees. Besides, I know what to expect in Detroit. I’m used to it. I’m not used to this.”

“I’ve been wondering how you avoided getting all tangled up in any of that stuff down in Detroit. No gangs? No violence? No marijuana?”

“Marijuana? What?” I started laughing. “That’s funny. And no, to all of the above. I stuck to myself and took care of Dad. That’s it. And if anyone wants an anti-drug campaign daily live with someone addicted to drugs. Thanks, but no thanks.”

Grandma had walked up close to me. I could see her eyes shining, even in the night. “You’re a good young man, Marco. You really are.”

My throat felt all constricted again.

“You break down every stereotype that’s out there, and I can’t tell you how glad I am that you came up here.” She pulled me into her arms and hugged me.

I froze, not knowing what to do. Other than an occasional hug from Dad, I’d been my own fortress of solitude. I didn’t respond at first. The other night I hugged her, but that was different. I was in control of it and was using it as a form of manipulation. This hug felt real. Eventually, I placed my arms around her. "I'm not that good."

"Stop talking yourself out of it."

Branches snapped behind me, and I jumped out of Grandma's arms and turned in the direction of the noise. "Oh, sweet Jesus."

I saw the bear's eyes before I heard his breathing and movement. The moon gave more than enough light for me to see how I was going to die. It stopped and stared right back at me.

Then it turned back into the woods.

"See?" Grandma whispered. "They're not even interested in us."

"Get me out of here," I said, out-of-breath. "I ain't got time to be bear stew." Had that bear looked right at me? I had to have been several yards away.

"Fine, all right, let's go back. I only wanted you to see where your Grandpa's ashes were scattered."

Knowing my grandpa's dead body was burned and thrown into this field was not helping. I kept thinking about the bear staring right at me. "That's nice. Let's go back."

Grandma led me through the woods. The creepiness factor only increased with the night noises of the forest, so I kept the conversation going. "So, bears don't usually attack?"

"Not black bears. If you don't antagonize them, they leave you alone. The only time they're a problem is when they go through my trash. That's why I leave the big can under the roof of the shed."

"It looked right at me."

"I saw that. It was on the other side of the meadow. We were fine."

Grandma had misunderstood what I meant. I swore the bear looked at me and saw me. Not the outside me, but the inside me.

"You know Indian legend says that we are brothers and sisters with animals. That certain species connect with us because we have that brotherly bond."

"Sounds like a bunch of mumbo-jumbo."

Grandma paused and listened. "It's still close."

I felt my blood run cold. Okay, so just because I felt a connection didn't mean I wanted a repeat encounter. I went to move, but Grandma stopped me.

"Just listen," Grandma whispered.

I tried to listen, and I could hear muffled sounds of something moving through the trees, but I mostly visualized a bear charging out of the trees chomping my head off. Maybe the connection was nothing more than he wanted me for an evening snack. "Please, let's go."

Grandma took my hand and continued pushing past trees toward the house. "He wasn't going anywhere," she eventually said.

"Yeah, I could tell that," I said sarcastically.

"In all my years of walking through these woods, I've never had a bear stick around like that. Where he was coming closer, but still keeping himself at a distance."

I couldn't say anything. Did she realize that she was completely freaking me out?

"The Cherokees believe that the black bear is a connection to the spirit world. The black bear would act as a guide or be seen as protection over the Cherokee people, almost god-like." Grandma stopped in her tracks again. "It's a good sign, Marco. It's a real good sign."

"If you believe in that kind of stuff." I was done talking about bears and spirits, and I was even more done with being in the woods. "Are we almost back? Did you get us lost?"

"What do you take me for? Drag you out here in the dark and then get us lost? Can't you see that speck of light ahead of us? That's the house."

I could barely make out any light through the trees. "We're still that far?" I kept glancing over my shoulder. We walked quietly for about thirty seconds, but the woods made too much noise. "How did the rumor start about you?" I blurted. "That you did something to your husband?"

"Since I didn't have a traditional funeral, I guess people became suspicious."

"He doesn't have any other family that would want to come to say goodbye? People who could tell others that you're innocent."

"Sure. We had a private service back in that meadow. Pastor Bob came and his wife, along with your grandfather's two remaining brothers and their families. I had a few friends from downstate that came, along with a few women up here from the book club I was in. But that's it. Maybe fifteen-twenty people tops. And most of them aren't from around here."

Grandma suddenly stopped.

"What? Is that bear still around?"

"Shh."

I decided to stay focused on the porch light that I could now see through the trees. That's when I heard it. And it didn't sound like a bear.

Someone was on the property. Not just someone, but *someones*. As in plural.

My heart started pounding, and I felt the panic rise in me. She tip-toed the rest of the way to the forest's edge, and I followed. Closely.

Grandma gasped as soon as she entered the edge of her yard. Her eyes narrowed, and her hands went into fists. Her rusted-out hatchback now displayed a multitude of colors. A group of boys lounged in the back of a pickup laughing and swigging from beer cans, while one stood at the side of the hatchback scrawling letters with the spray paint can.

The panic immediately vanished, but my heart still fell to my feet. The one with the spray can was none other than Ricky's spitting friend. Grandma pulled me down. Motioning for me to keep quiet, she began crawling across the outskirts of her yard.

Luckily the guys were oblivious to our presence. The stench of beer draped the air, and the boys swayed and staggered on and off the bed of the pickup.

"Hey, whaddya' think?" The spitting guy slurred to the few paying attention to him. They cheered him on, even though they probably didn't have a clue what it said.

I scanned the yard for Grandma but couldn't spot her anywhere. Then I heard the gunshot and glass shattering. I yelped in shock. The drunken idiots fell to the ground, and Grandma emerged from a bush beside her shed.

"That's what you get for busting my window!" she yelled with force. Another shot went off. The air in one of the truck's tires hissed in release. The boys begged and cowered, but Grandma kept on talking. "And that's for ruining my car! Now get off my property, before a bullet finds you!"

The thugs ran around in chaos until someone finally got in the front seat and started the engine. As it took off with a repeated thump, thump, thump of a flat tire, I heard someone complain, "My dad's gonna kill me!"

Once they were gone, I remained shocked on the ground.

"Marco?" Grandma called out. "It's clear. They won't be bothering us again."

Finding my feet, my wobbly legs stood up. "Could you put the gun away? You're making me nervous."

I didn't mean for it to be funny, but my grandmother laughed. She unloaded the rifle and set it beside her. "There," she said. "I never keep it loaded."

"You're pretty good at it," I commented, walking toward her.

I kept looking back at the road, wondering if they would come with their own guns.

"Don't worry," Grandma said soothingly. She touched my shoulder with her one available hand. "Boys like that only bully when they think they can get away with it. I saw all of them crystal clear tonight, and I'm going to be filing charges. They won't bother us again."

"Did you aim for their window and tire?" I glanced at the gun warily. I really didn't like those things.

"Of course, I did. I never intended to shoot at any of them."

"You're pretty good," I said again.

"Not too bad. Stanley enjoyed hunting, and he taught me a thing or two. It's like riding a bike, once you know how to handle a gun, the skill never leaves you. I should teach you some of the basics. Maybe we could go hunting together."

"I don't like guns."

"Well, we'd start you off with a bb gun, nothing fancy."

"They made a mess of your car," I pointed over at the hatchback. Now that I stood closer, I could see *Old Bat* written across the driver's side.

"Dumb kids," she muttered.

Thinking it would cheer her up I said, "The truck's in worse shape than your car. I hope I don't ever get you ticked at me."

"You are family," she said from inside the shed. "And I don't shoot family members."

As we walked back to the house, exhaustion hit me, but I didn't feel right leaving Grandma to take care of the mess. "Want me to start scrubbing your car while you call the police?"

"That's thoughtful, but it'll need a new paint job. That's spray paint, and it's not coming off. Let's go inside, and I'll make that phone call."

I hadn't slept great the previous night, and it had caught up with me. "Can I jump in the shower real fast? I can help as soon as I'm done."

The phone rang. "I'll get that. Go ahead and wash up."

I nodded, grabbed some shorts and a t-shirt, and shut the bathroom door. As I dropped my pants, I felt something in the back pocket. Mr. Harvey's gift card slid out. It reminded me that my birthday was coming up, but I was too tired to think about it. Instead, I thought of bears and forest, gunshots and bullies, dead bodies and meadows, coffee cans and cash.

When I shut off the water, I leaned my head against the shower wall. Until I heard the phone ring again. Suddenly I felt nervous. What if those guys were calling to harass Grandma? I dried off quickly and threw on some pajama bottoms and a t-shirt.

She stood in the hallway while the phone rang. She looked confused and worried.

"Didn't you get the phone?"

"I did. Three times. Whoever's calling keeps hanging up."

I told myself not to act scared. I needed to think about

Grandma. "Maybe I should answer it. It might be Tim. It sounds like something he would do."

"At ten o'clock at night?"

"Does anyone else have your number?"

"It's unlisted."

The phone continued ringing. I walked into the cluttered front bedroom and picked up the phone. "Hello?"

No one answered but whoever was on the other end didn't hang up either. I could hear the person breathing, and there was a lot of background noise, even some music.

"Hello?" I said again. "Who is this?"

Grandma took the phone from me. "Hello?" Then she set the phone back on the receiver. "They hung up again."

"Whoever it was didn't hang up. I could hear breathing. It seems weird that they hang up when you answer, but not when I do."

Realization must have hit Grandma the same time it hit me. "Lance?"

"Dad?"

The phone rang again. I nearly knocked it over to answer it. "Hello?"

No one answered, but I heard the breathing and the background noise.

"Dad? Is that you?" I look up at Grandma. "Are you okay?"

I heard the person suck in a breath and sniffle as if crying.

"If you're Dad, please say something."

Only one word escaped. “Help.”

And then the line went dead.

CHAPTER EIGHTEEN

Mr. Harvey said that the best thing I should do was to continue going to school while the authorities figured out what was going on with Dad.

Yeah, right.

Grandma called the police Saturday night. By Sunday evening, we received word that the number came from a bar on South Woodward Avenue in Detroit's Westside. The bar owner recognized a picture of Dad, even though he said the guy that came into his bar didn't look quite as good as the picture. He said he never gave him the phone to use, but he remembered him sitting in the back booth with two other men. He had no idea how Dad got to the phone to use it.

"He's in trouble. I know it."

"We have to trust that the police will find him." Then Grandma called Pastor Bob who stopped by and prayed over us.

When Monday morning came around, I sat up in bed well before Grandma woke me up. For two reasons: I couldn't sleep worrying about Dad, and it dawned on me that it was my birthday. It made me miss Dad even more. For all his imperfections, he never missed my birthday. In the early years, he would get me a cupcake, and I would always receive a small present. He'd wake up early and take me to the park and just spend the day with me. Once drugs took over, and we had to keep hopping from one place to another, he would still wake up enough on that day to spend time with me. He'd somehow have two individually wrapped cupcakes, and he'd sing to me. It wasn't much, but it was enough.

Was that why he called last night? Then why did he say, "Help?" Why didn't he say, "Happy Birthday, Marco. How are you?"

There was only one birthday present I wanted. Not that I prayed often, but that morning I asked God to protect Dad, even if meant the police catching him. I decided that at least he'd be safe with the police. "Please," I whispered, my hands clasped in front of me, the way I saw people on the T.V. pray. "It's what I want for my birthday."

I heard Grandma moving around and wondered if she even knew what day it was. I never got around to telling her. About twenty minutes later, when the aroma of bacon filled my bedroom, I had a strong suspicion she knew. Today wasn't going to be a cold-cereal-for-breakfast morning.

I opened my door and went into the kitchen. A big, chocolate cake sat at the table, already baked and frosted. And Grandma stood at the stove, flipping a pancake.

"Good morning," I said.

She turned quickly and smiled big. I could see the dark circles under her eyes. I wasn't stupid, she was worried about Dad, too. Had she been up all night?

"There's the birthday boy!" she said. "Do you feel thirteen?"

"Were you up the whole night?"

"What? No. Don't be silly. Besides, today isn't about me or anyone else. It's about Marco Fuller. Go, get dressed, and get ready for school. The pancakes and eggs will be done in a few more minutes."

I threw on clothes and grabbed my backpack. I stopped at the door of the other room and stared at the phone. My birthday would be filled with worry, thinking about Dad.

"Marco?" Grandma stood outside the kitchen, watching me.

I turned to her. "Yeah?"

"Breakfast is ready, and the bus will be here in fifteen minutes. Let's eat up, birthday boy." She smiled, but it didn't reach her eyes.

Before I passed her, I paused and threw my arms around her. Stupid tears started leaking out of my eyes and wouldn't stop. This wasn't manly. Thirteen-year-olds shouldn't cry, especially on their birthdays. But the worry suffocated me. The feeling of helplessness hurt my heart. I felt helpless down in Detroit too, but at least I could see Dad and make sure he was alive for another day.

Grandma wrapped her arms around me and let me snot all over her shoulder. We stood there for a long time. It was like a current of anguish had been released in me, and I couldn't stop. Eventually, I heard the brakes of the bus outside, but I couldn't move.

When I finally stepped back, I wiped at my eyes. "The bus left me. I'm sorry."

"Don't apologize. I'll drive you in this morning."

I nodded but wouldn't look up at her face. I was too embarrassed for slobbering like a baby. "Don't tell anyone you saw me cry."

"Of course not, but there's nothing wrong with crying. You're worried and scared, but--"

"But what?" I looked up at her.

"But…I trust the police. I do. They're going to find him, and he's going to get help. And if he contacts us again, we'll do what we can to help him. It's good that he called, Marco. It's really good."

"He said, 'Help.'"

"Yes, and he's reaching out. So, I'm encouraged. I'm still worried, but I think things are going to turn around."

"What will happen when they find him?"

"They'll probably arrest him. At least until they figure out how he left the rehab facility. Then you and I will drive down there."

I felt my heart expand at least to twice its size. "Really? You'll take me down there?"

"Yes. I want to see my son, and you want to see your father. I'll make sure he has a good attorney and that he gets put back into a rehab facility."

I threw my arms around Grandma again. "Thanks," I whispered.

"So, I think what needs to happen now is for you to enjoy your birthday breakfast and to enjoy the rest of the day. You can even invite Gertie over this evening to have some cake and ice cream. Sound like a plan?"

I nodded, feeling very hungry. "I hope the food's not cold."

"Nope. I have it in the warmer."

"How can you be so optimistic?" I dived in the eggs and bacon.

"A feeling I have."

After a delicious breakfast, Grandma dropped me off at school. It was as if a weight had lifted off my shoulders. The worry still poked at me, but Grandma said to be hopeful, so I decided that on my birthday, I would be hopeful. The warning bell for first hour sounded as I got to my locker. Gertie wasn't around, but considering the bell for first hour was only three minutes away, I figured she wouldn't be.

I opened my locker and was bombarded by several small balloons falling out and onto me. A card was taped to the inside of the locker. I opened it up and read:

Happy Birthday to the toughest guy I've ever met.

Love, Gertie

P.S. I was just kidding when I said you had puny muscles.

It was the nicest thing anyone who wasn't family had ever done for me.

"Marco, the bell's about to ring."

I turned to see Miss Dantsy bending down to pick up some of the balloons. I didn't know what to do with them all, so I started shoving them back into the locker, but they kept falling out.

"How about you let me put the balloons in a garbage bag while you get to class? I'll give them back to you at the end of the day."

"Are you sure?"

"First hour is my prep hour, but you don't have that luxury." She smiled, then said, "Shoo, get to class. I'll take care of this. Oh, and happy birthday."

After first hour, I hunted down Gertie. "Thanks," I said. "How'd you know?"

"Your Grandma whispered it to me when we were at the ice cream parlor. Did I surprise you?"

"Yes!" I practically yelled. "It was really cool. There were balloons all on the floor, and I couldn't get them back into the locker!"

Gertie started laughing. "It was difficult, that's for sure. But it's nice that we don't have those tiny, half lockers like they have up at the high school. I could stuff more in! Dana, and some of the other girls from the bus, helped me as soon as we got here."

"What would you have done if I had been on the bus?"

"I was planning on getting excused a little early from third hour to do it before lunch, but this worked out perfectly."

Teachers started yelling down the hall at everyone to get to class.

"Oh, we're having cake and ice cream tonight," I said before

I waved goodbye.

"I'll be there!"

During third hour, Miss Dantsy quizzed us on last week's review. No big deal. I aced it (of course), and Miss Dantsy gave this big announcement in front of the whole class that she was impressed with my scholastic skills. And she handed me another glitter pencil (if I kept this up, I could start my own store). And she said it was my birthday, so the class sang to me.

That's when the strangeness began. Tim passed a note in my direction (Miss Dantsy sat him close to the front). It fell on the floor by my desk. Allison, the girl in front of me, turned around and motioned that the crumpled paper was for me.

I glanced in both directions. That's when I noticed Tim staring at me. So was everyone else. It seemed no one was paying attention to Miss Dantsy's lecture on exponents.

I dropped my glitter pencil on the floor by the note and bent over to pick it up. Unraveling it, I could hardly make out the chicken scratch. It said (I think):

Meet me at my locker. Lunch. Don't be late.

Tim

When I looked up, he was staring intently at Miss Dantsy even though the glazed-over look in his eyes indicated that he wasn't listening to a word of it.

Where's Gertie when I needed her? As soon as the bell rang, I jumped out of my seat and headed for the door.

“Marco?” Miss Dantsy’s voice called out to me.

I cringed, stopped my rapid flight, and walked back to her. “Sorry, I’m running in your class.”

“Oh, I’m not calling you because of that.” She rested her hand on my shoulder. “I just want to tell you how proud I am of you. You’re in a new school, away from home, and yet you are not letting that interfere with your work ethic.”

My heart fluttered from her touch. She was proud of me? She turned back to her desk. “Keep up the good work.”

“Uhhh,” I mumbled, as I backpedaled to the door. ”Yeah, okay.” I turned around and left, giving her an awkward wave as I did.

I couldn’t focus on Senor Martinez even though he was trying to involve all the students in the singing of the Spanish alphabet. I kept debating whether or not to meet Tim. But when the bell rang, I knew it would look wimpy to skip out on him, so I headed toward his locker in full Arnold Schwarzenegger persona.

He was already there with Ray and Chump. For some reason, everyone in school called the big lug with braces and zits Chump, but in my opinion, they were all chumps.

“What do you want?” I asked as I approached them. I leaned against a locker and folded my arms.

“Easy does it, dude,” Tim said. He flipped his hair then extended his hand in a salute. “We come in peace.”

The other guys snickered.

I didn’t crack a smile.

"Geesh, Marco, lighten up!" Tim exclaimed, playfully punching my shoulder.

I wasn't sure how to react. Was this a trick? They seemed to be cool, but I couldn't put aside my full-of-bull meter. Not yet anyway. "Fine, I'll lighten up. But could we hurry? I'm hungry."

"Me, too," Chump said.

Tim said, "Fine. Meet us at our table once you get your lunch."

I stood there in disbelief. "Wh-what did you say?" Regaining my Arnold composure I added, "I mean, I thought the table wasn't for losers."

"It's not. You're not a loser. Are you Marco?"

What kind of a question was that? "No, I'm not, but I sit with Gertie. Is that going to be a problem?"

Tim and the other boys glanced at each other.

"Listen, she's my friend."

"I get that, but this is a guy's table."

"Then we can talk later."

"All right, fine, she can sit with us."

I left them and went to my locker. I opened it slowly, to make sure there were no more balloons, and grabbed my lunch. When I shut it, Gertie was leaning against the locker beside it. "I saw you talking with Tim. What's up with that?"

"They want me to eat lunch with them," I said, not fully believing it. "I said I sit by you, and they said you could sit by them too, but I don't know. I don't trust them, and today, so far, is going well. I don't want to jinx it."

"First skateboarding, and now this. Maybe they're trying to be friends."

We began to walk down the hall. "You think so?"

"You're a cool guy, especially with your attitude sometimes. Yeah, I can see why they want to hang out with you. It'll probably up their street cred."

That made me laugh.

"If we sit with them, and they're still jerks, then we ditch them. Easy. But I swear, if he makes one comment about me and Ray or about me being trailer trash, I'm going to punch him in the face."

"That'd be fun to watch."

As we rounded the corner, I spotted the police officer, standing outside the front office with Grandma, Ms. Wright, and the school counselor, Mr. Harrington.

"What's going on?" Gertie whispered.

But I didn't answer. I didn't move either.

They all seemed to notice me at the same time. I found Grandma's eyes first. They were red-rimmed and still shiny from tears. Mr. Harrington looked like he had eaten too much food and was suffering heartburn or something, and Ms. Wright had lost that mega-watt smile of hers.

Gertie grabbed my hand. She must have sensed something wasn't right.

Grandma came over to me. "Marco, we need to go. Your

teachers will get your homework together, and Gertie can drop it off. Will that work, Gertie?"

"Sure."

Something was wrong. I felt it in my bones. Grandma and everyone else wouldn't talk about it in front of Gertie, so I turned to her and said, "I'll talk to you later."

"I'll stop by after dinner."

"Call first," Grandma said.

Gertie acted like she was going to burst into tears, and she didn't even know what was going on. She squeezed my hand and walked past the adults to the cafeteria.

I followed Grandma, Ms. Wright, and the police officer outside. The school counselor stayed back. Once outside, I couldn't stand it any longer. "What? I know it's about Dad."

The adults stopped and looked at each other. Grandma nodded at the police officer. "Marco," he said. "The authorities downstate found him."

And just like that, I felt the earth give underneath my feet.

CHAPTER NINETEEN

They wouldn't talk about it until we got to Grandma's house. That ride lasted longer than when I first came up here.

Once inside, I couldn't take it. "Is he…alive?"

"Yes," Ms. Wright said quickly. "He's alive, but the police arrested him and took him to the Detroit jail for booking. They found drugs in his possession. I'm so sorry…"

"But he's alive?"

"Yes," Grandma said this time. "He's alive, and when they gave him the one phone call…" Grandma got choked up. "He called *me*."

I probably did the last thing they expected. I exhaled in relief. He was alive, and now he could go back to rehab. "What did he say?"

"He didn't talk much, other than to say he was sorry, and that he was glad you were with me."

"Can I talk to him?"

"Soon," Ms. Wright said.

"I've already contacted a lawyer, and I'm going to make sure he gets the help he needs." Grandma wiped at her face and smiled back at me. "He asked how you were doing. He told me to tell you 'Happy birthday,' and he loves you."

"I wish I could've talked to him. Maybe he can call back."

"I'm glad to see you taking this so well," Ms. Wright said and rested her hand on my shoulder.

"He's safer with the police than he is out on his own," I said. "Did they find the men he was with? Did he leave the rehab center by choice or by kidnapping?"

"They are still looking for them. I asked Lance about it, but he changed the subject. The police seem to think that he was set up with the drugs."

"Those men set him up?"

"That's what they're looking into."

"How long does it take police to find bad guys? I don't get it."

"I know it's hard to be patient, but we have to try," Grandma said. "Hopefully, by this weekend, we can head down there and visit."

"Oh, before I forget," Ms. Wright handed me a gift bag with tissue paper sticking out. "Happy birthday."

Inside were two Starship Enterprise books, numbers 11 and 15, and a chocolate bar.

"I know they're out of order, but I found them at the library's book sale, and I don't know, thought you might want to read them."

"Thanks."

"And everyone loves chocolate," she said with a smile. Then she walked to the door. "All right, I guess I'll get going, and Marco,

I'll see you tomorrow."

It wasn't until she left, that I asked, "What's tomorrow?"

"She's going to pick you up after school for your counseling session. We decided she should counsel you at her office, now that you've been here a while."

"Say what?"

"Counseling session. It's part of the whole social worker package."

"I'm not crazy." So, that's why Ms. Wright always showed up asking questions?

"It's not for crazy people. It's for everybody. All of us need to talk and get things off our chests. It'll be good, you'll see."

I looked down at the bag I was holding with my birthday gifts. It's not like Ms. Wright bothered me like she first did, but I wasn't exactly ready to tell her my life story. "Why can't Mr. Harvey do it?"

"You know why."

"We could do a telephone counseling session."

"Marco, give her a chance. Besides, it's part and parcel of this whole stay-with-your-grandma situation." Grandma came over to me and squeezed my shoulder. "I'm proud of you. You are taking this so much better than I anticipated. Maybe I should take you back to school."

"Ha, ha, nope. I'm here now. And I've got new books to read." I held up the bag.

"Only because it's your birthday."

I walked into the bedroom and saw the wrapped present on the bed. I grinned. Actual presents on my birthday? Yes, please! "Can I open it?" I yelled, holding it in my hands. It felt heavy.

"Or you can stare at it. Whatever works." Grandma poked her head into the room to watch.

I opened up the birthday card from Grandma, then I ripped open the wrapping paper. Then I might have squealed. "Is it…?" I covered my mouth and stared at Grandma.

"Mr. Harvey said since I refused to get cable channels, you might like one of those. He set it up for you on Friday before you got back from school. Which is good because I don't have a clue how to work one of them things."

I interrupted her by throwing my arms around her. "I *love* it!" I said, squeezing her for emphasis. "I've always wanted a laptop!"

"Good. I'm glad I listened to Mr. Harvey. He knows what he's talking about. He said you guys can chat on that internet any time once the servicemen come out and install it. And he said that when your dad is past the detox phase that it'll be a great way for you to communicate with him."

It was like I seriously couldn't contain the joy. I jumped around the room, whooping before falling on the bed out of breath. Grandma looked like she was enjoying the show. "Thanks," I said. "I mean it. I'll take real good care of it. I know how expensive they are."

"You're worth it. And I haven't had anyone to spend money on in a while. I probably enjoyed spending it a little too much."

I thought of the money hidden in the coffee can. Did she get the money from there? "I've never had that much money before." It had taken a lot to put the can back into the ground and not go back to it. My first instinct had been to grab wads of it and shove it in my pocket. If Gertie hadn't been there, I probably would have.

"I don't want you to worry about that," Grandma said, her expression suddenly serious. "The days where you go hungry are gone, Marco. I'm not saying you're going to be rich, at least not living here with me, but those dark days are in the past. Today, our whole family can be hopeful."

My only response was to squeeze the laptop box in a bear hug.

***

Three hours later, I was playing a computer game that came as a free trial on the laptop. I had wanted to set up accounts, but the internet wouldn't be installed until Thursday.

The phone rang, but I barely registered it. I was too busy killing a zombie.

Grandma showed up at my door, a peculiar expression on her face. "The phone is for you. Want me to tell him to call back?"

I paused the game. "Who is it?"

"He didn't say. It sounds like a boy your age."

I walked into the other bedroom and picked up the phone. To my surprise, Tim was on the other end. "You're hard to nail down, you know that?"

"Yeah, sorry I wasn't at lunch. I had an emergency at home."

"I know. What's up with that? Everyone said the police were there to arrest you. Dude, what'd you do?"

"They weren't there to arrest me." I couldn't think of a plausible lie.

"Did your grandma hurt herself? That's what Gertie said, but it sounded lame."

"Well, that's what happened." I paused. "Is that why you called?"

"No. Yes. No. I called because I've been trying to talk to you."

"So…talk."

"Did you do your math homework yet?"

"There wasn't any math homework."

"Yes, there was. For those who didn't finish the chapter in class."

"Well, I did."

"I was hoping you could talk me through some of the problems."

"It's just basic exponents. It's not complicated."

"It's math. To me, it's complicated."

"Do you need to pass, so you can be in football?" I snorted at my joke.

"No, I'm not into football, I'm into boarding. Listen, you know what, never mind. I told Ray it was a dumb idea."

"Wait, hold on a sec. I never said I wouldn't help you. Lighten up."

"Lighten up? This is coming from the kid whose facial expression always looks like someone took a dump in his breakfast every morning."

Then a weird thing happened, we both started laughing.

Gertie walked into the room about a half-hour later. I was sitting on the floor, leaning against the wall. "No, it's two and three quarters," I said. "How'd you get ten?"

"Because I guessed."

"I've got to go. Are we done yet?" It hadn't escaped my notice that I had given him every answer.

"Thanks, Marco," Tim had said. "It's going to be sweet having you for a friend."

I was so caught up in being called a *friend* that I didn't care about helping him with his homework. Even if it *was* cheating.

"So, that's why he wants to hang out," Gertie said. "It makes sense. Last year, I practically did all of Ray's work in science."

"Come on, you two!" Grandma called from the kitchen. "Let's have some cake!"

"Should I say something?" I asked Gertie before we went to the kitchen. "Should I tell Tim to get a life?"

"Let's see if they really want to be friends with you, or if they're being jerks. We can dump them in a minute." She snapped her fingers to prove her point.

"All right. Sounds like a plan. Thanks for coming over."

"Thanks for getting me out of my horrible house. Now let's go get some cake."

CHAPTER TWENTY

I turned around and glanced at the small clock that hung on the wall behind me.

"Only five minutes have passed," Ms. Wright said across from me.

I pressed my lips together and blew out air. "So, how's your diet going?"

Ms. Wright raised her eyebrows, and her smile faded slightly.

"I don't mean anything bad by the question," I said quickly, trying to backtrack. I couldn't have her telling Grandma I was bad. Then I'd never get out of these things. "Just that you told me a while ago that you couldn't have chocolate because you were on a diet."

"My diet's fine, thank you, but let's talk about you."

"What's there to talk about?"

"How's school?"

"Good."

"Want to elaborate?"

"Nothing to elaborate about. I get up, go to school, go to classes, come back to Grandma's house, eat dinner, go to bed. The end. Then I do the same thing the next day."

She nodded, made a face, and wrote something down. *What'd I say?*

"What'd you write down?" I asked, trying to keep my attitude in check, but she was making it hard to do. "Every time I see you, you ask questions, then write stuff down."

"I'm only taking notes."

"About what?"

"Things I observe. Or, things you say. It helps me put a picture together."

"What'd you write down? I haven't said anything yet."

"Why don't you tell me about living with your grandma? How's that going?"

"Fine." There. One word. Let's see her write that down. I crossed my arms and glowered at her. I was starting to not like her again.

"Want to elaborate?"

"No."

Ms. Wright's smile tightened. "Marco, the only way these sessions will work is if you allow yourself this time to let down your walls and be open with me. Consider this your safe zone."

I turned and looked at the clock behind me. It hadn't even been another five minutes! At this rate, the hour would never end!

"Time will go faster if you open up and tell me about your day."

"I already did!"

"Do you like school?"

"No."

"Why not? Are other students bothering you?"

"No." I huffed out a breath. "This really sucks. How come I don't get to interrogate you?"

"Fine." Ms. Wright set down her notepad. "You ask me a question, and I will answer fully. Then I will ask you one, and you answer me fully. Deal?"

At least she put the stupid notebook down. "Fine. Do you have a family?"

"I have parents," she said. "I don't have any children of my own. My ex-husband had a daughter from a previous relationship, but since the divorce, I don't see her as much as I would like." She smiled and extended her hands. "What about you? Why don't you talk about your parents?"

"I don't know my mom," I answered. "It's only ever been me and Dad. And now there's Grandma. My Grandpa's dead apparently, so that kind of sucks, but Grandma's cool." I smiled and extended my hands to show her I could play along. "Do you have a boyfriend?"

"No, I don't. My work consumes a lot of my life. Do you have a girlfriend? I see you with that Gertrude girl quite a bit."

I could feel the heat in my face. When Ms. Wright picked me up, Gertie had opted to miss the bus to wait with me. "Gertie is the nicest girl I've ever met," I said simply. I didn't want to say too much, but that part was the truth. "She likes me, and I don't even have to try to be someone I'm not."

"That's a rare find," Ms. Wright said quietly. "To find someone who cares for you no matter what. That's a friend to keep. Have you told her about your dad?"

"Hey, wait! It's my turn!" I paused, thinking. "Um, so, why do you live up in Northern Michigan?"

"Because there was a case overload. My home is normally in the Detroit area. That's how I know Mr. Harvey. Since I've recently divorced, I volunteered to live up here for a while."

"Do you like it?" We were interrupted by a knock at the door. A young woman peeked her head in. "Ms. Wright, I'm sorry to disturb you, but there's an emergency on line one."

Ms. Wright furrowed her eyebrows and waddled over to her desk. "Hello?" She was quiet while the other person talked, then she glanced over in my direction, the alarm apparent on her face.

"What?" I stood, already braced for the bad news.

She set the phone down. "Mr. Harvey's on the other end. He'd like to speak to you."

I nearly jumped over the couch to get to the phone. "What's wrong?" I asked him.

"Hey, Marco. How are you?"

"What's wrong?" I repeated.

"Nothing, exactly. I have some news about your father."

"How is he doing? Did you tell him I'm coming to see him in

three days?"

"I went to tell him, but when I got over here, I was surprised to find out someone had posted his bail."

"Say what?"

"Someone paid to get him out."

My stomach dropped to my ankles. "He's out of jail? Why didn't they put him back in rehab?"

"They gave him another court date because of the drugs on him when they found him."

"Can I still go see him?"

"We don't know exactly where he went."

I thought I might get sick. "Doesn't he have to leave an address?"

"Yes, the address doesn't pan out."

"So, you've lost him?"

"Someone by the name of Joseph Ricci paid his release money." Mr. Harvey was quiet. Finally, he said, "Marco, it shouldn't have happened. He should have never been awarded bond."

I set the phone down. Going over to the window, I stared outside and tried to calm my stomach down.

"Let's take you to your grandma. We'll continue next week."

"There's never a day I'm not worried," I said, still looking outside. "Never a day that I can just be a kid. Never." I turned and glared at Ms. Wright. "And bringing me up here and away from Dad only makes it worse. Do you all want to help me? Then take me back to him!" I shouted at that point, but I didn't care.

"Your safety comes first," Ms. Wright said quietly. "I know it's tough."

"No, you don't know. You don't get it. Nobody does. Nobody. Not even Grandma. Just pull the kid away from his father. It's for his safety. He'll be fine. He'll make friends. He'll forget about his father!"

"We don't want you to forget."

I didn't stay to hear the rest. I barreled down the stairs, knowing that she'd never keep up. Slamming out the doors, I began to run. I sort of knew where Grandma lived. It wasn't too far out in the country. Just a couple of roads off the main one. I ran in that direction.

How could everything go from so right to so wrong in a day? In my heart, I knew Dad was in danger. He didn't have close friends. Not real ones. That meant that whoever paid to get him out of jail had an ulterior motive. And I could tell from Mr. Harvey's voice that he thought so too. He was horrible at masking his worry and concern.

So, the plan was simple. Get the coffee can. Take the money. Head down to Detroit.

But first, I was going to stop and pick up Gertie.

***

By the time I made it to Gertie's, I was close to hyperventilating. I had already slowed to a jog and stuck to the side of the country roads. If I heard a car, I'd duck in the woods, only to reemerge when the coast was clear. I couldn't even think about talking to an adult. I only wanted to grab Gertie and convince her to go with me.

Two police cars zoomed by at one point. I thought they might be headed toward Grandma's, which complicated things. But as I got closer to Gertie's, I saw that they had stopped there. Gertie's Mom was talking to the officers and acted freaked out about something. I ran across the road to the woods. I'd have to brave them.

Suddenly, I heard, "There's that boy she hangs with!" Gertie's mother screeched it so loudly, I jumped like I was caught. But I didn't stop.

"Halt!"

"Stop!"

I kept running. My heart felt like it would explode in my chest at any second, but I couldn't afford to stop. I didn't even have enough time to think about me running through the woods all by myself. Which was probably a good thing. I ran past that dirt bike trail Ricky and his friends had been on a few weeks ago, and then I started to see the markers Grandma said she posted to signify her property lines. Good. At least I moved in the right direction.

Before I got to Grandma's backyard, I had already decided that I wouldn't have time to wait for Gertie. I could come back and get her after I made sure Dad was all right.

My plan quickly morphed into grabbing the coffee can of cash and hightailing it back into the woods and to the bus stop. I wasn't sure where the bus stop was, but I'd figure it out.

That's when I heard sirens. Luckily, I ran through the last cluster of trees and out onto her back vegetable gardens. I would have been impressed that I completely ran through the woods without being scared, but the sirens were already pulling into Grandma's yard.

I opened the garden gate, fell to my knees, and started digging. I hit the can's lid and hurried to pull the can out from its hiding spot. I had just yanked it out and was in escape mode again when I heard, "Freeze!"

I would have kept going, but I heard Grandma's voice. "Marco?"

My heart froze. Not again. "I can explain," I said, turning to her. Well, at least, I tried to say the words. I was super out of breath.

Grandma eyed me then the coffee can. "Hon, we've been worried sick. Did you run from Ms. Wright's offices?"

Ms. Wright walked alongside a police officer, whispering to him.

"I've got…to go…find… Dad," I said, emotion hitching onto my words. "The police lost him. He wrote the word *help* in my book. He…needs me."

"What's in the coffee can?" One of the police officers walked over and stepped up beside me.

I glanced over at Grandma, and my face crumpled. "I was only going to borrow it. I was going to put it back. I needed money for a bus ticket."

The police officer took the coffee can from my arms and pulled back the lid. His eyebrows bunched together. "What's supposed to be in here?"

"Money," Grandma and I said at the same time.

That's when the police officer showed us. The coffee can was empty.

CHAPTER TWENTY-ONE

What bothered me more than having my escape to Detroit foiled again was the look of distrust in Grandma's eyes. "I'm telling the truth," I said for the umpteenth time. "Why would I carry an empty coffee can? I thought the money was in there."

"How much would you say was in the can?"

"It was stuffed full," Grandma said, pacing back and forth in the front room, where we all sat. "Twenties, fifties…"

"Who else knew where the can was located?"

Everyone turned to me. Could I rat out Gertie? No. Besides, I trusted her. I doubt she took all that money. "I don't know."

"His friend knew," Grandma said sadly. "They both came from around back with their hands covered in dirt."

"Gertrude Blackstone?" the police asked.

"And you were going to steal it?" The police looked at me and motioned with his hand for me to continue.

"I was going to buy a bus ticket to Detroit."

"Do you know where Gertrude is?"

"Gertie…and no, I don't. The last place I saw her was at

school. She decided to skip the bus home and wait with me until Ms. Wright showed up."

"Did she make any indication where she might go? Has she ever mentioned a place that she would want to run away to?"

I shook my head. "No, not that I can remember."

"You weren't going to meet her?" The police asked suspiciously.

"No," I said with attitude. The guy was getting under my skin. "How many times do I have to repeat myself?"

"That's enough," Grandma said to me. "He's doing his job, and he wouldn't have to question you if you were honest."

"I *am* being honest. Forget this. I'm going for a walk."

"No, you're not," Grandma said. "Go to your room. I'll call you out if we need you."

I pressed my lips together really hard so that I wouldn't snap at Grandma. She was acting sad and upset, and it bothered me knowing that I was a big reason for it. So, I huffed to my room, but first I made sure to glare at the police officer. And Ms. Wright.

But my room was boring. I couldn't shut my mind off. From Dad to Gertie, it kept jumping around. Now I was worried about both of them.

I found my notebook in the backpack and scribbled a note:

Don't worry. I'm not running away. Just going for a walk. And I didn't take the money either.

But I couldn't leave out my window. One of the police officers stood right outside of it. Then I thought of the window in the front bedroom. I felt so caged in, I was willing to risk it. As quietly as I could, I opened my bedroom door. The police officer was asking Grandma and Ms. Wright questions. Good. I tip-toed to the front bedroom and had to maneuver through it without making a sound, but it was like a minefield. It didn't help that it was closer to the living room than my bedroom. It would have to work. I needed to get out.

The screen nearly hit the desk, but I caught it in time. I paused and listened. They were still talking. It sounded like it was about me, but I had no time to be curious. I set the screen down and jumped out the window.

I stood and briefly contemplated where to go. I came from behind the house, which is where they thought I would probably go again, so I decided to take the path to the lake. It wouldn't work if I was running away, but I wasn't. Every time I tried, I failed, so I had to come up with a better plan. Besides, I needed Grandma to believe I didn't take the money. The money was gone, and it wasn't me.

When I made it to the lake, I saw Gertie sitting beside the water, her backpack next to her. My heart leaped. "Hey," I said, relieved to see her. "Everyone's worried about you."

She didn't turn around, only kept staring in front of her.

I sat next to her and saw her face puffy and splotchy from crying. "You didn't get very far."

"I was waiting for you to get back from your doctor's appointment."

I had to tell Gertie that I had a doctor's appointment because it felt weird saying I was going to a counseling session. But now I felt bad for lying. "Well, I'm here. What's the plan?"

"Get as far away from here as possible." She had yet to look over at me.

"What happened?"

"They released him," she whispered, fresh tears forming. "He didn't even serve three full years. They are letting him go for good behavior." She wiped at her face, but it wasn't helping.

"It'll be okay," I said. "If he gets near you, call the cops."

Gertie adamantly shook her head. "No one believed me. Even my own mother thought I wanted attention because she dumped my dad to go back to Ricky's dad. That I was being temperamental. My dad was too busy partying to listen."

"Someone listened."

"Yeah, my face and all its bruises were pretty hard to shove under the carpet. And that wasn't the only place he hurt," she said without looking me in the eyes. "They promised he would go away for a long time. That he wouldn't hurt me anymore. Mom even got back with my dad to keep an eye on me. And now they're going to let him go. Ricky told me that he and his dad were going to make me pay."

My gut clenched at what Gertie endured. What did Ricky's father do to her? More than just physical abuse from what she said. "I don't know why bad men do what they do," I said quietly.

"My mother acts like she cares," Gertie kept going, stopping to suck in breaths. "But she keeps doing it. She brings home these jerks."

"I thought you said that your dad is around now."

"Yeah, but just recently. He went to rehab for a while to help with his drinking problem." She sniffed and wiped at her nose. "My Dad doesn't get that she's not the only one these men like. I've tried to tell her. I've told my social worker, too. No one listens! Mom smiles and says everything they want to hear."

"You have a social worker?"

Gertie nodded. "Yeah, I got sent away for a while. Honestly, leaving that trailer was the best thing that ever happened to me." Now her voice became steel. "I'm leaving now. I don't care that I'm not sixteen yet."

"My dad's not a pilot."

Gertie didn't say anything.

"He's a drug addict in Detroit who was arrested. I thought it would be better for him to be with the police where he could get off the streets and get some help, but someone paid his bail. Everyone thinks he's in danger. Like the person who paid it needed him out before he gave names or something."

"Is that why you came to your grandma's?"

"Dad told them to take me up here. I'd never been up here before."

"Who was that guy that came from your place last weekend?"

"My social worker." I smiled.

Gertie smiled. We stayed quiet for a minute before Gertie asked, "Do you believe in God?"

The question surprised me. "Yes," I said, surprised my answer popped out so fast. "Dad would tell me stories from his Sunday School classes. Not often, but now and then."

"That's why?" Gertie didn't sound convinced.

"We're getting into some personal stuff," I started to tease.

"I'm serious," she said and nudged me. "I want to know why you'd believe that something out there exists who gives a crap about us."

I thought about her question, but I hesitated to answer. But as I watched her, I knew I could trust her even with my secrets. "I know it sounds weird," I began, "but I keep praying and asking God to make Dad not addicted to drugs."

"Isn't he still addicted?"

"Well, yes. But if I stop believing in him now, I don't want him to get mad and not do it. I know that seems dumb."

"No, it doesn't. I'm kind of clueless about all of it. It's hard to believe in something or someone who would let bad things happen. But then," she paused, then continued, "Well, never mind."

"When I would get bored of reading, I'd turn on the television to those preachers who'd be on there, and I would listen."

"No way!" She started to laugh.

"Seriously. I'd place my hand on the T.V. and everything. I

think I've been saved about a hundred and twenty times."

Gertie kept laughing. "Stop kidding around!"

"I'm telling the truth!" I acted indignantly.

When Gertie's laughter subsided, she shook her head. "I guess I can tell you something weird about me. Ever since I was a little girl, Mom would make me say evening prayers. When all that bad stuff was happening to me, I'd pray that God would make it stop. But that was years ago. I hadn't prayed in a long time." She paused, then continued, "But I prayed the night before I met you."

It felt like someone released a thousand butterflies into my stomach.

"I prayed that I wouldn't feel so alone anymore." She didn't say anything else, only scooted closer to me, resting her head on my shoulder.

I didn't know what to say to that. I eventually said, "You're not alone anymore."

"I know. And you at least have your grandma."

"Yeah, but now she's mad at me because she thinks I took the money."

"Oh." Gertie took her backpack, unzipped it, and showed me the money. "I'm sorry, Marco, I was going to repay her. But I needed money to move away. I was going to share with you." She paused, then closed the zipper. "I can't go back home. I can't."

I heard the desperation in her voice. She leaned her head onto my shoulder and started to cry again.

And we stayed like that for a long time.

CHAPTER TWENTY-TWO

Unfortunately, we were busted before we could make a break for it. A part of me was glad Grandma discovered the removed screen, and they found us at the lake. I was kind of tired and wanted to sleep in my bed.

Gertie acted resigned. She apologized to Grandma and gave her the backpack full of money. I knew Gertie would try to run away again. I only hoped that she would talk to me first so that we could figure out a better plan.

"Be on the bus tomorrow," I whispered to her before we both headed home.

Grandma didn't say much other than to go to bed and please stop climbing out of windows. I was too tired to think about running away again. I took a shower and crashed within minutes of lying down.

Now, as I ate breakfast, I watched Grandma stare vacantly out the front window. I finished my milk and set the bowl in the sink. "Are you still mad at me?"

"I'm worried," she admitted. "You don't seem to understand

how important you are to me. If you want to go downstate, talk to me about it. We can make something work. But running…and stealing…you're better than that, Marco." She turned to look back out the window.

My stomach felt sick. "I'm not better than that," I said. "If I wanted to survive, there were two things I had to get good at. Running and stealing."

Grandma turned back to me. "You don't need to do those things anymore, especially because it breaks down trust. How can I trust you if you keep trying to sneak out from under me?"

"Aren't you scared about Dad?"

"Yes, but I trust law enforcement. They are keeping a close eye on the situation."

"Grandma, no offense, but you don't get it. Dad is in danger. Whoever paid his bail did it because they didn't want him to give names. That's why those guys broke him out of rehab. Dad knows something."

"Let the law enforcement do their job. We can still go down this weekend if you'd like."

I swallowed the lump in my throat and nodded. The bus got there before I could say anything else. I ran outside to the bus, feeling bad about my actions. Not only that, but my muscles were sore. Running from town to the house ended up being three miles, and my legs felt it.

Gertie climbed on soon after and slid in beside me.

"Did it get any better?" I whispered.

"My dad said he'd kill the guy if he came near, and then Ricky overheard that and said he'd kill my dad if my dad killed his, so I ended up locking myself in my room."

"I don't like your brother. I'll figure out a way to take him down."

"Let's just figure out a way out of here."

I thought of my grandma. I couldn't risk running away again. But Gertie was determined. "Hey," I said, thinking of a great idea. "How about if you come with me and Grandma downstate for the weekend? It'll get you out for a couple of days, and we can come up with a plan."

Gertie jumped at the idea. "Definitely! I'll endure until Friday. Thanks." She intertwined her fingers with mine.

I glanced down and felt the heat flood my face. We held hands the entire bus ride. When we got off the bus, Tim was waiting for me. Gertie quickly dropped my hand.

"Hey, we need to talk." Tim glanced at Gertie. "Privately."

She rolled her eyes. "Bye, Marco."

I turned to Tim. "What's up?"

"Tried to call you last night to get help with the homework."

"Yeah, last night was crazy. Why don't you sit by me in class, and we can do the problems together? That way, you won't ever have homework."

Tim's eyes widened. "I never thought of that. Good idea. Until then, help." He thrust the textbook at me.

"Right here?"

"Look, I did the problems. I only need you to make sure they're right."

I walked over to a brick ledge that led into the building. I flipped open the book to the pages his notebook had been crammed between. I sighed. "You didn't do the problems."

"I tried with the first one. Come on, man, I need your help. Just do this for me until we can sit by each other in class. Then you can, you know, tutor me…or whatever." Tim flipped his hair out of his eyes.

I sloppily did the ten advanced exponent problems because it was easier than trying to explain it. And really, what did it matter? "There. Next time, I'm charging you."

Tim laughed. "Thanks, dude. You're awesome."

"You think I'm kidding," I said and walked away. "Five bucks for every time I help."

Gertie waited at the locker. "Let me guess. Tim wanted your help."

I told her I was going to start charging them.

"That's a good idea. Then we won't have to steal your grandma's money. But don't get caught. That would probably turn out bad."

"I'm not going to get caught. As far as anyone's concerned, I'm helping Tim in math. What he chooses to do with the work is his business."

"Hey, I wanted to make it up to your grandma. I feel bad about stealing. Do you have any ideas what I can do?"

"I don't think she's too angry. She seems worried about Dad."

The bell rang and we split to head to class. I wasn't in gym ten minutes before some kid approached me, "Hey, is Tim trying to get your attention?"

I looked up and saw Tim outside the gym doors. He motioned to go to the guys' locker room. Mr. Oliver wasn't paying any attention. He was setting up basketball teams. I slipped away easy enough. When I got around the lockers, I saw Tim. "What's going on?"

He handed me his phone. "Quiz in math today."

"Who took a picture of the quiz?"

"Ray has it first hour. He's freaking out. He's got to pass, man."

"Ms. Dantsy doesn't have math first hour. It's her prep period."

"Yeah, he's got Collins, and they all give the same tests and stuff. It's like mandatory."

"Five bucks," I said. "I'll do it for five bucks."

"Are you serious? I thought we were friends."

"Do I look serious to you? If I'm going to do this, I'm not doing it for free."

"I don't have the money on me. I'll give it to you tomorrow."

"Per person. Five bucks per person. I'm not just helping you, and you know it."

"Fine." He watched me with what seemed like slight reverence and annoyance. "Is this what you did back in Detroit?"

"No, but I should have." If I would have thought about this *tutoring* business, it could have kept me fed. Maybe I could still be down there taking care of Dad.

The picture of the quiz was clear enough, and I did the twenty problems in minutes.

"You should get a phone," Tim said. "It would be easier."

"When I save enough money, I will." I left him in the locker room with a plan formulating in my mind. Sure, it nagged at me that cheating was wrong and blah, blah, blah, but this could be a way to make some serious money. I wouldn't have to steal from Grandma.

And, who would ever find out?

CHAPTER TWENTY-THREE

Another two weeks had passed, and life had fallen into a semi-normal routine. Gertie made Grandma a slightly burnt cake to say she was sorry, and after Grandma lectured us both, she hugged us and said that all was forgiven.

But Grandma also acted distracted. Her hatchback was at the mechanic's, which delayed any visit to Detroit. And she was on the phone a lot, and not sleeping enough. I'd wake up to the floor squeaking from her pacing back and forth.

One morning, she told me, "They're dropping off my car today, so we can drive downstate this weekend."

"Finally! I'll tell Gertie. She wants to come too."

"As long as it's all right with her mother. Make sure she gets permission. We'll leave early Saturday morning and return that evening or on Sunday. It depends on what we find out."

All I had to do was get through Friday at school. Easy enough.

Until first hour when Tim handed me an envelope full of money.

"What's this?" I counted a bunch of five-dollar bills. "There are sixty dollars in here."

"Yep. I've worked out this sweet gig," Tim whispered, glancing around to make sure no one heard. "When word spread that we had answers to the quiz, a bunch of kids started texting me for the answers. So, I told them 'Five bucks or no deal.' I think you and I've got a pretty sweet thing going. You do the math work, and I'll be like your bodyguard who goes around demanding the money." Tim smacked my shoulder. "And our first unit test is next week. Do you know how much you're going to be raking in this school year?"

My eyes lit up. Dollar signs swam in my vision. Why *hadn't* I thought of this before? "And there's no way to get caught, right?"

"No way, especially because you don't even have a phone. And I delete every text, the minute I hit send. It's brilliant."

"As long as everyone else does," I said.

"Good point. I'll spread the word that every text has to be deleted. Or I won't do it from text anymore. I'll think about it, but don't worry. You're free and clear from all of this, especially since Ms. Dantsy already knows that you're helping me."

I didn't need to give Tim any more homework answers because Ms. Dantsy thought it was a great idea for Tim to sit beside me.

"Fuller!"

I turned to see Mr. Oliver standing on the other side of the lockers. I shoved the envelope into one of my books and shut my gym locker. "What?"

"You're getting a zero in participation if you don't get out there right now. And you, Daniels, aren't you supposed to be in first hour…somewhere else?"

Tim nodded and left without another word. I walked past Mr. Oliver and headed to the gym. "Why do I have a feeling you two are up to no good?"

"I'm helping Tim in math with Ms. Dantsy's permission." I made sure to have an attitude. Mr. Oliver had way too many muscles for any middle school kid to not feel intimidated.

"I'll check with her on that. Now get on your basketball team."

The gym teacher worked fast because Ms. Dantsy called me to stay after class. Tim and I made eye contact. "Mr. Oliver came and talked to me."

I wasn't worried, but it made me dislike Mr. Oliver all the more. "Yeah, Tim was telling me he was nervous about the unit test, and Mr. Oliver yelled at us. I told him that I was helping Tim, but he didn't believe me."

"All right. I thought so, but Mr. Oliver overheard something about texting answers, which I know you would never do." She looked at me pointedly.

I disliked Mr. Oliver. "I don't even have a cell phone!"

Ms. Dantsy slowly nodded. "I know you wouldn't cheat on purpose, but be careful."

It felt weird that Ms. Dantsy truly thought I wouldn't cheat. Why would she think that? I thought of Grandma and her telling me about people trusting others. Then I thought about the money that I had transferred to my main locker by the classrooms. I said goodbye and was relieved to find Gertie there waiting for me.

I showed her the envelope of money. Her eyes widened. “Is it wrong?” I whispered. “What I’m doing?”

“Technically, yes, but it’s for a good cause, right? If we’re going to skip out of town, we’ve got to have money, and I don’t want to steal from your grandma.”

“If we keep this up, we’re going to have some money in no time.” I paused. “Maybe you should keep the money and hide it. That way I don’t have it on me. Just in case.”

“Okay, but I don’t want to take it home. My family would snatch the money in minutes.”

“Let’s get a coffee can of our own and hide it in the woods or something,” I said. “No one will know other than us.”

Gertie agreed. She placed the money in her purse that she always had dangling diagonally from her left shoulder to her right hip. “Don’t worry. I never take the purse off until I get home.”

At lunch, we took our spots at Tim’s table, which is where we’d been sitting. Tim and Gertie had become grudgingly polite. But I saw the way he looked at her. My theory about him liking her was a strong possibility. And it bothered me. I didn’t want him to like her. As we took our seats, the plan for the unit test was already in motion. “It’s easy. Ray is going to--”

“Stop.” I held up my hand. “It’s better if I don’t know.”

"Right. Okay, next week, we need to schedule a meet-up. I'll take care of the rest."

Suddenly everyone hushed. Gertie motioned that someone was behind me. The teacher on lunch duty said, "Marco, you're needed in the office."

No one said anything at the table. I stood, shrugged at everyone so they knew I wasn't bothered, and followed the teacher out of the lunchroom. I told myself that there was no way anyone could know, but my palms were sweaty by the time I got there.

Then I saw Mr. Harvey standing outside of the principal's office, and all thoughts of cheating left my mind. "Is it Dad?" I asked as soon as I walked in.

Mr. Harvey signed me out, waved at the principal, and motioned for me to follow him. I did. My stomach immediately rolled. I couldn't say anything until we were in Mr. Harvey's Taurus. I knew he was worried. He kept rubbing his chin and his forehead. But it wasn't until we were out of the school parking lot, that I asked, "What? What's wrong?"

He didn't say anything at first, only kept rubbing his chin and then his forehead.

"Tell me, Mr. Harvey. I can handle it."

He glanced over at me. "Your father's first court date was this morning."

"Yeah, so? We're heading downstate tomorrow morning."

"He never showed up."

My guts were churning in overtime. Something warned me that the bad news wasn't over. "This is ridiculous! This doesn't sound like my dad. I mean, yeah, we would run from authorities, but only from one squat to another, and we mostly ran from motel managers and truancy officers. Not this."

"The police believe he's gotten involved with the wrong people. Scary people."

"Most of the drug dealers are scary, but most of them liked Dad."

"These guys are scarier. The police have investigated enough to know that he owes money to someone who doesn't take not getting paid lightly."

"How much does he owe?" I asked quietly as if all the air had been sucked out of my lungs.

"They don't know, but considering the quality of drugs they found on him when he was arrested, probably in the tens of thousands."

I tightened my arms around my stomach. "He's never done stuff like this before!"

Mr. Harvey turned right, heading north.

"Where are you going?" I asked. "I want Grandma. We're going downstate, and we're going to find him."

Mr. Harvey pressed his lips together. "You're going to have to wait to go downstate."

"N!" I slammed my fist on the seat. "You don't get to tell us what to do, remember? You left me up here! And I'm going down there to find my dad, and Grandma's taking me!"

"That can't happen right now."

"Why not?" Anger and despair swept through me like hot lava on a mission. I was so angry at Mr. Harvey; I could barely stand to be in the car with him. I might have gotten to meet my Grandma, but none of it mattered with my father in danger.

Mr. Harvey slowed as we approached a small hospital. He put on his turn signal and turned into the parking lot. He didn't have to say a word.

"Why are we here?" I thought of Grandma. Her restless nights and constant worry. "Is she okay?" I unlocked the door and jumped out of the car before he had come to a complete stop.

"Marco!" he yelled. "Wait!"

But I didn't listen. I was already running through the hospital doors.

CHAPTER TWENTY-FOUR

"Marco, you can't go in." Ms. Wright stopped me.

"I have to see her."

"She's fine, but she's changing. You can't go in while she's undressed."

"She's fine?" Emotion started bubbling up, and I started taking deep breaths.

"Yes, she had an anxiety attack, so they ran some stress tests, checked her heart, that kind of thing, but she's fine."

I covered my mouth and focused on not crying in front of Ms. Wright or anyone else. Grandma was okay. But I wouldn't rest until I saw her for myself.

Mr. Harvey ran in and stopped beside us, panting. "You…" he said to me. "Don't…do…that."

"Is that Marco out there?" Grandma called from the room. "Send him in. I'm dressed now."

I pushed past Ms. Wright before she could say anything and ran into the room. Grandma sat on the edge of the narrow hospital bed, lacing up her shoes. I went over to her and hugged her hard.

"Don't ever do that again," I said, my voice catching in my throat. "I thought…What would I do…I couldn't…" but the words were all jumbled on my tongue. I didn't know how to express that I needed Grandma. I might have only met her a short while ago, and I might push to go downstate to help Dad, but Grandma had become my rock, my constant. I didn't know how to say that, or if it sounded too weird or mushy, so I hugged her neck for a long time instead.

Eventually, Grandma released me. "Hey, I'm all right." She touched my chin and gazed into my eyes. "I got a little too worried about Lance and got a little short of breath. I'm sorry they even pulled you out of school. I was hoping to be home before you and sweeping this whole thing under the rug."

I gave a half-smile because she seemed like she expected it, but I couldn't help observing the dark circles under her eyes and that her skin seemed paler. Grandma was trying to keep strong for me, but I wasn't fooled. This situation was hurting her hard.

There was a knock at the door before Mr. Harvey poked his head inside. "May we enter?"

"Of course," Grandma said.

I folded my arms across my chest and glared at Mr. Harvey. I wasn't sure why I was taking my frustrations out on him. The mess wasn't exactly his fault, but I had to glare at somebody. I was angry inside at a lot of things, so he became the target.

"I heard you got a clean bill of health." He smiled at both of us.

Neither Grandma nor I said anything. It's like we both expected bad news and didn't want to pretend our way through niceties.

"The police arrived," he said quietly to Grandma.

She nodded and sighed. "Well, now's as good a time as any. Send them in."

"Are you sure?" I asked her, grabbing her hand.

"Yep, we'll get through this together. But we have to hear what they know, so let's be brave." Her voice shook a little, so I squeezed her hand.

Two police entered, one from the other night. I looked away, not making eye contact. I had set my chin to look tough, but on the inside, I didn't feel like being brave. I wanted to lock the door to my bedroom, throw my blanket over my head, and wait until everything worked itself out. But I was starting to realize that I might be one of those unfortunate people where things don't work out.

The one stepped forward and began to speak. "There are several things that we need to bring to your attention." He glanced over at me. "Should the boy leave the room?"

"He's fine," Grandma said, squeezing my hand. "He needs to know what's going on."

The police officer nodded and continued, "From what the investigator at the Detroit precinct has conveyed to me, your son, Lance Fuller, has been borrowing money and drugs from Joe Ricci, the son of Carl Ricci. The family owns several dry cleaners on the east side, but it's well known that Carl and his son have many businesses in the black market. It's also well known that Carl's ruthless, which is why he's not in jail. Rumor has it that Carl broke Joe's arm one time because Joe lost some of his money in a gambling bet. Joe's not a lot better. They have no mercy. It's probably one of the biggest crime rings in the Detroit area that they've struggled to crack. Nobody lasts long enough to talk against him or his son."

Grandma took in a shaky breath. "How'd he get involved?"

"We're not sure. From what he said when first arrested, he's been involved with Ricci for almost a year, mostly for drugs, and that he started fearing for his life and that of his son's about three months ago."

"It's probably why he called us to pick up Marco," Mr. Harvey said to Grandma and me. "He wanted to make sure he was safe."

"Exactly. His earlier account was that threats were made against the boy's life, and he needed him as far away as possible," the police officer agreed.

"Wait," I said, trying not to act afraid. "Somebody wanted to kill me?"

It was Mr. Harvey who spoke, "If your father owes this man money, the Ricci family will resort to all kinds of things to get him to pay. Hurting you would be a motivator to get what they want from him."

"So, is Marco safe here?" Grandma asked.

"He should be," Mr. Harvey said.

"Not so fast," the police officer said to Mr. Harvey. "The investigator questioned the bar owner where Lance made the call to his son. The bar owner would not admit this, but his fear of Ricci was so palpable, and the surveillance camera at the bar indicates, that there's reason to suspect Ms. Fuller's phone number, and now Marco's location, have fallen into the wrong hands."

"Are you implying that Joe Ricci is coming after Marco?" Mr. Harvey stood straighter and began pacing. "If that's the case, he needs to be removed immediately."

"I'll start checking available homes," Ms. Wright said.

When it finally registered what they were talking about, my panic went into overdrive. "No way. I am not leaving Grandma."

"Marco, please do not fight us on this," Mr. Harvey said. "The situation is grave. You need to be safe until this situation is resolved."

"So, that Grandma can fight the bad guys by herself? What are you smoking? No way."

"You don't have a choice," Ms. Wright said, just as firmly.

"Listen, I will run from wherever you put me. That's a promise."

"Marco, they're right," Grandma said without raising her voice. "You're not safe right now at my place. This will only be temporary."

I began shaking my head back and forth. "No, not another home. No, I'm not doing it. You can't make me." Mr. Harvey stepped toward me. I immediately moved past him. "Get away from me."

Feeling like a caged bird, I pushed past everyone to the door. Ms. Wright tried to grab me, but I threw open the door. The other police officer that had been in the hall blocked my path. "Going somewhere?"

Every negative emotion hit me like a freight train, so I shoved at the guy with everything I had and started running down the hall. But he was fast. Faster than me. He grabbed at me and held my arms, so I started kicking my legs. "Let me go!" I yelled. "Help!" I knew I was making a scene, but I couldn't stop myself. I was tired and worried and scared and wanted the craziness to end. So, I threw the tantrum. I fought the police officer with all the strength I could muster.

"Don't make me put you in cuffs," he said through his teeth. "Now settle down. We're trying to keep you safe."

But I was too worked up to hear him. "Grandma!" I bellowed. "Help!"

Before I knew it, I was surrounded, but I didn't stop my screeching. Somehow, they got me into an empty room down the hall. I heard the police officer ask someone. "Do you want me to cuff him?"

I wasn't sure of the answer because I was still carrying on, but suddenly Mr. Harvey placed both of his hands on my face and stared me down. "Marco Fuller. Enough. Don't make them restrain you."

I took in shaky breaths and stopped screaming long enough to reason I had lost my voice some time ago. But the scream had come from inside, and I now felt depleted like a balloon that had lost its air. I felt the police officer's grip on my arms relax a bit and saw Mr.

Harvey step back. “Give him room to breathe,” he said to whatever crowd was in the room.

All I could do was lie there on the hospital floor and suck in breaths. My chest heaved, my lungs burned, and my heart ached.

At some point, the room emptied, and I became cognizant of only Mr. Harvey kneeling on the floor beside me. “I hate you,” I whispered in a hoarse voice.

“I know you do,” he said quietly. “But I don’t hate you. I care about you and your safety.”

“Now you’re taking me from my grandma.” The tears were there, and they burned. I wanted to go home. For the longest time, I didn’t know where that was. I thought it might be in Detroit where my dad was, but that was only because I had become familiar with it. The devil I knew. But I now knew better. That wasn’t home. Jumping from vacant, condemned houses to stale motel rooms, trying to find food when Dad was passed out.

It had only taken a couple of months, but the feeling was powerful, especially knowing they were going to take me away from the only place where I had ever been able to let down my guard. Sure, the place freaked me out when I first saw it. But it was the only place where I had truly felt safe. The only place I ever felt like myself. Why had I tried so hard to run away from the first place that had ever felt like home?

CHAPTER TWENTY-FIVE

"Shirley has an idea," Ms. Wright stood in the room, wringing her hands, watching me like I was a ticking bomb and detonation could happen at any moment.

I had finally sat up and leaned against the wall, but I had yet to get up from the floor. Mr. Harvey had stayed with me, and a nurse came in occasionally to monitor me, asking if I needed to be checked in as a patient for some calming medicine. Mr. Harvey had told her he'd let her know, but I think he thought I had lost my fight. What he might not have realized was that I only needed to gather my strength. I had every intention of running away from wherever they placed me. Maybe Gertie could hide me somewhere until the whole mess blew over. But I'd let them think they'd won for the time being.

"She wants to know if she and Marco can leave town for a while. They could stay in a hotel somewhere close by. That way Marco could still go to school here."

"Wouldn't they be monitoring the school?" Mr. Harvey asked.

"Maybe they could go out of the area, and Marco could do his work remotely."

"Yes," I said with no voice. "I can do that." I tugged on Mr. Harvey's sleeve. "Please."

He watched me for a minute, then stood up. He stretched his back and told me to wait there. "I need to make a few calls." At the door, he motioned for the police officer to stay outside the room. Even he knew Ms. Wright was no contest against me.

Eventually, Ms. Wright got called out of the room. That left me alone with the police officer right outside the door. I pushed myself up and checked the window, but there was no opening it.

I had been left alone for quite some time. I thought about turning on the room's T.V. but didn't feel like it. I wanted to see Grandma. What happened if they had her leave before I could say goodbye?

I opened the door and peaked out. Mr. Harvey stood down the hall with Ms. Wright, the police officers, and a new lady in a pantsuit. Mr. Harvey's face was beet red, and he acted angry. "He's not going to be used as bait. No. I won't allow it."

The new lady said, "This is how we nab him. There will be 24-hour protection. It's a win-win situation."

Mr. Harvey was adamantly shaking his head, and Ms. Wright kept looking from Mr. Harvey to the new lady like she couldn't make up her mind. Someone from behind me said, "Get back in the room."

I turned to see a third police officer staring me down. "How many of you are there?"

"Enough."

"I want to see my grandma. I won't freak out anymore."

He sized me up then quickly nodded. "All right, but no more shenanigans."

"What are they talking about?" I asked while we walked, pointing at the group behind us.

"None of your business."

"Well, technically, it's about me, so it is my business."

We made it to Grandma's room.

"Do you want to see your grandmother or not?"

I nodded and knocked on the door before entering. When I heard her say, "Come in," I pushed open the door.

Grandma sat in a chair with her head resting in her one hand. I stepped inside the room but stood off because I felt embarrassed for my earlier breakdown. Here she was battling with her own anxieties, and I act like a lunatic. "Hey," I said.

She looked up. "There you are," she said and outstretched her arms. "I was hoping they'd let you back in to see me."

I walked over to her, leaned down, and hugged her. "I don't want to go."

"I know."

"I wish I hadn't have tried to run away. That was so stupid."

"You've been through a lot. Everyone knows that. We're trying to figure out a way for you and me to take a little hotel vacation somewhere. Maybe with a pool and continental breakfast."

I released her and sat on her bed. "Do you think that Ricci guy is coming?"

"I'm not sure. Law enforcement seems to think so. They're trying to keep you safe. It's what I want, and it's what your father wants too. That's why you're up here to begin with."

"If I tell you something, do you promise not to tell anyone?"

"I promise to listen and not say a word, so long as it's not imperative knowledge that the police need."

"It's not really Mr. Harvey's fault. I act angry at him, but it's not fair." I stared at my hands. I needed to say the next words. "It's Dad's fault. This whole mess. All he cares about is stupid drugs. He stopped caring about me a long time ago."

Grandma got up from the chair and sat next to me on the hospital bed. "There's a lot of blame to go around, but don't think he doesn't care about you. Drug addiction is a very warped world. No matter how much you love someone, the drug takes control over your mind and body. It's like you can't even think without the drug in your system. It gets so bad that you'd do just about anything to get some more of the drug, even it means inadvertently hurting someone in the process."

"I hate drugs."

"I do, too."

"Drugs are going to kill Dad."

"Don't say that. There's always hope. As long as the good Lord gives breath in a person's lungs, there's always that hope of recovery. God helped me, and I believe He's going to help my son."

The hospital room door opened, and several people entered, including Mr. Harvey, Ms. Wright, and the new lady. She stepped over to me and Grandma. “I’m Detective Mueller, and I’ve been sent up here to assess the situation and the threat of possible harm. I’ve been told that Officer Muzinski filled you in about our concerns regarding Marco’s safety?”

“Yes,” Grandma said. “I’m more than willing to get away for a couple of days until this all blows over, as long as Marco can come with me. I don’t want him sent to live with someone else. He’s already been through so much.”

“Of course.” Detective Mueller smiled at me. She had a beautiful smile. It reminded me of Gertie’s. “I do have an idea, and I’d like to run it by you.”

“Please know that not all of us agree with this idea,” Mr. Harvey said. He had his arms folded, and his face was scrunched up like he ate something he didn’t like.

“Yes, I will discuss that,” Detective Mueller said, smiling at Mr. Harvey, which seemed to ruffle him up even more. I couldn’t tell if it was because he thought her smile was pretty too, and he was embarrassed, or if he didn’t like her idea. She turned back to us. “My partners and I, along with local law enforcement, believe that we need to stare this threat head-on. Finding out ahead of time that Ricci is possibly planning on coming up here is a Godsend. We can catch him in the act. If not him, then at least those working closely to him.”

“He could go to jail?”

"Yes, if we catch him—and I believe we will—he would go to jail for a very long time."

"I'm the bait," I said simply, thinking back to what I overheard in the hall.

"What?" Grandma asked, now catching on.

"Not technically."

"Yes, technically," Mr. Harvey interjected. "It's too risky and too dangerous."

"There would be 24-hour protection. We would set up cameras. Give you both cell phones that directly contact us. Marco could keep going to school. He could stay with you. The minute there's any trouble, we're there, and Joe Ricci is arrested and thrown in prison, along with his father, Carl."

"Why do we have to be at the house? Couldn't you set all that up without us there? They'll come to get Marco, and then you arrest them?" Grandma asked.

"Ricci has slipped through our fingers way too many times because we were sloppy. If he knows or suspects that either of you has any idea, he'll bolt. We need it to look like you are going about your everyday lives."

"Yes," I said. "I'll do it."

"Marco," Grandma said. "We need to talk about this."

"This is the hope you were talking about, Grandma. This is the hope we need to get this guy and save Dad."

"I am not about to risk your life, young man. You were sent

up here to be safe. I don't see how putting you in harm's way is keeping you safe."

"How safe would I be at a hotel? Or even in another home? If this Carl guy is as dangerous as everyone says he is, and I'm the prize, he's going to find me. At least this way, we have the police watching our every move."

Grandma studied my face for a moment, then turned to the detective. "Marco would have protection 24-hours a day, no matter what. No donut breaks, no bathroom breaks, nothing. My grandson would have security throughout the day and night."

"Yes, we would set up the cameras at different locations on the property. We would set up shop in an undisclosed location with patrols surrounding him and you day and night. We would need to make sure that we are hidden from them as to not scare them off, but with the cameras, the police detail, and the cell phones already programmed, you would be safe."

"There is no guarantee," Mr. Harvey said to Grandma.

"There's no guarantee we'll be safe anywhere," Grandma said to him. "At least this way Marco can stay with me and keep going to school. He needs normalcy. If we are going to have surveillance and 24-hour protection, I don't see how we can lose."

Mr. Harvey glared at the detective. Okay, so he must not be as wowed by her smile as I was.

"I should add something," Detective Mueller said, after making eye contact with Mr. Harvey. "Ricci is ruthless. He has no problem torturing, kidnapping, or killing, even children. When he feels trapped or lied to, he snaps, and it gets ugly. So, there is an element of danger that you should be aware of, not only for the both of you but for Lance. But," she added, "he's kept him alive this long. That must mean he wants the money enough to keep him around."

No one said anything for at least a minute. Finally, I said, "If this is what I need to do to help my dad, I wish everyone would let me have this chance."

Everyone shifted and gazed at Mr. Harvey. He threw up his hands and said, "As his social worker, I'm supposed to find the safest place for him. Don't make me the bad guy."

I stood and approached Mr. Harvey.

"Yes, Marco, I know you hate me, but I am looking out for you. And I am concerned…very, very concerned…about using you to lure in a criminal mastermind."

"Remember when you told me that you wished you had someone in your life when you were a kid like my grandma?"

He stopped pacing and stared at me. "Don't bring my words back up like that. It has nothing to do with this."

"Remember what it was like to not have anywhere to call home? Well, Grandma is my home."

"What good is finding home if you're kidnapped, or hurt, or not alive?" he asked quietly.

"How good is living when you have no home? Because I'll tell you, it's not living."

He studied me for a second, then pressed his lips together and closed his eyes.

"I know you care about me, and…" I paused, but I knew that I needed to say the words. "And I don't hate you, Mr. Harvey. I know you're trying to protect me. But I need to do this."

He opened his eyes, turned to Detective Mueller, and said, "You better do everything in your power to protect this kid." Looking at me, he added, "Because I see a lot of potential in him. I'd like to see what he does with it." Mr. Harvey left the room with Ms. Wright following at his heels.

Detective Mueller took a deep breath and said, "All right, let's go ahead and get started."

CHAPTER TWENTY-SIX

The weekend came and went, and my life still felt like chaos in overdrive. Now I slid over on the bus to make room for Gertie. She'd demand answers, and unfortunately, I could only tell her half-truths.

She sat beside me, leaned her head back, and sighed.

"That bad, huh?" I took her hand. I decided I liked holding her hand and wanted to hold it as much as I could.

"I thought I would be away from my family this weekend."

"I know, and I'm sorry." I couldn't tell her everything, so I only told her about Grandma being in the hospital.

"I'm not mad at you. Your Grandma got sick. I'm disappointed, that's all. You couldn't even hang out Saturday or Sunday."

Those two days were spent fixing up Grandma's house and secretly meeting with Detective Mueller. She had even given me a silver necklace with a thin device attached in the shape of a cross. One press on the jewel inside of it, and the authorities would be notified. It also monitored my heart's beating and rhythm, so if it got ripped off of me or something like that, they would be alerted, as well. I also had a device on my shoe that was a locator. Talk about feeling safe. And wired. Sheesh.

Gertie moved closer and whispered in my ear. “When are we running away? I’m getting desperate. Ricky’s acting weird, and I keep catching him staring at me. I hate to say I’m scared of my own brother, but I am.”

Her breath tickled my ear, which brought warm fuzzies to my belly. “Soon. I can’t leave my grandma after her episode.” Detective Mueller said that no one could know what was going on. That would put that person in danger. I was already worried about Dad and Grandma. One more person would be too much.

“Can’t I at least come and stay with you? I can sleep on the couch.”

“Grandma snores in her chair. You wouldn’t get any sleep.”

“I don’t care.”

“We’ll figure something out. I promise.”

She nodded and acted pacified. “How much do we have saved?”

“Almost a hundred dollars, but we have a big unit test this week, and Tim said he thought I’d make some big-time cash.”

“I feel bad that you’re cheating so that we can have money to run away.”

“It’s not the worst thing I’ve done. Besides, as soon as we have enough money, we can head out.” And that was another half-truth. I wasn’t completely sold on running away. I felt bad that Gertie didn’t think she was safe in her own house, but I loved my grandma too much to skip out on her, especially with everything she was going through. Hopefully, I could keep Gertie from leaving until things settled down, both in her life and mine. Until then, I would keep up pretenses.

When the bus arrived at school, I noticed Ray and Chump loitering around the brick ledge. “Something’s up,” I said to Gertie, as we stepped off the bus steps.

“Need me to stick with you?”

“No, I’ll fill you in later.”

She glanced down at our intertwined fingers and acted hesitant to release me. Before I registered what happened, Gertie had closed the distance between us, leaned forward, and kissed me softly on the cheek. “Bye,” she said, and then took off.

Once it hit me what she had just done, my hand flew to my cheek as if to keep the kiss there. Gertie had kissed me? In front of everyone?

I grinned. My heart soared. For weeks, I had pushed down the crush I had toward her because I thought she only wanted to be my friend. Could it be that she liked me the way I liked her?

I nearly forgot about Ray and Chump. At least until they called me over.

“You act like you never got kissed before,” Ray said and rolled his eyes.

“Whatever,” Chump said, defending me. “Ray’s jealous that Gertie never kissed him last year.”

Ray huffed out a breath. "Shut it, Chump." To me, he said, "Meet Tim in the bathroom by the gym lockers. That way, butthead Oliver doesn't catch you guys again."

They both left me standing there.

Gertie wasn't at my locker, so I headed to the bathroom before the first bell. I kept thinking about how she snuck that kiss on me! I walked right into Mr. Oliver. "Marco," he said in a way that showed he was not surprised. "What are you doing in the bathroom on the other side of the building from where your locker is located?"

My smile left and annoyance took its place. "I'm using the bathroom located right next to the gym lockers where I need to be for my first hour."

"First hour isn't for ten minutes. Normally you are running into first hour right at the bell."

"I'm early today." I went to walk into a stall.

"Your buddy, Tim, was just in here. He got called down to the office." Mr. Oliver threw away a wadded-up paper towel.

I watched Mr. Oliver leave as the first signs of panic started to settle in. All of a sudden it seemed like such a stupid idea. Take five bucks from a bunch of kids I don't even know and do the homework for them? Someone was bound to tell. Now I'd get busted, Grandma would get called in, and she'd be upset again. "Stupid," I said to myself and let the stall door slam shut. With the whirlwind already spiraling around us, I added *cheating ring* to it.

First hour I was useless in dodgeball. I kept waiting for the principal to drag me out and to the office. When she showed up, I felt relieved. I nearly walked over to her before she called to me. “Marco.” She motioned for me to follow her.

Mr. Oliver watched me with a smirk on his face.

I followed Ms. Snyder, the principal, to her office. I noticed two things. First, I noticed Tim sitting in a chair off to the side, then I noticed Miss Dantsy sitting next to him. Neither one appeared happy. Tim wouldn’t even look at me.

“Sit down,” Ms. Snyder said.

I sat in the only available chair. Ms. Snyder watched me over her glasses. She was an older woman with a tight bun at the base of her neck, and more importantly, she was built like a freight car. Seriously, the woman could be a professional wrestler. It didn’t matter that she had some gray mixed with her dark hair. She could take a grown man down. I could even envision her in the wrestling ring body-slamming some poor sap. I thought of her wrestling Mr. Oliver and pinning him. Now *that* was something I’d pay to see.

“Marco?” she was saying. “I’m talking to you.”

I snapped to attention. “Sorry.”

“Miss Dantsy informed me that you are tutoring Tim, is that correct?”

I glanced over at Miss Dantsy. She nodded in encouragement. So, at least she wasn’t glaring at me. That had to be a good sign. “Yes, I help Tim. Miss Dantsy even put us next to each other in class.”

“Did you know what Tim was doing with all the correct

answers you were helping him with?"

I licked my lips and looked over at Tim. He still wouldn't look at me. "Uh…"

"He's selling them. We found over a hundred dollars in an envelope in his locker. A student came forward and made us aware of this cheating ring he's established. I need to know if you had any idea about the money or what Tim was doing."

"I told you he doesn't know," Tim said to Ms. Snyder.

I stared over at Tim and didn't mask my shock. He was covering for me? Why?

This time our eyes met briefly before he flipped his bangs out of his face and looked down at the ground again.

"I can't have you sitting next to each other anymore," Miss Dantsy said to me as if apologizing. "Tim will stay after school and get help from me."

"That's all," Ms. Snyder said and motioned that I could leave. "Just be careful of kids who want to take advantage of you. They will use your good intentions for their wrong motives."

I stood to leave, but guilt weighed heavily on me. Tim had covered for me. Yeah, he asked me for the answers, but I had freely given them, *and* I had been the one with the idea about the money. Before I could talk myself out of it, I blurted, "I knew."

Ms. Snyder's eyes turned into slits. "Knew what?"

"I knew about the cheating and the money. It's not Tim's fault. It's my fault."

It was like all three of them gasped at the same time.

"Tim asked me for help. It was easier sometimes for me to do the problems for him. When he mentioned that other kids wanted my help too, I said only if they paid me. At first, it was a joke. It kind of took off from there. We didn't know what to do with the money because a lot of kids wanted in on it. But nothing has happened yet. I haven't even given out answers. It just sort of blew up. But it's not Tim's fault. He was just covering for me."

"And why would he do that?"

"Because he's my friend, which is why I'm not letting him…Because I'm his friend."

"We'll have to call your grandmother. Please take a seat."

"I am disappointed," Miss Dantsy said to both Tim and me. "Cheating is wrong." She left the office.

"I'll be right back," Ms. Snyder said. "No talking."

When she left, Tim shook his head. "You didn't have to do that."

"You didn't have to cover for me either, but you did. I wasn't about to let you take the fall."

"You didn't tell them about the other money I gave you," he whispered.

"I didn't see the point. Did they take the cash?"

"What do you think?" he said with a snort. "They said they were going to give it back to all of the kids' parents, but I'm not telling who paid."

"And I don't know who paid, so I'm in the clear on that one."

"When I find who ratted, he'll be sorry," Tim said, shaking his head. "Do you think Gertie would tell?"

"No," I said. "Why would you think that?"

"I know she's your girlfriend and all, but she also hates me. I thought maybe she ratted me out without bringing your name into it."

"No, she wouldn't do that. Besides, she doesn't hate you anymore." It didn't escape my notice that I didn't refute the *girlfriend's* reference.

Ms. Snyder came back into the room. "Tim, go sit out in the office waiting room until your mother shows up." When he left, Ms. Snyder said to me, "Marco, you stay here. Your grandmother will be here momentarily."

My heart pounded. And not in a good way. Now I decide to get a conscience? How inconvenient.

Ten minutes of torture. I sat by myself and thought of all the ways I was a horrible person. Then the door opened, and I heard Grandma's voice with Ms. Snider's, and I wanted to hide under the chair and pretend to be invisible.

"Hello, Marco," Grandma said. "What's this about?"

I kept my eyes lowered.

"Explain to your grandmother what you explained to me," Ms. Snider barked.

I stared at my hands.

"Marco?" Grandma asked. "Whatever it is, you can tell me."

I shook my head.

"He's the mastermind of a cheating ring," Ms. Snider said in a huff. "He and his buddy have been charging students five dollars for correct answers that he has been supplying. We found an envelope with a large sum of money."

"I hadn't cheated yet," I interrupted. "At least on that. It only happened one time. Don't make such a big deal about it."

"Marco Fuller, do not speak to an adult like that," Grandma said in a low voice.

"Well, she's making it sound like a bigger deal than it is!"

"Did you cheat? At all?" Grandma asked.

I didn't say anything at first.

"Did you?"

"Yeah."

"Then it's a big deal. Did you take money from other students?"

In a quieter voice, I said, "Yeah."

"Then it's a big deal. Cheating, stealing, and lying are all very big deals."

"Marco is not the only culprit. He was approached, and no doubt pressured, by another boy. As it stands right now and given the current situation surrounding the boy's life, Marco will serve one day of out-of-school suspension, starting immediately, and then two weeks of after-school detentions."

"That sounds more than reasonable," Grandma said in a

clipped tone. "We will have a long talk about this. Marco, do you have anything to say to your principal?"

I swallowed hard, the apology leaving a bitter taste in my mouth. "I'm sorry," I mumbled.

"All right, well, the other boy's mother is here, so if you can escort your grandson out, I'll send the disciplinary forms in the mail."

Grandma stood and exited the room without saying a word to me. I got up and quickly followed. Tim and I made brief eye contact. He didn't look too happy either.

Not a word was spoken on the walk to the car or once in the car. I thought of a million things to say, but none of it would make what happened go away.

At the cabin, Detective Mueller came from around the back. Grandma ordered me, "Get to your room. I'll be there in a minute." To Detective Mueller, she said, "What's going on? You said you all were done."

"I'll occasionally walk the perimeter to see if anything's out of line. I was hoping to be gone before you got back." Detective Mueller smiled over at me. "What are you doing home so early?"

I kept my head down and walked inside. I overheard Grandma questioning, "But you said that you were not going to be seen. That Ricci can't know you all are here. So, why would you be walking around in the open?"

I paused and watched from the door. Grandma's mouth was set in a deep frown, and her hands were planted at her hips. But I couldn't figure out if she was angry at Detective Mueller or me, and the poor detective was receiving the brunt of it.

The detective tried to appease Grandma that they had already deemed the property secure before she entered the premises.

"Then why are you here? If the police said the property is secure, I don't see why you are here."

"I'll get going then."

"You said this would not interrupt our lives. Having you here is a constant reminder of danger. I want you to keep us secure, but I don't want Marco's life disrupted any more than it has to be."

"Understood," the detective said.

I watched as Detective Mueller glanced toward the backyard before she headed to her car. "Don't worry," she said to Grandma. "You all are safe. The minute anything happens we will be here."

"A minute is all it takes for someone to get hurt," Grandma said and turned to head toward the cabin. At the porch, she stopped. She glanced over her shoulder and watched as the detective pulled out of the driveway and took off down the dirt road. Then Grandma made her way to the backyard.

I went to my room, so I could see from my window. I watched as Granma studied her gardens. Her brow had furrowed, her lips had pursed, and she scanned the area as if searching for a clue.

Suddenly she turned and went around the front. I stayed in my room, wondering what Grandma was looking for. After a few minutes, she showed up at my bedroom door. "Your computer, please."

"Say what?"

"Your computer. Hand it over."

"Why? What were you doing outside?"

She entered the room, unplugged my laptop, and picked it up.

"Wait! You can't give someone something, then take it back. That's not cool." I reached for the laptop.

"Neither is cheating," Grandma said. "You're grounded. You are to come straight home from school. You are to give Gertie back her games. You are to think about your actions. After a week, we will see if you've learned your lesson. Then you can negotiate the laptop."

My mouth hung open. No games? No computer? "You can't do that." Grandma was acting like I took millions from a bank.

"Yes, I can."

"Why are you making it such a big deal?"

"Because it is, Marco. And that's the problem. You don't see it as a big deal."

"I've got thugs that are chasing me down. I've got a father who is not only addicted to drugs but is now involved with these thugs, and you think me cheating on a couple of math problems is a big deal? We've got other things to worry about!"

She stared at me as if in shock, only to shake her head. "You are not responsible for the actions of other people," she said quietly. "But, you *are* responsible for your own. At the end of the day, that's what matters."

"Whatever. Fine. Take it. I don't want it anyway." I turned my back on her and threw myself onto my bed. My blood boiled, and I clenched my fists and pressed my lips together to try to rein it in. I knew better. I wasn't a dummy. I had made Grandma upset. After everything that had happened and all that could still happen, I threw cheating into the mix.

I had to be the worst grandson ever.

CHAPTER TWENTY-SEVEN

The next day, Gertie waited by my locker. Her creased forehead and the frown that played on her lips showed me her worry without her having to say a word. Great. First Grandma, now Gertie.

"What happened?" she asked. She moved out of the way so that I could get to my locker.

Gertie had stopped over yesterday after school. Grandma and I were eating an early dinner. I've learned that when Grandma is worried, frustrated, angry, or pretty much any other emotion, she cooks. The apology sat on my tongue, but I went through all of dinner without saying anything.

When Gertie knocked, Grandma told her I was grounded, and I could only hang out with her at school.

Unfortunately, I couldn't tell Gertie all that was happening. I had to keep certain things a secret. "I got one-day suspension, and all this week and next week, I have detention."

"I'm talking about between you and your grandma. She acted sad when she came to the door, and have you noticed the dark circles around her eyes?"

I slammed my locker shut. Of course, I'd noticed. She also paced all last night. Again. I hadn't slept that great either. At one point, I even heard her get up and go outside. No doubt to make sure no criminals had decided to show up. That made me sad on so many levels. Here she was with a punk grandkid who got in trouble all the time, and she still wanted to protect me.

"Tell me," Gertie whispered. "Is it about your dad?"

The bell rang. "I've got to get to class."

Gertie took my hand and led me to the choir room area. There sat a set of outside doors, leading directly to the back of the building. She quickly glanced around, saw that the choir teacher was busy talking with students, and opened one of the doors. We stopped along the brick wall of the building. "Hurry. Tell me what's up."

"We're just going to stand here out in the open?"

"Nobody checks back here. Trust me, I'm in choir. We'll come talk out here the last five minutes of class. Now talk."

"I'm upset that I made her upset. That's all. I didn't think I'd get caught. It's not even that she took everything away. It's the way she looks at me. Even this morning, we barely said two words."

"Did you tell her you were sorry?"

"Not yet."

"Why not?"

"Because I've got a lot on my mind. Because I don't think it'll matter. I screwed up. She probably doesn't even want me up here anymore. Ever since I've come, I've been nothing but trouble. And now it's even worse."

"I've seen you two together. She loves you. Tell her you're sorry. Everything will go back to normal."

But it wouldn't go back to normal. Not as long as there was some bad guy out there searching for me. Grandma had already been to the hospital for not handling stress. How much more could she take? "You're right. I have to tell her I'm sorry."

"Yep. No worries." Gertie smiled at me.

But I was worried. Still, I would play along that I was fine because that's what was expected of me. And the minute I got home I would tell Grandma how sorry I was. Maybe I could talk her into staying in a hotel until this blew over. When I agreed to be the bait, I didn't think about her peace of mind. Had I ever thought about my grandma's needs before my own?

Since Gertie had choir first hour, she slipped into the classroom, and I headed down the hall to the gym. I thought of all the times, just since I've known her, I had thought about myself and not her.

**I'd tried to run away at least a dozen times.*

**I stole 17 dollars, even though I technically did work it off.*

**I accused her of murder.*

**I was about to steal a bunch of her money a second time, even though there ended up being none to steal.*

**I cheated and got in trouble at school without thinking about how it would hurt her and how disappointed she would be.*

I had to stop my mental list because Mr. Oliver stood outside the gym, staring me down. “Look who decided to show up for class.”

A sarcastic comment nearly came out of my mouth. Something along the lines, *Look who decided* not *to show up with his brain.* Or, *Look who decided* not *to show up with a personality.* I mean, really, the comebacks could be endless. Instead, I walked past him.

I heard him mutter, “Nothing but trouble,” under his breath. It took all my willpower to keep walking. During dodgeball, I imagined hurling the ball at him with lightning speed. Nothing like a good dodgeball sting to shut someone up.

By the time lunch came around, my mood had tanked even more. Part of it came from the fact I had slept so little, most of it came from the fact that I itched to get home and talk to Grandma.

Pretending to be normal was hard, but I had to make Gertie convinced I was fine. Ray walked over to us, “You guys coming to the table?”

Gertie and I turned to each other, surprised. “I’m not helping you cheat anymore.”

“So? You’re still our friend, right?”

“I guess…sure. Where’s Tim?”

“He got a longer suspension because they think he started the whole thing. He’ll be back tomorrow. He told us what you did.” Ray punched my arm, then walked back over to the table.

“I never thought I’d see the day,” Gertie said. “The day where

I am sitting at Ray and Tim's table, and I don't hate them."

"Don't worry. Your secret's safe with me."

We made our way through the lunchroom, but I didn't get very far. Ms. Snider herself stopped me. "Marco, you're needed in the office."

"Oh, my word, what now?" Gertie whispered in my ear. "This will be the third time in a row you've missed your last two hours."

"Get my homework, okay?" I kind of hoped that Grandma decided to get me out early. The idea of a nap—after I told her how sorry I was—dangled in front of me like chocolate on a stick. "Is my grandma here?"

"No," she said as we left the cafeteria. "Your aunt called and said that your grandmother had to go to the hospital." She stopped right outside the office door. "But nothing alarming. I've been told that she is fine, that she was having some irregular heart palpitations."

"Grandma is in the hospital?"

"Your aunt will be here soon."

"My aunt?"

Ms. Snider frowned. "Vanessa Mueller? She said you would be able to identify her."

Detective Mueller! "Yes, I can identify her."

"Good. And Marco? Be good to your grandma. I realize that you are going through a lot right now, but I know Shirley. I want it to work out for the both of you."

I didn't realize she was friends with my grandma. "I'm

trying," I said honestly. "I really am. I think I'm just a horrible person which is why I do horrible things."

"You're not a horrible person. Don't believe that lie for a minute. Just start making better choices. It's your life. You choose what path you're going to walk down."

All I did for the next ten minutes was contemplate my actions and how I was making it worse for my grandma. And I worried. I kept looking out the window from Ms. Snyder's office to watch for Detective Mueller. Then I would demand her to take me to the hospital. Then I would apologize. It would be the first thing out of my mouth.

But when the front office door opened, it wasn't Detective Mueller who came walking through. It was Dad.

CHAPTER TWENTY-EIGHT

My heart seized, and time stood still. Before I thought it through, I opened the door and ran straight to him. I flung my arms around him and held on. "You're here. You came for me."

He hugged me just as tightly but whispered "Shh," in my ear.

"Who are you?" Ms. Snyder asked from behind the office counter. "You don't look like a Vanessa Mueller."

"I'm Robert Mueller," Dad said and released me. "Marco's uncle. Vanessa stayed at the hospital with Marco's grandmother." He gave Ms. Snyder his most disarming smile.

Even though I wondered why he was lying, I still took in the sight of him. He had showered and looked fresh-faced and clean. He looked pretty good, but I could see how thin he still was and the sallowness around his eyes.

The truth smacked me right across the face. Why was Dad here? How did Dad know about Detective Mueller?

"Come on, Marco," Dad said after signing me out. "I need to drop you off at the hospital."

I shoved the worry and panic aside. Dad would never hurt me

or Grandma. That wasn't his style. He must have escaped the Ricci guy and came up here to see us. "It's so good to see you," I whispered as we walked outside. "I've missed you."

"I've missed you too. We'll talk later. Right now, we have to get out here, and no matter what, I need you to trust me. Got it?"

I noticed Grandma's hatchback parked in front of the school. "Grandma was probably so happy to see you. She's been worried about you. Did she faint or something? Is that why she's at the hospital?"

"Shh," Dad said. "We'll talk about this later. Just get in the car."

Dad walked around and opened the driver's side. As I opened the passenger side, I noticed the man in the back seat. I stopped.

"Get in the car," Dad said, his eyes frantic. "Please." Dad dunked into the car and quickly shut the door.

I was frozen. I didn't know what to do. I raised my hand slowly to press against my chest, knowing that would alert the police, but now that I saw Dad, I wasn't ready to turn him in. But who was the guy? And why was he crouched in the back of my grandma's car?

His eyes blazed in my direction, and he motioned for me to get in.

I quickly slid inside Grandma's car. Whatever was going on, Dad might need my protection. I still had the necklace and the device on my shoe. I should be safe for now.

Dad pulled away from the school. "It's good to see you."

I couldn't say anything. I turned around to make sure I had really seen a guy in the backseat. Yep. He watched me with this hungry look, and it made my stomach hurt. He had on an expensive suit, and not a hair was out of place. The whole car smelled of his cologne.

"It's good to see you again, Marco," he said in a low voice. "You probably don't remember me, but I've been friends with your dad for a while."

"What are you? His drug dealer?"

"Marco, don't," Dad whispered.

In a swift move, the guy yanked a semi-automatic out of his suit pocket. He started playing with it. He even brought it up to his nose and sniffed it.

"Put it away," Dad told him. "You promised."

Suddenly, he pushed the gun against my arm.

"Joe!" Dad jerked the wheel, and the car swerved.

"Just drive," the guy ordered. "Your son needs to understand the direness of the situation." He looked back over at me. "Ever heard the name, Carl Ricci?"

The gun had taken away my words and my sarcasm. There were so many emotions running through me, I couldn't make sense of any of it. All I could do was nod.

"He's the one you need to worry about. If we don't give him what he wants, you and your dad and the old lady are toast."

I must have looked confused because he added, "You

cooperate and everything will be just fine. Sound good?"

"Don't freak him out," Dad snapped at Joe. "You're making him nervous."

"Good. I want him nervous. That way he doesn't get any ideas. One wrong move and my dad will do what he promised."

"Where's Grandma?"

Dad glanced at me then made the turn in the direction of the cabin. "She's fine. She's secure, and she knows I went to get you."

"Is she at the hospital?"

Dad didn't answer.

"Is she at the cabin?"

"She's fine."

"Dad? Where is she?"

"She's not at the hospital. I needed a reason they'd release you. That part was your grandma's idea. And she's not at the cabin right now either, but she's secure. Trust me." Dad took his eyes off the road to make eye contact with me. He raised his eyebrows as if I was supposed to understand something. But I didn't. I was confused. And I was concerned. If Grandma wasn't at the hospital or the cabin, where could she be?

My heart beat heavily in my chest because I knew what I had to do. I reached up and held my hand over my heart. I pressed as hard as I could. I loved my dad, but I no longer trusted him.

I didn't want to believe Dad would be involved in criminal activity, but it was starting to look like he and this Ricci guy were in it together. I kept pressing down on my chest, hoping I was pressing the cross necklace hard enough. Then I started out the window.

"Hey, stop that," Dad gently chided. "Don't look at me like I'm the bad guy. I borrowed something from his father, and we have to pay him back. That's all. What we need to do is find some coffee cans that your grandma has buried out back." Dad patted my arm. "Everything will be fine."

"Why do you keep referring to her as my grandma?"

"That's what she is, isn't she?"

"Yeah, but she's your mom. You haven't one time called her mom."

Dad stayed quiet.

"Why do you want Grandma's money?" I asked. "Besides, the one coffee can I know of is empty."

Silence descended upon the car. Dad's eyes widened, and he gripped the wheel.

"They're empty," Joe snarled in my ear.

"Just the one. I don't know about any others." I swallowed and tried not to look at the end of the gun, pointing at me.

"Don't point that at him!" Dad yelled.

"You promised me the kid had it," he said, pointing the gun at Dad. "Then your mother swore it was in the coffee cans."

"It is. She already told you what you needed to know. Leave my son alone, or all bets are off."

"I hedge my bets," he said to Dad fiercely. "And they're never off."

Dad slowed at the stop sign near the cabin. I knew what I had to do. While we had been talking, I had unlocked my car door. There was one place I knew I'd be safe. As soon as Dad came to a stop at the sign, I swung open the door and jumped out.

I heard the Joe Ricci guy swearing.

But my feet kept sprinting toward the woods.

The one place where at the beginning I thought might house murderers was now the one place I knew would protect me from them. So, I ran into the woods and didn't look back.

CHAPTER TWENTY-NINE

Don't get me wrong, the woods still freaked me out, but not as much as that Ricci guy. And if his dad was even meaner, forget that.

I sprinted in zig-zags, jumping over fallen logs, pushing past low-lying bushes and branches, and around as many trees as I could. I wanted as much distance and as many obstacles as possible between me and them.

It would have helped if the detective had given me a cell phone! She gave one to Grandma. The only other phone I knew of was the landline.

My options were limited. I'd have to risk going to the cabin.

I kept hearing Dad call for me. It was growing fainter, and he'd probably give up soon. And there was no way I was faster than a car to get to the house. The question that kept playing over and over was: Where were the police and Detective Mueller? Where was Grandma?

Shouldn't I have heard sirens by now? Wouldn't the police have protected Grandma? Maybe that's what Dad meant. Maybe Grandma was secure with the police. Maybe Dad couldn't tell me with that Joe guy in the backseat.

Maybe they were all at the cabin waiting. But if Grandma was there, would I be leading the bad guy right to her? I shoved that thought down. No doubt the police were probably there too, so I pushed myself to run faster. I had to tell them that Joe Ricci was on his way. Maybe they'd ambush him and arrest him. I wondered if they would arrest Dad, but I stopped myself from thinking about that. Too much was happening, and my concern had changed from worrying about Dad to worrying about Grandma.

I tripped over an exposed root and went flying. I thought about just staying on the ground and hiding. Now that I had paused, I tried to catch my breath. I pushed myself up and onto my knees. Suddenly, my neck hair stood up. I wasn't alone.

It ambled out from behind a tree, stopping directly in front of me.

I couldn't move. The bear didn't either. Both of us seemed frozen at that moment. I tried to keep quiet, but my lungs were burning. I heaved breaths as if I couldn't catch any air.

What freaked me out more? Bear or bad guy?

Grandma had never told me what to do in case I encountered one. And that whole the bear is a connection to the other world doesn't matter for squat when one's staring at you deciding if you'd taste better with barbeque sauce.

Eventually, I heard a car engine start. Crap. They'd be heading to the house.

The bear grunted at me and continued ambling in the direction it was going. As soon as I thought I could, I took off again, but not as fast. I hadn't realized my knees were knocking as hard as they were.

The car drove past on the other side of the trees. I pushed myself.

Sweat trickled down my back to my butt crack, and my thighs felt like they had rug burns from the uncomfortable rubbing combination of jeans and skin. But I was almost there.

The car engine turned off.

I stumbled through the last of the trees and ran to my bedroom window. *Always keep a window prepared*, Dad had taught me.

Yeah, it would come in handy trying to escape him. A part of me was so angry and hurt at him. Why was he involved with Ricci? For drugs? Were drugs more important than my safety or Grandma's? But another part of me didn't want to blame him. There had to be a reason he was with Joe Ricci. Most of the time Dad was drunk or wasted from drugs, but violence wasn't his thing. If anything, he endured the violence of others without ever dishing any out himself.

As I jimmied the screen off and slid the window open, I remembered the time when I was around eleven and Dad had come back late one night with a black eye and a bloodied lip and I had asked him why he never fought back. "Nothing good comes from using your fists."

Everything seemed too quiet. Then I heard them talking out front.

I pulled myself up and through the window. I shut the window, so they wouldn't know I was in the house and hurried into the other bedroom. "Grandma?" I whispered. I hoped I hadn't led Joe right to her, but I quickly observed the empty cabin. Wherever she was, it wasn't here.

Dad and Joe argued outside. I grabbed the phone and dialed 9-1-1.

"9-1-1, what is your emergency?"

"There are bad people at my house trying to find money. My address is…" I opened up drawers to find an envelope addressed to Grandma. "274 Lake Harvey Road. In Otsego County. Please hurry."

I hung up before dialing again. I hoped he picked up his phone.

"Hey, I'm not supposed to be talking on the phone," Tim whispered. "I'm grounded."

"Are you at school? I need to talk to Gertie," I whispered back.

I heard Joe say he was going to check the perimeter and for Dad to check the house.

"No, I'm suspended for another day. Why?"

"Listen. It's an emergency. Contact the police. Someone's kidnapped my grandma. I'm serious. Please." I hung up as soon as I heard the screen door shut.

I scrambled to the closet and slid inside of it.

"Marco?" Dad called.

The door to my bedroom opened. He had to be checking the window.

The phone rang and I nearly yelped in the closet. Was that the police? Grandma? Mr. Harvey? I wanted to grab it, but I couldn't risk it.

As I sat in the closet listening to the phone ring, the weight of everything finally fell in its entirety on my shoulders. Why was I running from my own Dad? The answer that I didn't trust him scared me. I told myself that it wasn't that I didn't trust him, but that I didn't trust the guy he was with. And what did he do with Grandma? What kind of person would do something bad to their own parent? Sure, I might have turned Dad into police, but it was to help him. I wanted him to be free of drugs. And even though he looked all put together today, there were no mistaken signs of drug use.

I covered my face with my hands and took in slow breaths. I couldn't cry. It made too much noise. Besides, what good are tears? They wouldn't give me a new life.

"Hello?" Dad said into the phone.

I held my breath and listened. My heart still pounded from the run. I pressed a hand to my chest, hoping it'd quiet down.

"No, this is his father. Who is this?" Dad paused. "Hello, Tim. Did he just call you?"

I gritted my teeth in frustration. *Tim!* I had no choice; I opened up the chest and squeezed myself into it. I didn't know whether I should be glad or sad that I actually could squeeze myself into the wooden box. Talk about claustrophobia! Plus, I was pouring sweat so badly I could have bathed in it.

He hung up the phone. "Marco? I know you're in here. You couldn't have time to run to the house and run out of it."

I heard the closet door slide open and Dad push aside some clothes. Luckily the chest had been shoved on the other side of the closet. Unless he investigated, he probably wouldn't even see it.

"Marco!" he called, sliding the closet door shut. I heard the bedroom door shut.

The front door opened. I lifted the chest lid so I could breathe.

"He contacted the police," Joe said and punched the wall.

I jumped and nearly slammed the chest lid down.

"From inside the house?"

"Yeah, have you searched?"

"I've checked everywhere. And there's not a lot of places to hide in this cabin. He probably slipped in and out through his window. The screen's popped out."

"So, he's in the woods again?"

"I guess. Look, we don't need him. Just leave my son alone and let's start digging for the coffee cans. Your family wants the money, so leave my family out of it."

"He wants more than the money, and you know it. And that kid knows where they are, that's why. We don't have time to dig holes around acres of land!"

"Yeah, but the money will buy us time."

"It'll buy *you* time. Don't drag me into this. You're the thief who's been blackmailing him."

"I already told you. I don't where it is."

"Save it. You've been jerking my chain all day. First, with your mother, and now with your son."

Grandma?

"She told you where to look!" Dad yelled. "Why are we

wasting time?"

"All I can say is that you better have enough money to pacify him, or you can kiss your family goodbye."

"Don't you touch my son."

"Or what?"

"Or I'll have nothing to lose but to tell the cops everything."

"What makes you think you'll be alive?"

The front door opened.

"Where are you going?"

"To start digging."

The front door closed, and I heard them both outside. Dad covered for me. He knew I was in the house. Or at least that I was. Maybe he wanted to keep me hidden. Joe Ricci had threatened to kill me. Suddenly, I felt sick. I grabbed my necklace and mashed it on it. Why wasn't the stupid thing working?

Then Joe Ricci's words hit me. *He contacted the police.*

How had he known that? I contacted 9-1-1 minutes ago. He wouldn't know that fast. I studied the cross necklace. Who was at the receiving end of this signal? I'd watched enough movies to know that criminals and drug lords often have someone on the inside, but how could the Riccis have someone from the police force in Northern Michigan working for them? I clenched my fist in frustration. Who could I trust?

I had no idea where Grandma was. I could call Ms. Wright, but what could she do? Ms. Wright might be nice and had good intentions, but it wasn't like she could move fast. Tim was obviously out. I couldn't get ahold of Gertie while she was at school. Then I figured it out.

I knew the one man I could count on for anything. I slid out of the chest, and as quietly as possible crawled back to the phone.

He picked up on the first ring. "Ms. Wright said you got in trouble at school. Want to talk about it?"

"Mr. Harvey," I whispered. "I need help."

It was like I sensed his immediate attention. "What is it?"

"My Dad came and picked me up at school today."

"Your Dad?" Mr. Harvey swore under his breath. "I knew this was a bad idea."

"He had Joe Ricci with him."

"Oh my God. Where are the police? Did you press the necklace? I know he's your father, but we have to stop this, Marco."

"I did, and no one came. Dad and Joe are wanting Grandma's coffee cans, but I don't know where the cans are. And Joe is scaring me. He says if his father doesn't get the money then we're dead. I don't know what to do. I keep pressing on the necklace, but no one is coming, and I don't know where Grandma is, and I'm really scared, and someone in the police is helping them, and what am I going to do--"

"Take a deep breath. You're at the cabin now?"

"Yeah, but Dad and that Joe guy are right outside looking for the cans of money."

"How'd you get away?"

"I jumped out of the car and ran into the woods. They think

I'm still in the woods."

"No one has responded to your distress call?"

"No, and I even called 9-1-1."

"Oh my God. Marco, they probably have the phone tapped. You need to find a safe spot until the proper authorities get there. Don't worry. I'm on it, and I won't stop until you're safe."

"Aren't you four hours away?"

"No, I never left. Got a hotel room. There was no way I was letting them use you as bait. What kind of a detective does that? Just get out of there, Marco, until I can get there with her."

As soon as I hung up the phone, I heard the sirens. But it didn't make me feel as relieved as I thought it would have.

CHAPTER THIRTY

I peeked out the bedroom window and saw Detective Mueller stepping out of the car. She had her gun drawn, scanning the property. My heart felt immediate relief. But it was short-lived. Joe Ricci suddenly came around from the back of the house.

"What are you doing with the sirens? Want to alert everyone that we're here?"

The detective put her gun away. "The kid is around, I need to keep up pretenses. Which doesn't matter now since you just shot our pretense to toast."

Joe Ricci pulled the detective into his arms and began kissing her.

Detective Mueller was a *bad guy*?

I scooted from the window, suddenly feeling afraid. Maybe I should have felt fear when I first saw Dad come through the school doors, but it was Dad. Now, I finally connected that there were a lot of people who I couldn't trust. Could I trust Mr. Harvey? One minute ago, I would have said yes, but what if everyone was bad?

I backed up, deciding I needed to get out and pronto. As I

turned to leave, I saw Dad standing at the bedroom door. “Where were you hiding?” he whispered.

“The chest in the closet.”

“Good. You need to get out of here.” He came over to me and put my face in his hands. “Please don’t look at me like that. I will do whatever I can to protect you. That’s why I intercepted your grandma’s phone. I had to change the plans.”

“Lance?” Joe called from the front. “Come out front. I want you to meet someone.”

“Go,” Dad said, grabbing my arm and pulling me to my room. “Do you still have the book?”

“What book?”

“The book with the numbers?”

“Yeah, it’s in the drawer in my nightstand.”

He opened the drawer, grabbed the book, and flipped to the back. He breathed a sigh of relief and shut the book. Then he shoved the book in my pants. “Where’s the Stephen King book?”

“Still in the duffel bag.”

He hurriedly went to it and snatched it. He shoved that one in my pants too. “Whatever you do, do not let anyone get ahold of these books. Hide them in the woods if you have to.”

Dad opened the window and pushed me to it. I was so confused. And there were two books in my underwear. That, too.

“I’ll keep them distracted. Go back to the woods, and get help from someone you trust. Your Grandma is at the One Choice Motel off Old 27. It’s right next to Otsego Lake.”

"What about you?"

"I'm fine. I've just got to find enough cash to pacify them."

I stopped and studied his face. I couldn't help it. Dad didn't look or act fine.

The screen door opened.

Dad practically shoved me out the window. "I'm right here! Just checking inside to see if he snuck in."

Once my feet hit the ground, I ran. I heard him talking but I couldn't risk looking back. I ran into the forest and didn't stop until I was covered by trees.

By the time I reached Gertie's, I was winded, exhausted, confused, and anxious. She had to be coming home soon, so I tucked myself in some bushes over by her garage and gathered my thoughts and my breath.

Once I could breathe semi-normally, I thought about all the developing information.

Dad is working with Joe Ricci? Or, Dad is pretending to work with Joe Ricci? They were talking about Dad owing money, so Dad doesn't work with him. He needs to pay him off.

Dad kidnapped Grandma? Maybe he lured her to the motel. If she knew he would be there, she would go see him. In either case, why would Dad do that to his mother?

Dad told me where Grandma was so I could help her, but maybe he told me so that I could be kidnapped too. Then why would he help me escape now?

Dad shoved two books down my pants. He said to keep them

safe. That means the messages he wrote in the books are important.

The detective is crooked and works with the bad guys, so I couldn't trust her. This means everything she gave us or was a part of can't be trusted.

Could I trust Dad?

The bus snapped me back to the here-and-now. I pulled the book out from my pants and flipped to where the numbers were written. What was up with them? Were they to a bank account?

Gertie ran up her driveway. I said, "Psst! Gertie!" then ducked back into the bush.

She stopped and turned all around.

"In the bushes."

Gertie walked slowly over to the bushes. "Marco?"

I brought my head up and motioned for her to join me.

She did a quick survey of the area before pushing through the bushes and ducking down. "Are we leaving now?"

"I'm in trouble, and I need help. I'm not supposed to tell you, but I don't know who else to tell."

"You can tell me anything."

"Promise? You'll keep it a secret forever?"

She crossed her heart. "I swear it."

"My Dad picked me up from school today."

Gertie's eyes lit up like it was good news.

"He brought the bad guys up with him."

"How bad are we talking?"

“It’s like a crime lord or something. Dad owes him money, and they are up here because they know about the coffee cans!”

Gertie’s eyes widened, and she covered her mouth. “This is bad. Are you in danger, too?”

“Yes. And so is Grandma. They took her somehow. She’s at some motel by Otsego Lake.”

“There’s the Waterfront Cabins, or there’s a dive called One Choice.”

“Yeah, that’s it.”

“It’s a strip of dingy motel rooms. Nobody ever stays in them. I didn’t even know it was still open.”

“Yep, that sounds like just the place my dad would go to. Anyway, I need to make sure Grandma’s okay. I’d wait for Mr. Harvey, but I don’t know who to trust anymore. The detective is one of the bad guys!”

“This is like a suspense movie!”

“Except it’s real, and my family’s in real danger.”

“Yeah, that. Sorry. Okay, I’m thinking we should borrow Ricky’s dirt bike. He’s let me ride it a time or two, so I know how to handle it. We can head to the motel, save your grandma, then go to the police.”

“The police are all corrupt. I don’t know who to trust.”

“They can’t all be corrupt.”

“But how would we know which one to trust?”

“Well, let’s at least go and get your grandma. Maybe she’ll have ideas about what to do next. But we need to hurry. Ricky will be done with football practice soon."

"Wait a sec," I said, thinking fast. "Can I borrow your necklace?"

Gertie glanced down at her silver necklace that held a small green jewel. "Will I get it back?"

"Of course, I just need to wear it for a while."

She shrugged and took it off, handing it to me.

I took off the necklace the detective gave me and threw it into the trees. Then I ripped the page out of the one book with the numbers on it and set the book on the ground. I studied the Stephen King book, not knowing if I should take the book or leave it. I think I could remember H-E-L-P, so I set that book down too. I clasped it around my neck and tucked it in my shirt. "Don't tell anyone. It's really important."

Just as we slipped into the garage and pulled out the dirt bike. Multiple sirens filled the air.

"We need to go and now!"

"Shouldn't we wait and talk to them?"

"No, the detective's a crook. They might all be crooks."

I slid onto the back of the dirt bike as Gertie started it. She handed me a helmet, which smelled like nasty sweat, and told me to put it on. I did, but I had to hold my breath while doing so. Holding on to her waist, she revved the engine. We nearly crashed a few times as she tried to maneuver the bike, but eventually, she corrected it and we sped down the road.

The sirens blared, as we flew past the police cars.

But the police didn't keep going toward Grandma's. They turned and started chasing us.

"Why are they coming after us?" Gertie yelled over the dirt bike's engine.

"Because they must be the bad guys! Go faster!"

One of them had sped up and was right on our butt.

"We're almost to the trail! How do they know it's us? We have helmets on!"

The necklace was gone, so that couldn't be it. Then I glanced down and sighed. My shoes had a locator device.

Suddenly, Gertie turned onto a dirt bike trail. We once again nearly spilled, but she corrected it enough that we managed to hold on.

I looked behind us and saw two police cars stop. One jumped out and had a gun drawn. But we were already in the midst of trees and moving too fast. I promised myself never again judge trees. They had protected me more than once.

My heart still pounded in my chest. "I've got a locator chip in my shoe."

"Then get rid of it! Or they'll just keep following us!"

"But I'd have to find it! It's tiny."

"Get rid of the shoe!" she yelled.

They never told me which shoe had the device. I groaned and kicked off both shoes. And they were my new ones, too!

With one hand, I touched the key that now hung around my neck. That's why Dad had wanted me out of the cabin. It probably wasn't his idea to come get me at school. Joe Ricci gave him no choice. Whoever these bad people were, they wanted me. That's why Dad sent me up here. And that's why they came up here to get me. It wasn't for some stupid coffee cans. It was for the numbers. Dad must have thought I'd be safe. That the numbers could stay hidden. Whatever the numbers were for, it was important.

I vowed to keep them with me and away from everyone else. No matter what.

CHAPTER THIRTY-ONE

I had to hand it to Gertie. She knew the backwoods' trails pretty well. We didn't come out to a road until we reached the large Otsego Lake. She drove around the lake, then cut through some more trails. She eventually slowed.

"What's up?" I asked. We were still in the middle of the woods. The only difference was the massive lake to our left and in plain sight.

"If they know we're on a motorbike, then it's probably not a good idea to just zoom right up to your grandma's room. There might be people there."

"Good point." I slid off the bike as Gertie turned it off. "Where's the motel?"

"Right in front of us. Just past the trees."

We both heard someone approach. Luckily the person stayed on the other side of the thicket of forest. The sound of the man talking silenced both of us. He didn't seem happy.

I could faintly make out a building and gravel parking lot. And there, almost right next to the woods, was an older man. Not as old as

Grandma, but he had to be at least fifty. He had on a fancy suit. Joe Ricci resembled this guy a little bit, except this guy was bald. Bald and very, very angry. Even though he was trying to whisper into his cell phone, I could hear him from where I stood in the woods.

"Where are you?" He paused to listen. "So, you have the boy in your custody?" He paused again. Then he laughed. Not a joyful laugh, but a bitter, I'm-super-evil laugh. "The boy ran away. The boy who supposedly has the account number. Fine, I'll go in the motel and get the old bat and bring her over. You should have just kept her with you… That is the stupidest thing I've ever heard." He brought the phone away from his ear and sighed. Someone was on the other end still talking. He brought it back to his ear. "I swear to God when I find you, I'm going to skin you alive and leave your body for the birds to devour!" He paused. "I don't care what pathetic excuse Lance has given you. We wouldn't be in this mess if you would have taken care of the situation back in Detroit! Find the boy…" All of sudden he gripped the phone and squeezed it with a fierce intensity while yelling through clenched teeth. When he brought the phone back to his ear, he said, slightly out of breath, "Someone is going to die. Today. Do you understand me? Find those numbers, or it might be you." He put the phone in his pocket and turned toward the motel.

I felt Gertie's hand in mine. "I'm scared," she whispered. "He's going to kill you, Marco."

"Or my dad."

"Or your grandma."

"I've got to get to that motel room before he does."

"How are you going to do that?"

"I'm going to see if Dad helped me out at all." I pushed through the trees. "Stay here, Gertie. That guy isn't one to be messed with."

"What about you?"

"Stay here by the bike and have it ready to go. I might come running."

"All right. Wait!" She grabbed me before I left the trees for the back of the motel. I turned to her and raised my eyebrows. She leaned forward and kissed my cheek. "For good luck."

I nodded and told myself to think about what just happened later. I left her standing in the woods while I snuck toward the back of the motel, looking for a back door or another way inside a room.

Suddenly, I heard a car door slam and an engine in the front of the motel startup. It sped out of the parking lot. I pushed myself against the side of the building, as the black SUV peeled away. The guy had left in a hurry.

I peeked around the corner to the front of the motel and saw no cars in the parking lot. Did he have my grandma?

I tested all the motel doors until I saw the one that was still open. He hadn't even bothered to shut it. I swallowed and prayed that Grandma was still alive and that he hadn't taken his anger out on her.

When I stepped inside, I saw a chair beside the front window (which would be no help whatsoever). There was ripped duct tape all around it.

Had Grandma escaped? Or had that guy taken her?

I walked over to the motel phone and dialed Mr. Harvey's number. It rang and rang.

That's when I heard the ringing of a cell phone outside of the room. I turned to see if Mr. Harvey was here when the bald man who had just left stepped inside. "Funny thing…" he said, playing with the phone. "If you're going to play search-and-rescue with an old lady, it's good to remember your phone…I'm assuming this belongs to someone you know."

I froze, the phone still in my hand. "How'd you get back here? I saw you speed away." It was probably a silly thing to ask, but it was what came out of my mouth.

"One of my informants called right when I found this phone on the floor by that chair." He pointed to the empty chair that I had investigated. He continued to talk conversationally. "I told her that the old woman who was supposed to be in here had somehow escaped and that this phone might help us find out who helped her." He walked over to me, real slow. Then he took the phone from my hand and hung it up. "So, I have this old woman on the run and a boy that fled into the woods. Only now, according to the informant, the boy had sped away on a dirt bike. That he no longer had a locator chip on him, but that the chances were good that this is where he was headed. So, I turned around. Lo and behold, I saw you walk into the room. I parked the truck across the street and decided to surprise you… Surprise…"

"What do you want with my grandma? She's innocent."

"I know she is, which is why I will feel sort of bad when I have to kill her."

My stomach churned, and I thought I might puke right there on his shoes.

"Maybe I'll let her live. But you have to help me."

I nodded.

"Good. I thought we could be friends, Marco." He must have noticed my surprised expression. "What? You didn't think I'd know your name? I know all about you. I know how brilliant you are. That you've been taking care of a drug-addicted father for years. Your potential just rotting in Detroit."

"What do you want?" I could feel the ripped paper with the numbers on it burning a hole in my chest. I should have memorized the numbers and ripped them up. If he searched me, he'd easily find them.

"Your father stole something that belongs to me. Something very special. I have a feeling he gave it to you…for safekeeping. But I want it back."

"Money?" I whispered. "Is it money? How much does he owe?"

"More than he could ever repay. No, this something is even more important than money. And my patience has reached its limit. I'm done with his games. I asked nicely. I wasn't going to involve him in anything shady. But he has brought this upon himself. Now, Marco, I need you to tell me where to find the account information."

My knees shook. I didn't know if I could tell the lie convincingly enough. It didn't matter if this man got the numbers or not. Chances were likely that I was going to die. "I…"

He grabbed my arm in an iron grip. I yelped. "Where is it? Don't tell me you don't know."

Suddenly, his face contorted in pain, and he let me go briefly. He turned, and he and I saw Gertie standing behind him, a large tree limb in her hands. She swung again at his head. He tried to duck, but the limb smacked him right across the forehead. The wood against the skull made a "wump" sound, and he fell to his knees.

I grabbed Mr. Harvey's phone that had fallen from his hands. "Run!" I yelled to Gertie as I jumped over the bed and out the door.

I could see that he wasn't quite unconscious, so I slammed the door, took Gertie's hand, and began to run toward the trees where the dirt bike was.

"Hurry," I told her, as I picked up the bike.

But her hands were shaking. I also noticed tears trickling down her cheeks. "I thought he was going to kill you. I saw him drive back, and I knew. I thought you might be dead."

I took her hand. "Gertie, I'm alive. Because of you. But we have to get out of here."

She wiped at her face and nodded. We put on the helmets and got on the bike. The engine roared to life. "Where are we going?"

"I don't know yet. Just away from here."

As she sped away, I thought of where we could go. Mr. Harvey and Grandma could be anywhere, but I doubted it would be the police station. "Ms. Wright!" I yelled over the engine. "They would have gone to Ms. Wright's!"

"Can we trust her?"

"We have to try."

We would have to drive through a portion of the town, but Gertie said there was no way to avoid it. Ms. Wright's office sat right on the east side of Main Street. Gertie tried to stick to the side streets to avoid too much attention.

Once there, we parked in the back. "Take the keys," I told her, as we jumped off and set the bike against the kickstand.

The blast of air conditioning hit us, and I was tempted to let it air me out.

"Which way? Up or down?"

Ms. Wright's office building had a small foyer with stairs that went either to the upper floor or the lower level. "Up," I said, and we climbed the small set of stairs.

Racing down the hall, we ran past the secretary's desk that no one manned. Ms. Wright's door was ajar. I opened it all the way and walked in. And noticed Ms. Wright loading a pistol with a clip of bullets.

Gertie sucked in a breath, which made Ms. Wright snap her head up.

"Marco?" she asked, her mouth semi-full with chocolate.

"You, too?" I asked, walking backward.

"No, no, no, no," she said, swallowing the chocolate and wiping her mouth with her available hand. "It's not what it looks like."

"Run," Gertie whispered.

"Marco!" Mr. Harvey said from behind me. "I am so glad you're all right. I don't know what I did to my phone, and I was nervous because there was no way for you to get ahold of me."

I turned to him, then back to Ms. Wright. "Where's Grandma? Did that guy pay you off too?" Too much was happening. I didn't know who I could trust. All I knew is that Ms. Wright had a gun in her hand. And Mr. Harvey was with her. "How'd you know I was here?"

"I didn't. I dropped off your grandma at the property."

"Why would you do that?"

"She demanded it! We thought you were there, remember? She's trying to save all of you. She was willing to pay whatever the debt was, so she traveled to the motel room to see Lance. But I guess they're not just here about money. Which means they must be here for you."

"That detective lady is a bad guy. They all are, and I saw the older man. He was at the motel. Gertie helped my getaway."

"Carl is here?" Ms. Wright asked.

I hadn't noticed how close she had walked to me while I had been listening to Mr. Harvey. I stepped away. "How do you know him?"

Not willing to take a chance, I pushed past Mr. Harvey and ran out of the room, dragging Gertie with me.

"I've got to get to Grandma," I said as we ran outside.

"They'll hurt you."

"What choice do I have? I can't let them hurt her."

Suddenly we came to a complete stop. A black SUV sat idling between us and the dirt bike. The passenger window rolled down.

"Get in," the man from the motel said. His forehead had a massive welt on it, which might explain why he looked royally unpleasant. "Or I make the call, and they kill your father and your grandmother."

Mr. Harvey busted out of the door. "Marco, please stop running out on me. You know I can't keep up."

The man—Carl—acted annoyed. "Get in, now."

"Stay here," I told Gertie.

"No."

"He doesn't want you. He wants me."

"Oh my God," Mr. Harvey said, as he now saw the man in the SUV. He grabbed my arm. "No, you can't have him. You'll have to go through me."

Carl sighed. "I don't have time for this." He raised a gun and pointed it at Mr. Harvey. In broad daylight.

Gertie's clinging to my one arm, sobbing, and Mr. Harvey's gripping the other arm.

"It's too late," Mr. Harvey said. "Even if you kill me, it's too late. The proper authorities know now."

"Know what? What have I done? Do you even know why I'm up here?"

"Well, I know you're pointing a gun at me, so you're not trying to pass me a religious tract."

"Let Marco go."

The three of us turned to see Ms. Wright step up behind us. She had no smile on her face. And she still held the pistol.

"I knew it," I said. "I knew I shouldn't trust you."

"Just shut up and get in the SUV."

Mr. Harvey stared at Ms. Wright. I saw her give him a weird look, but who knew what that was about?

But none of it mattered anymore. I was tired, I didn't want Gertie or Mr. Harvey to get hurt, and I wanted to see my grandma. Maybe I could work out a deal if I gave the guy the numbers. No offense to my dad, but I couldn't care less if the stupid numbers led to this guy's riches. "All I know," I said, as I walked to the SUV. "Is I'm tired of adults letting me down. Isn't anyone good anymore?"

I slid into the SUV, glaring at Ms. Wright and Mr. Harvey. Gertie stood there sobbing, but I couldn't look at her without my heart hurting. If Ms. Wright was evil, what would she do to Gertie?

But before I could change my mind and have Gertie come with me, Carl gunned the engine, peeling out of the office lot. He kept the gun in his hand. "So, let's get this out of the way," he said. "Where's the account information?"

"I'm not sure what you mean."

"Stop the act. Yes, you do." He zoomed past stop signs, not even remotely slowing down.

"If I give you whatever this account information is, will you leave us alone? Just leave us up here? We're not bothering anybody."

He made a hard right turn down the road to Grandma's house. "You know too much. Sorry, it's nothing personal. I clean up messes to make sure no dirt remains. If you know what I mean." He placed his large palm on the back of my neck and squeezed tightly.

I forced myself not to flinch even though it hurt. He flew past the stop sign by Gertie's house.

I started to feel sick. There was no way out of this. Whatever mess Dad had gotten us into, it wasn't going to end well.

CHAPTER THIRTY-TWO

Carl Ricci now pointed the gun at me.

He parked outside the cabin. The detective's car was still there. "Don't make any sudden moves. There are many ways to maim you without killing you." With one hand he opened his glove compartment, took out handcuffs, and secured them on my wrists. He opened his door and slid out while grabbing my arm. "Come out my side."

Once I had slid out of the SUV from the driver's side, he shut the door.

"Take me to the account information, and I promise your deaths will be quick and painless."

"When I ran away the first time, Joe and my Dad were digging in the gardens, looking for coffee cans."

In one swift move, Carl brought up the butt of his gun and hit me across the temple. I fell to my knees and cried out in pain. Stars exploded in my head, and I couldn't open my eyes. I could barely gather my breath, the pain demanded everything.

"Where is the account number? I know you know. He said you

did!" He paused. "What's this?"

I felt the paper from my back pocket get lifted.

He opened the paper and laughed. "Thank you, Marco. I knew you'd help." He took out his phone and made a call. "I've got the numbers. Make sure to transfer all of it to secure locations and then delete the account." He read the numbers. After a moment, he looked in my direction. "Pin? Hold on, let me ask the kid."

Pin? I thought of Dad's letters on the bottom of each page. H.E.L.P. I felt some relief that I didn't have the book or any of the pages with me.

Suddenly, I felt a blow to my stomach. "Where is the pin? And don't play dumb."

While my insides exploded, I heard a voice say, "Don't ever touch my grandson again."

No. Carl had a gun. I tried to move, but pain consumed me.

"Where are you, little old lady?" Carl asked.

I saw his back was to me as he searched for Grandma.

"I took care of all the others, and I'll take care of you, too. That's a promise."

Grandma was near the front of the SUV. I sensed it.

Carl must have figured it out, too, because he spun around. This time with a raised gun.

No. I lunged at him, tackling him to the ground. The gun exploded in my ear, and I felt a rip through my shoulder like burning volcanic coal had just detonated inside of it. I fell back in agony.

I blacked out. Seconds before, the commotion had escalated.

There was another gunshot and maybe some sirens. Definitely screams. I heard those. I also heard someone yell, "We got him!" I must have been delusional because it sounded like Ms. Wright.

CHAPTER THIRTY-THREE

"Marco," Grandma's face hovered over mine.

When I came to, I felt pain. I scrunched up my face and started breathing through clenched teeth.

"They're increasing the pain killer, hon," Grandma said. "They had to wait until you were semi-conscious."

I must have blacked out again, and this time I awoke gradually. People were talking in the room. "They have him in custody. He'll most likely serve time."

"What about the account information? Won't that help prove his innocence?"

"Not really. He was blackmailing him for drugs. When he realized how dangerous Ricci was, it was too late. Plus, he still has to go to court for the drugs on his person with the last arrest."

"How long are we talking?"

"It could be anywhere from three to twenty years. But hopefully, with his testimony against the Ricci crime ring, his sentence will be more on the shorter end of things."

There were too many drugs in my system, making me feel

loopy. I registered they were talking about Dad, but I couldn't open my mouth to say anything. I eventually fell under a blanket of darkness again.

Several times I'd come in and out of consciousness. I noticed Grandma in the room, and once I saw Mr. Harvey. But I could never stay awake for long.

One time I woke up to the feeling of a cool hand in mine. I blinked open my eyes and squinted. My eyes had to adjust to the light, but eventually, my sight focused on Gertie. "The doctors said you're not going to die." She wiped at her eyes. "So, don't do it, or I'll be mad."

"Hey," I croaked out. My mouth felt like someone dumped a pound of sand in it. "I'm…not…dying."

She smiled her pretty smile.

"Yours is prettier than the detective's," I said before closing my eyes again.

"Are you going to sleep again?"

I forced my eyes open. "I'm kind of awake."

"What were you saying about mine being prettier than the detective's? Are you talking about Ms. Wright or the other woman?"

My eyebrows scrunched together. "Ms. Wright? Why would I compare you to her?"

"She's a detective, and you said--"

"Wait. What?"

"Yeah, it surprised me too. I think Mr. Harvey might have known."

"Tell me what happened."

"As soon as you left with that Ricci guy, Ms. Wright ordered us into her SUV. She gunned it down some back roads and two tracks. She called in what happened to her squad and ordered an immediate backup. She said something about luring the criminal into a trap. Then Mr. Harvey blew up at her and was like, 'You're using Marco to trap Ricci?'

"And she said that Marco would be all right because they would get there before anything happened. She said that Ricci needed you alive because he needed to use you as an incentive for Lance to tell where the key was. Or something like that."

"Ms. Wright is a detective?" I tried to laugh, but oh no. Stopped as soon as I tried. "That's crazy. And she was wrong. Something did happen. If Grandma hadn't shown up, that guy would have kept beating me. And I got shot."

"I know. Ms. Wright's acting quietly. Mr. Harvey barely speaks to her. Even your grandma has acted cool toward her." She acted like she wanted to say something else.

"What?"

"It's about your dad."

"Is he okay?"

"He was arrested. Right there at your grandma's house. So was Joe Ricci and the other detective woman. When your dad saw you on the ground and all the blood…" Gertie paused again. "He started freaking out. Like really freaking out. Started yelling 'No," and 'Not Marco,' and he pushed against the cops to try to get to you. Then he fell into their arms, sobbing. When they shoved him in the police car, he kept murmuring, 'What have I done? What have I done?'"

I turned away from Gertie and stared out the window of the hospital room. "I still don't understand why he got involved with those guys." But I knew. The answer hurt more than the bullet wound. "Drugs. They had the quality drugs."

"Yeah, but he stole the account number that exposes a bunch of laundered money. Like from politicians and stuff. It's big time. That's got to count for something."

"Dad stole the account information to double-cross him. For drugs."

"He's the one who found Ms. Wright. He wanted someone who wasn't touched by the Ricci family. And I guess she has quite the reputation of hunting down drug rings. Or something like that. It's kind of hard to believe."

"This is nuts."

The hospital room door opened, and Grandma entered. When she saw I was awake, she smiled. "There he is. Look, I brought ice chips."

There she was. Grandma. Looking like her normal self with a bright t-shirt and skirt and a cardigan that didn't match. "You're alive," I got out the words while she fed me spoonfuls of ice. I suddenly blurted, "I'm sorry."

Grandma's forehead creased from raising her eyebrows. "For what, hon?"

"I'm sorry I cheated. I've been wanting to tell you."

Grandma took my other hand and squeezed it. “Stop that. Of course, I forgive you.”

“I thought…if I never saw you again, and I didn’t apologize…”

“Well, thanks to the good Lord, we both have second chances.”

“Did Ricci shoot you?”

“No, honey, you blocked the shot. Then I shot him. He’s not going to be bothering us anymore.”

“Dad?” I asked. “Where was he?”

“Once I had tied up and secured the young man and that evil, double-crossing detective, I had him stay with them in the shed to keep him safe.”

“Wow,” Gertie said. “That’s incredible. You stopped a crime family and double-crossing detective by yourself!”

“No, I had a little bit of help.”

“Who helped?” I asked, feeling too tired to figure out the answer.

“Lance. I shot Joe in the leg, which dropped him. That detective lady raised her gun and pointed it at Lance. Told me to drop the gun or my son was dead. Then I said to her, ‘You’ve never seen me shoot before, have you?’”

My eyes widened. “You’re kidding me! You really said that?”

“Yep. I was able to shoot the gun out of her hand.”

“That’s crazy,” I said.

“Crazy awesome,” Gertie agreed.

"When I did that, Lance lunged for the gun. It was that simple. I walked over, disarmed them, and tied them up. I was worried Lance was too shaky, but he held that gun steady enough. They both told us we were dead. That Carl was coming and was going to kill our whole family. And I said 'Over my dead body.'"

"You did it," I said. "You stopped a criminal mastermind."

"You stopped him, Marco. Not me. He would have shot me if it wasn't for you. I'm just so sorry you got hurt. I was trying to make sure you didn't get hurt."

"He would have killed me if you hadn't shown up."

"And yet, you were brave enough to tackle him."

"I didn't want you hurt," I said. "I guess we were protecting each other."

"I guess we were."

"So, he's dead?"

"Yes. I made sure of it. He is never going to harm anyone ever again."

"People are going to know not to mess with you, Ms. Fuller."

"Yeah, well, don't go spreading any rumors that I cut up his parts and am using him for fertilizer."

Grandma and Gertie laughed.

I fell asleep again not long after that. Thirst had me waking up.

I heard whispering, but turning my head just wasn't going to happen. It seemed the only body part I could move without hurting was my fingers. Even my feet ached, no doubt from running all over the place with no shoes on. Bandages now covered them, so my socks must not have been super protection.

Someone gingerly squeezed my fingers. "You alive?"

Blinking my one good eye, I saw Grandma watching me with worry still lining her face.

"Yeah," I croaked. My mouth felt like the Sahara Desert, but Grandma already had a cup of water waiting to bring to my lips.

"The doctors said you need to try to sit up."

"It hurts to even move my head."

"The more you push past the discomfort, the more your body's going to heal."

She handed me the bed's remote, and I pushed the button that raised my head. Once up, I used my hands to reposition myself. I pressed my lips together to keep the groan in place, but pain shot up my right shoulder where I'd been shot. Grandma helped me plump the pillows behind me to rest against, then sat at the edge of my bed. "There."

I was sweating and panting. "Not so bad," I said with a slight grin.

"Can I join?" Mr. Harvey poked his head into the room.

"He's been here every day," Grandma whispered in my ear. "Even reassigned his other cases downstate to be at the hospital for you." Then Grandma called, "Come on in, Tom."

He took a chair by the bed and scooted up next to me.

"Tom?" I asked.

"Yes, but you can call me Mr. Harvey," he said with a grin.

But it didn't reach his eyes, which had dark circles under them. "How's the hero?"

"Grandma's the ninja," I said.

"Yeah, she's something, but I saw you tackle Carl Ricci. That was something too."

"I got shot."

He nodded. "I know. I saw that, too."

His mouth fell into a deep frown, and I wondered if he was choking up. "I'm all right, Mr. Harvey. I didn't die."

He nodded but wouldn't look at me. Now I could tell from his contorted facial expression that he was trying to keep the emotion in place. "This could have turned out so much worse. When I think of what would have happened, it gets me all worked up again."

"But it didn't. You went and rescued Grandma, and she came like a predator and attacked the bad guys. If it wasn't for you, things would have turned out so badly."

"I knew better though. I knew that using you to lure them was a bad idea. I should have put my foot down."

"Look, Joe Ricci and that fake detective are arrested, and Carl Ricci is never going to hurt anyone again. Can we just be glad that things turned out the way they did? No more blame. I don't even blame Ms. Wright, even though I still am having a hard time with her being a detective, or whatever she is."

"She's a private investigator."

"Did you know?"

"Yes. After I secured your home with your grandma. I made

some calls, and they gave me her name. She's been after the Ricci family for a long time. Anyway, she jumped at the chance at protecting a child from the family and seeing if she could find any clues."

"So, that's why she grilled me all the time? That was so annoying."

"Yeah, she fooled a lot of people. I guess she's really good because no one thinks she could be working for the police. She's so nice and sweet. Isn't that crazy?"

"Well, I can't believe it either. What if there's a high-speed chase? And I'm not talking with a car."

Mr. Harvey shook his head, but I saw his grin. "Marco, that's not appropriate."

"It's funny, admit it."

"She's faster than you think. She was acting the part and was in costume. She had us at your Grandma's cabin in five minutes, and she was out of the car with her gun drawn before I could even unbuckle my seatbelt."

"All right, all right, that's pretty impressive."

"Besides," Grandma added. "You shouldn't make fun of people's appearance. How would you feel if someone made fun of you?"

"So, I shouldn't pick on Mr. Harvey's ugly ties?" I asked. His current one was Bart Simpson saying "Hey, dude." It was yellow and orange and tacky.

Mr. Harvey looked down at it. "I like my ties."

Grandma sighed and shook her head. “Don’t worry Mr. Harvey, he thinks I need better style too.”

Mr. Harvey lifted his eyebrows but remained silent, but Grandma caught on. “I have fashion style!”

Mr. Harvey and I broke into a grin.

We were quiet for a minute. I watched the unspoken communication between the two of them and knew there was something that they weren’t saying. They’d look at each other, then dart their eyes back to me. Grandma would set her lips in a tight line, then remember herself and soften her face. Mr. Harvey would fiddle with his tie by rolling it up then rolling it down. Then they’d do it all again.

“If you two don’t tell me what the heck’s going on, I’m going to toss you both out of my room.”

Grandma smiled and patted my hand. “Whatever it is can wait until tomorrow.”

Mr. Harvey crinkled his eyebrows together and acted like he was going to say something.

“I know it’s about Dad. Gertie told me he was arrested.”

“He’s been sent back downstate for continued rehab until the next court date. But first, he needs some medical treatment.”

“What kind of medical treatment? Did he get shot?”

Grandma and Mr. Harvey glanced at each other. Grandma spoke. “He went into shock after seeing you on the ground. He has yet to fully recover from it.”

“Don’t worry,” Mr. Harvey said. “This isn’t life-threatening, but we were hoping that when you felt better, you could go down there and talk to him. I've already contacted the proper authorities, and we can arrange a meeting. It will do him good to see you alive and well."

"Yes," I said quickly. "Let's go now."

"Easy there," Grandma said. "You need to be a hundred percent. I did drive down there a couple of days ago, once the doctors said you would pull through just fine. I told him that you would make it and that Carl Ricci was dead and wasn't going to hurt our family again. It did seem to help."

"Wait a sec, how long have I been in here?"

"Ten days," Mr. Harvey answered.

"Say what?"

"Getting shot is a massive shock to your system. Your body needed to adjust and repair itself."

"That's too much time. We need to leave. I feel much better."

"Just twenty minutes ago, you could barely sit up," Grandma said.

"I'm not saying I'll be running, but I need to see Dad. Please."

"How about if we rest tonight, and we'll see how you feel in the morning?" Mr. Harvey offered.

I nodded, determined to make it work.

That evening, I pushed myself to stand and walk around the hospital ward. My appetite had partially come back, so I ate some of the dinner, then pushed past the discomfort and walked around the ward a second time.

I must have overdone it because I fell into a deep sleep as soon as my head hit the pillow.

When I woke up, the sun shone through the window, and I felt a lot more like myself.

The nurse took my vitals and determined that I had no fever and my heart rate was strong. Due to the circumstances, the chief doctor agreed to release me for the day and that if there were any concerns to get readmitted immediately.

While we waited for the hospital to get my discharge papers, Ms. Wright knocked on the door and stepped inside. “How’s the patient doing?”

I had to shut my mouth, but she looked so different, I’m sure I didn’t hide my shock. Her red hair that was this huge mess on her head was gone. She still had red hair, but it was more brunette and cut to just past her ears. No gaudy earrings. No hula hoop skirts. Her round shape had disappeared too. She had on a navy-blue pantsuit with heeled black boots. Not knowing what to say, I blurted, “Where’d it all go?”

She looked down at herself, then said, “It was a fat suit. I needed to strategically alter my appearance. It was for your protection.”

“A fat suit? Like in the movies?”

“I’m pretty thick still, but yes, I added a little bit of an extra layer.”

“That’s pretty cool,” I admitted. “So, you’re technically not a social worker?”

“No, I’m not, which explains why I’m not too good at it.”

"You won't hear me deny it," I teased.

Ms. Wright laughed, then turned serious. "I'm sorry you were taken by Ricci. I've been pursuing him for years, and he was right there. All I could think was that I couldn't let him get away. I thought you'd be safe. I had found a backwoods route to the cabin weeks prior, so I thought it'd be no problem." She shook her head. "I risked your life needlessly, and I'm sorry."

"Even if you tried to stop me, I would have gotten in his car anyway. Grandma and Dad were at the cabin. They needed me."

Ms. Wright still acted torn.

"And I've got a battle wound," I added. "It all worked out."

"So…we're cool?" She gave me her fist. "Come on, pound it."

I laughed that time. Even though it hurt. Then with my good hand, I pounded her fist with mine. "I would have never thought you were a cop."

"Good. Then my disguise worked. Can I steal your grandmother for a few minutes?"

"Sure, but hurry. We're leaving in a few."

I watched Grandma and Ms. Wright leave the room and start whispering out in the hall. Grandma did not appear too happy. In the end, they shook hands. When Grandma came back in, she said, "It's a good thing, you came out alive. The thought of you being used in such a dangerous situation doesn't sit well with me."

I held out my one good arm. "I'm alive." She came over and hugged me on my good side.

"Are you saying I should forgive her?"

"Oh, so now you don't like Ms. Wright? I see how it is. Now that I think she's cool, you've got to change your mind. Just don't start in on the cookie jokes. They're not very nice."

Grandma chuckled. "What did I do before you came into my life?" She kissed my forehead and finished getting my belongings together.

After signing discharge papers, Grandma went to get the car while Mr. Harvey pushed the wheelchair. "I can walk now," I said testily.

"Everyone leaves the hospital in a wheelchair," he said. "Relax. It's a miracle they even agreed to release you."

Once outside, I breathed in the fresh air. The air calmed my nerves.

Grandma pulled up in Mr. Harvey's Taurus. Gertie waved from the passenger seat.

I could feel my smile stretch across my face.

She got out of the car and walked over to me. "Surprise! My mom said since you're famous now, I can officially hang out with you. She even agreed to let me take a day off school so that I can go downstate."

"I'm famous?"

"It's all over the news. Teen boy takes a bullet to protect his grandma. Your grandma's pretty famous too. She single-handedly caught a crooked detective and Joe Ricci."

"No more rumors about body parts buried in the backyard?"

"I can't make any promises on that."

"All right, everyone, let's get this show on the road." Grandma came over to me and wheeled me to the passenger's seat. "You'll sit up here with Mr. Harvey. I'll take the back seat with Gertie."

Once we were all inside, Mr. Harvey pulled out of the hospital's parking lot and asked if anyone wanted a burger and fries.

When he drove through, he ordered me a chocolate milkshake. It seemed a long time ago that I hated him for taking me away from the only person I knew.

But this time, he wasn't taking me away from him. He was bringing me back to him. And nothing was going to be the same.

CHAPTER THIRTY-FOUR

The Henry Ford Hospital in Detroit was this massive structure, and they kept Dad in the mental evaluation wing of the facility.

I had slept most of the way down, and I still had to push past the light-headedness.

“Are you sure you’re all right?” Grandma asked as we stood outside his room.

I nodded and allowed the guard to unlock the door. Only Grandma and I were allowed to enter because we were family. The room was much different than mine was up north. There was no window, no devices, and the bathroom had no door.

Dad sat on his bed, writing furiously in a notebook. He looked freshly scrubbed and wore matching blue bottoms and a shirt.

“Lance?” Grandma said.

Dad’s head came up, then he froze. He stared at us and didn’t move a muscle.

“Marco came to say hi.”

But I had frozen too. Every feeling I had ever experienced my entire life came flooding back: hopelessness, hunger, despair, envy, anger, resentment, bitterness, and love. Yes, I admit it. I was conflicted.

"You're okay," he said in relief. He dropped the notebook and pen and walked over to me. Hesitant at first, he rested his hand on my hurt shoulder. "When I saw you on the ground…" His eyes filled up.

"I lived," I said. "Grandma was there to protect me."

Dad nodded and glanced up at Grandma. He hugged his mother's neck, and Grandma hugged him in return. "Thanks, Mom," he whispered to Grandma. "I knew he'd be safe with you."

"Always," Grandma said.

When Dad released Grandma, he looked back at me. "I know that words are empty," he said. "I've been working with a psychiatrist here who's been helping me see the truth. I'm not going to give you any empty promises."

I couldn't say anything.

"I'm going to show you," he said. "I'm going to show you how sorry I am by changing. And one day, I'm going to be completely clean. And when that day happens, I'm going to show you. I'll show you what I should have shown you a long time ago. That I love you more than anything. Even drugs."

Now. I had to speak before I lost my nerve. "You chose drugs over me," I said, finding my voice, even if it still sounded like a toad. With clenched hands, I started again, "For the last couple years, it was drugs first, then Lance, then Marco."

Dad gave me his attention. His hands shook, but his eyes were focused. Finally. Finally, his eyes were on me. "For as long as I can remember it's been me and you against the world. And we were losing. Bad. I don't know how many nights I went to bed hungry. Or how many nights I went to bed alone. They all blend into one never-ending nightmare.

"But I never stopped believing that you'd quit. Eventually, you'd realize you had a son, and then everything would be okay. It wasn't until I met a grandmother I never knew I had that my eyes were opened to what my life could be like. You robbed me of that."

I stopped and breathed. I said it.

"No more empty promises," he whispered. "Give me a chance to make it up to you."

But then it was done, and the floodgates were emptied. I wrapped my one good arm around him and whispered the very last thing I needed to say. "I love you."

The three of us sat together, making small talk. Grandma acted a little shy with Dad, and he acted as if the shame weighed heavily on him.

Grandma asked about what he was writing in the notebooks. Dad got quiet, not looking her in the eye. "I've been writing down memories. For you. Memories of Marco when he was young. Memories of me with Dad. Memories of us. I'm writing down all the things I should have said over the last thirteen years." He handed her one of the notebooks that rested beside him. "Here. This one's done. I'll send you more as I finish them."

Grandma reached for the notebook and held it tenderly in her hand. She opened it to the first page and quietly read. A tear ran down her cheek. She glanced over at me then back to the page. She began reading.

It was September 15th, 2009. The bar finally closed around three in the morning. I finished cleaning, counted out my share of tips, and stumbled to my truck. I was tempted to sleep right there in my truck, but I shared an apartment with four other guys from work, and they relied on me as their transportation. I opened the door and saw something in the driver's seat. It looked like a small mound of blankets. At first, I thought I might be hallucinating, especially when the blanket began to move. That was the first time I laid eyes on my son.

The note read something about not being ready to be a mother and that she hoped I'd be a good father. Even though she and I barely knew each other, I remembered the evening together. At first, I was angry. This child couldn't be mine. I wasn't ready to become a father. I didn't have my life together. I was all alone in the big city. Instead of calling you, Mom, I drove the baby to the hospital. I walked in and handed him to the first employee I saw. "Someone left him in my truck."

They somehow convinced me to stay. They had questions, and they said it would be simple and not take long. Later they offered a paternity test. "Don't you want to know if he's yours?" the doctor asked. A part of me didn't want to know. That was the boy still in me, not wanting to take responsibility. But a bigger part of me not only wanted to know but needed to know.

When the test came back certain that I was the father, I couldn't speak. They kept asking me what I wanted to do with the baby.

I ran. I ran out of there so scared. What was I going to do with a baby? But I couldn't leave the parking lot. Dad had been such a good father to me, and he wouldn't want me to abandon this baby. So, I walked back inside, signed papers, asked for resources to help with baby necessities, and 24 hours later, walked out with Marco Lance Fuller.

"Mom left me?" I asked.

"I went and found her. We decided to try and raise you together. I wrote about it. It's in the notebook."

"Where is she now?"

"I don't know. She was a struggling addict too."

Before I knew it, our time was up.

"I won't let you down, Marco."

He reached out to Grandma and kissed her tear-stained cheek. "Thanks for giving him what I never could."

"Can we write letters back and forth?" I asked.

"Definitely," Dad said. "And I'm going to keep writing memories to you both."

Grandma and I walked out of the room and headed outside

where Mr. Harvey and Gertie were waiting. “So, Marco,” Gertie said. “What’s your next move?”

I simply answered, “I’m going home.” And I knew exactly where to find it. In a little cabin in the middle of the woods. Too small to comfortably take a shower, but large enough to fit all the love I would ever need.

The End

Thank you for reading ***Marco's Next Move***.

Here are more great titles from the author:

Tubbs and the 200 Dares

The Road Back Home from Here

The Secret Heir

The Runaway Heir

Broken: Macy's Story

Visit Janice Broyles online at

www.janicebroyles.com

Made in the USA
Las Vegas, NV
21 February 2023